T0344546

DEATH BY DESIGN AT ALCATRAZ

DEATH BY DESIGN AT ALCATRAZ

a novel

ANTHONY POON

goff
BOOKS

GOFF BOOKS

Published by Goff Books. An Imprint of ORO Editions
Gordon Goff: Publisher

www.goffbooks.com
info@goffbooks.com

Text, drawings, and jacket design by Anthony Poon
Book design by Pablo Mandel
Proofread by Kirby Anderson
Managing Editor: Jake Anderson

Photos of Alcatraz Island by Anthony Poon
Author photo by Mikel Healey
Silhouette of falling man inspired by Pexels photo, Pixabay

10 9 8 7 6 5 4 3 2 1 First Edition

ISBN: 978-1-954081-28-4

Color Separations and Printing: ORO Group Ltd.
Printed in China.

Goff Books makes a continuous effort to minimize the overall carbon
footprint of its publications. As part of this goal, Goff Books, in
association with Global ReLeaf, arranges to plant trees to replace
those used in the manufacturing of the paper produced for its books.
Global ReLeaf is an international campaign run by American Forests,
one of the world's oldest nonprofit conservation organizations. Global
ReLeaf is American Forests' education and action program that helps
individuals, organizations, agencies, and corporations improve the
local and global environment by planting and caring for trees.

For Ella and Lily

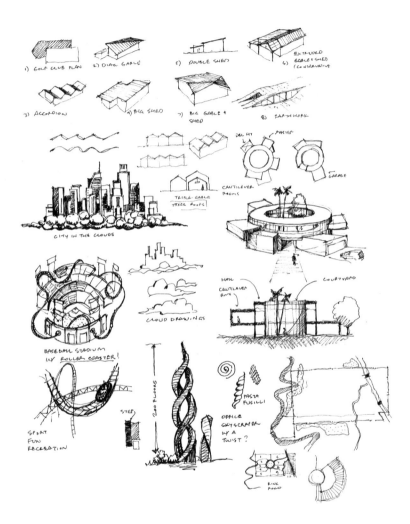

1) GOLF CLUB PLAN 2) DIAG. GABLE 5) DOUBLE SHED 6) EXTRUDED GABLE & SHED (CONSERVATIVE)

3) ACCORDION 4) BIG SHED 7) BIG GABLE & SHED 8) EARTHWORK

DBL HT MASTER

CANTILEVER ROOMS

GARAGE

TRIPLE GABLE THREE ROOFS

CITY IN THE CLOUDS

CLOUD DRAWINGS

HALL COURTYARD

CANTILEVER RMS

BASEBALL STADIUM W/ ROLLER COASTER!

SPORT FUN RECREATION

STEP

200 FLOORS

PASTA FUSILLI

OFFICE SKYSCRAPER W/ A TWIST?

RING ROAD

Table of Contents

THREE-QUARTER
LENGTH COAT
W/ BLASÉ SCARF

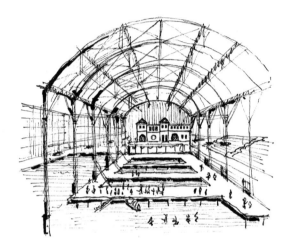

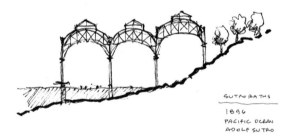

SUTRO BATHS

1896
PACIFIC OCEAN
ADOLF SUTRO

The Architect Who Couldn't Fly

S IX A.M. AND DELIVERED FROM A RED-EYE FLIGHT, the Dutch architect eyes his construction site blanketed in the cold veil of San Francisco's coastal fog. Here and there through openings in the swirling heavy mist, Lars von Meester glimpses his latest architectural design in progress on a cliff overlooking the Pacific Ocean.

Forties, tall and thin, he is either handsome or lanky and bald, depending on who you ask. It is unknown if he is balding due to genetics or simply making a fashion statement with a close-to-the-scalp haircut, as Lars mimics his older colleagues in Rotterdam and Paris.

Like many architects, Lars von Meester is tightly groomed, well-dressed, and put together in a hyperconscious manner. He prides himself on his standard black uniform, predictable as it is cliché, stylish as it is practical. He arrives in a black turtleneck, black jeans, and black boots that are as hip as they are protective, at a site of concrete and steel. His three-quarter-length black-wool coat is noticeably trimmed with a hand-stitched blue thread. His loose, gray scarf aims to present a touch of blasé, but the apparent indifference is well-rehearsed.

Out of competitiveness or perhaps disdain, Lars's design colleagues often wonder how such a young architect has already bested those twenty years older in landing numerous prized commissions. On top of that, how does this influencer get his outrageous ideas built, ideas that some architects accuse of being lifted from the images of comic books and graphic novels? Many architects and design students alike have fantastical design visions in their heads, from cities hovering in the clouds to stadiums wrapped in roller coasters. But it is the rare few architects that have the courage, opportunity, and presence to convince a client to fund and build such wild and whimsical structures.

The industry of architecture suggests, unfortunately, that one's career doesn't launch until age 50 at least, unlike the twenty- and thirty-somethings who abound in tech, banking, law—and pretty much any field that isn't architecture. It takes a while for architectural talent to season and for relationships to forge before an architect can be considered for a significant project. But Lars has risen to the top with his boyish face, clever salesman turns-of-phrases, and majestic plans for his clients. He has already completed projects of enviable substance, from massive housing projects to twisting skyscrapers, from sculptural cathedrals to mega-hotels with ski slopes descending off the roof.

Lars von Meester is known as "the Flying Dutchman," and although he does not like this nickname, it is apt because his international projects require him to rarely port for long. Today, he arrives in the almost-too-perfect hilly city by the bay to inspect progress on the construction of his latest project. Lars has been hired to re-envision and reconstruct the famous Sutro Baths designed by Colley and Lemme in 1896. Then, a cavernous, five-story-high steel and glass shell magnificently enclosed a public complex of seven saltwater swimming pools. But over the past century, the Baths, situated on the edge of the ocean, had fallen into complete disrepair, appearing like ancient ruins at best, forgotten body parts at worst. Lars's redesign of the unique and historic property is an ambitious project for San Francisco, a town often accused of fetishizing nostalgia. The nearby Cliff House restaurant, still in operation for locals and tourists, having been reconstructed four times over the span of 140 years, stands tall in the distance.

It would be a welcome plan if the project was just to rebuild the Baths, but as with some clients who are developers-for-profit, there is a grander commercial agenda. Adjacent to the Sutro Baths, the client of the Flying Dutchman has also hired him to design what the developer is marketing in glossy PR material as a "new city Mecca" and a "hillside lifestyle center"—in plain English, yet another shopping mall.

With no small amount of controversy, opponents have so far failed to halt the construction of the mall adjacent to the Baths. The disputed project has already desecrated a small portion of Lands End, the beloved grounds of Point Lobos. This vista-embracing western boundary of the Golden Gate Recreational Area ends in cliffs a few hundred feet above heroic ocean waves.

The ego of the developer is matched by the ambition of the Dutchman. For better or for worse, most architects want to change the face of cities; and desire and arrogance begets enemies.

Lars is expecting a call to confirm a breakfast meeting with a local architect, before they both head over to a press conference. Billionaire art collector Magnar Jones, the developer of these projects, is to soon announce an elite design competition for a career-capping project: the redesign of Alcatraz Island, the historic federal prison, into a new museum of art. Yet another project that will doubtless beget enemies.

The cloak of fog has not burned off quite yet, leaving Lars von Meester to discern construction progress as best he can. He stumbles a bit around piles of debris, stacks of steel beams, and coils of electrical wires. Any clear view of half-completed structures at Lands End only alludes to the haunting and skeletal quality of a building shell being erected, awaiting a soul to come.

Despite years of comfortably gliding through construction sites, from balancing on the I-beams of office towers to navigating machinery and underground labyrinths, Lars finds himself hesitant as the morning light fails to earn its way through the haze. He feels the menace of the ghostly white pea soup and, having read the news on the plane, also feels the unwelcome of the community for his "lifestyle center." Local residents were calling it yet another project of consumerism and poor tastes captured in brick and mortar.

Lars's arms are full. One hand is attempting to take photographs documenting the field work, which is a valiant but wasteful effort in these murky conditions. Under the other arm are several rolls of drawings—blueprints as they were once called for the chemical process using a blue ferric ferrocyanide compound resulting in the trademark and romanticized prints of the past.

The Dutch architect sees the shapes of a few first-arriving construction workers gathering at a coffee wagon in the distance beyond the arms and legs of copper pipes, galvanized ductwork, and rebar. For balance in taking photographs, Lars places the rolls of drawings against the construction site fencing running intermittently across the rock boundary of the site near the cliff.

A fresh breeze comes up and satisfied with his photographs, he reaches for his drawings. They aren't there at first grasp. He reaches out farther and farther, like a blind man desperately looking for a cane that has fallen to the ground. He gets on one knee, his three-quarter black jacket tails grazing debris and rock. He finds one roll and feels around for the other, which can't be far. His cell phone buzzes.

Perturbed and disoriented, he stands up to reach for his pocket while he takes a few steps in the gloom peering for the other roll. At the same time, a voice calls out, asking if he needs help.

Lars's bulky black boot meets a flat but slick rock, and his practiced balance and vanity is gone. He stumbles a bit, and moments later, realizes this Dutchman doesn't know how to fly. Lars von Meester falls twenty stories to his death at the base of the rocky cliffs, where he is united with the rolls of drawings he was so anxious to retrieve.

The city's signature fog has finally lifted. The construction pace is in full force as concrete foundations are being poured, as trusses are being lifted in place, as welders weld. The sounds of construction reach a harmonic vibration resonating with the rhythm of progress. Work goes on.

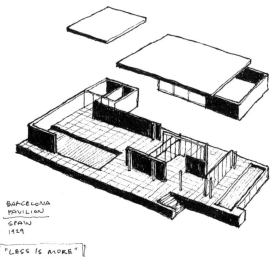

BARCELONA
PAVILION
SPAIN
1929

"LESS IS MORE"

- MIES VAN DER ROHE

BARCELONA
CHAIR

CHAPTER 1

The Puppet Master: Magnar Jones

W ITH BOUNDLESS GREED, Magnar Jones collects things: art, people, press clippings, media links. An absurdly wealthy commercial developer, he possesses a lifelong passion for collecting modern art, most notably the works of Abstract artists. His favorites include the usual suspects: Rothko, Pollock, Klee, and Kline. Magnar chooses Rothko for the wash of rich colors and indescribable atmospheric passion, Pollock for the excitement of the artist ferociously swinging his arms and paint brushes, Klee for the innocence and playful musicality, and Kline for the primitive black-and-white markings of calligraphic freedom.

Mr. Jones, as he likes to be called despite his overt narcissism, treasures his cloak of common Oklahoman roots. But he is no common voice in the world of art.

With a stern face, he often argues with colleagues, "I see life as my blank canvas where I can manipulate a composition, like a game even. People are my medium, and money my brush strokes."

Magnar's business vision is driven by the theoretical ideas of the Abstract Expressionist art movement, where independence of mind and body can be achieved by abandoning the predictable visual and physical world and its historical content. He regards representational subjects such as still lifes or countryside haystacks as banal and tired—unchallenging and too obvious for his soul, unnecessary to his elevated existence. He devours subject matters not easily described—geometric patterns or extracted textures. In the Abstract art movement, the participant sees what he wants to see, applies his own set of rules to the content, and rarely is judged for whether the interpretation, or even a new construct of reality, is right or wrong, benevolent or malicious.

His evolving interpretations of right and wrong have helped him turn the world of bland shopping-center development into groundbreaking territory, including his latest, the unpopular lifestyle center at Lands End with architect Lars von Meester. Magnar steamrolls local ordinances and pays off whoever must be paid off. And he pays top dollar for architects who offer him bold visions, brave forms, colors, and materials.

Now however, pushing past sixty, he is bored with it all, not wanting to be remembered as just another commercial developer. He'd call off the Lands End project if he could. Who cares about a mall with a view of the ocean? Anyone else but Magnar Jones.

Perched high above the city in his luxurious snobby Nob Hill penthouse, Magnar takes in the sweep of the bay every day, from bridge to bridge, and his eye has more consistently targeted Alcatraz Island of late—known simply as The Rock.

Months ago, an idea had come to him in a coffee shop meeting, and since then he has formulated an impressive project for himself, a culmination of his life's work. On the site of the abandoned island prison, he would build a new temple to art, to his beloved Abstract art, and it will be *the* museum of Abstract art. He won't even need to add his name to it, he thought. Everyone will know it is his creation.

In short order, he has filled in more of his plan. He will summon the world's top six architects and gift them with the opportunity to compete for the prize, his prize: a new internationally acclaimed museum.

Museums are especially prized by architects for their prestige, holding an elevated status over a library or a stadium. A work of art that holds art is ensured a place in history. Think of Gehry, Pei, Wright.

As much as Magnar is looking forward to the final structure, he is going to love the famous architects fawning at his invitation, and even more than that, the game, *his* game, that will take place to decide the winner.

A tall, large, and convincing presence, Magnar dons various shades of brown suits coupled with a crisp white dress shirt, never a tie. He contrasts his minimal ensemble with a selection from his cowboy-boot collection, each pair handcrafted in his native Oklahoma. Black calf-skin, brown ostrich, and burgundy alligator. A full house of boot chic. All to draw attention away from his too-fast graying hair and skin.

Also in an effort to combat his undeniable aging, he supplements his art collection with a collection of attractive women usually half his age. He dates incessantly, a new sexed-up candidate monthly. He doesn't care if all they see is his money. The date of choice, as it is for many old, privileged, white males is predictable: the slender (read flexible) Asian female, considered by Magnar to be exotic (read erotic). But really, anyone different from his Tex-caucasian self will do.

He's been dating Celadonna Kimm longer than most women. She is a tiny beauty in her late twenties, part Korean and part Filipino.

She met Magnar in Los Angeles at a launch party she set up for an up-and-coming fashion designer. Celadonna manages public relations and social media for several boutiques and indie designers. In that town, it usually translates to doing little more than constantly playing on one's phone with the pretense that having many Instagram followers was some sort of valuable currency, but Celadonna's clients adore her aggressiveness on their behalf. A few resent her, as she became a brand of her own, and is often the brightest light at any party. Celadonna accents her black locks with streaks of blonde, earning her the label, "Blondasian." Her laugh and profanity-laced conversation can be heard above any rooftop poolside din.

Many were surprised and disappointed when she left Southern California, their center of the universe, for Northern California. And for Magnar Jones and her new appointment to his board.

For now, he adores her, finds the sexual attraction addictive, and without a missed beat, appointed her the Director of Marketing for his newest project, leaving his board of directors to assess the situation. Will this new woman be true love, another plaything and accessory, or an unfortunate femme fatale? Magnar Jones, the shrewd capitalist, doesn't care whether Celadonna Kimm, or any past flings for that matter, falls into one of these categories or all three. He prefers to focus on his two, and only two, passions: business and art.

From his penthouse view, he gazes defiantly at the island that once imprisoned infamous criminals such as Al Capone, then was devastated during Native American occupation, often considered haunted by evil spirits, even once a nature sanctuary, and now a tourist attraction. Magnar believes he can conquer this project, redefine the island's dreadful history, and reshape how the mass audience would view Alcatraz. Indifference to failure, alongside an egomaniacal self-importance, drive the billionaire to *abstract* the contents that arrived in the baggage of Alcatraz. And make up new rules. He is convinced that he could reposition this land-form surrounded by the bay as his new canvas.

Fond of pompous lectures to his board, Magnar asks, hands strongly on his hips, "You know the expressions 'less is more' and 'form follows function,' don't you? From the Bauhaus architects, these two mere phrases of three words each, demand utilitarian simplicity and design abstraction. Discarding classical themes and traditional rules, I have learned to pave my own path starting with 'Ground Zero,' as the Bauhaus teachings mention. Yes, make my own rules—however I want, whenever I want."

An arrogant developer, he has a knack for seeking out challenging opportunities that could reap spectacular if not controversial results. But equally disconcerting, he has also enjoyed manipulating people, regulations, costs. But people the most, enjoying an almost sadistic enjoyment in watching politicians, builders, and creatives squirm. Jump at his every command. Pulling strings. Pulling the strings. This Alcatraz project would be a present to himself for his sixth decade, his greatest accomplishment. He'd make the architecture world and its greats bend to his will, like a puppet master.

He rationalizes the merciless thoughts with a comment he once shared with Celadonna. "We'll make front page news many times over."

With his un-businessman's thirst for art and beauty, he had committed to his board with smugness and a grin, "I will allocate my vast wealth to constructing a world-class institution to present all the hidden glories that lie in Abstract paintings, sculptures, textiles, writings, and even music," he paused for effect "and institute an architectural competition amongst legendary architects in an international-news-making sensation. Yes, I will."

In a mad rush, Magnar worked with, or more correctly intimidated, officials to re-zone the island to be a cultural and educational institution. The island's owner, the U.S. Army, and the operator, the National Parks Service, gave Magnar a land lease for a large sum of money. He negotiated a significant clause: He is unrestricted from what he does with the island.

With his cash and intimidating reputation behind his vision, the endeavor launched with the developer proudly announcing his museum's ambitious name, the "World Museum of Abstract Art at Alcatraz." Alongside this announcement, and an acknowledgement of too many awkward syllables, Magnar's booming voice roared in the boardroom. "I call it WoMA!"

Mr. Jones's new arts campus would join the prestigious list of art house acronyms like MOCA, MOMA, LACMA, SFMOMA, and the like. With phone never detached from her hand, Celadonna was already at work branding WoMA as "the commission of the century."

In short order, six fortunate, or so they'd think, architects were chosen from a long roster of premiere international names and letters were sent out by FedEx. No email. A box with a scrolled invitation, and a surprise.

In accepting the invitation to compete, each architect and their supporting creative team would have to make their way to San Francisco, and quite unexpectedly and unconventionally, the architects would have to work out of designated galleries in the San Francisco Museum of Modern Art. Not in their offices around the globe but on-site, sequestered in downtown San Francisco. He hasn't decided yet if he'll take them all on a boat ride around the island or not. Less is more, perhaps.

Fondly called SFMOMA, Swiss architect Mario Botta designed the monumental building in 1988. The overall shape of this massive building is like that of two giant childlike forms. The first mass is the size of an entire city block, then wrapped in red bricks stacked 75 feet high. The second, at the building's center, a large cylinder of white marble—the museum's rotunda lobby at 50 feet in diameter and standing tall at 120 feet. Topped with an angled-glass roof. Within this lobby, a glass suspension bridge.

In 2016, Norwegian firm Snøhetta created a stunning 10-story-building addition clad in 700 uniquely individual panels of white fiberglass-reinforced polymer, layered at various angles. The exterior design presents a bizarre rippling skin in contrast to the original building's stately red bricks.

The invitation letter made the ground rules clear to each participant:

Congratulations to a world class architect,

You have been selected for an exclusive architectural competition to re-envision the infamous Alcatraz Island of San Francisco, redesigning it into my new World Museum of Abstract Art at Alcatraz—which I fondly call, WoMA.

This design contest will take place over four continuous days where your creative process will be monitored. You will bring your top three associates to a designated gallery space in the San Francisco Museum of Modern Art, also known as SFMOMA.

You will design open book, publicly displaying your work in real time—day by day, hour by hour—your research, sketches, models, and drawings. This demonstration of your usual private artistic journey will be made evident to a general audience, and your competitors as well—and video recorded for posterity.

Stationed within SFMOMA, *you will be brought design tools, resources, computers, office furniture, beds, and all such accommodations. There will be access to staff locker rooms, and meals will be provided by the Michelin-rated restaurant within the building, In Situ.*

Congratulate yourselves for being chosen to participate in my project to offer to this city, and the world abroad, a new monumental institution of art.

With Admiration and Anticipation,
Your Esteemed Magnar Jones

Magnar has devised a fishbowl approach that requires each architect to live and labor in assigned rooms turned into design laboratory and theater. Yes, even theater. All the creative steps, side steps, and missteps will be scrutinized by the visiting citizens as they watch architects design a landmark structure for their city. Like children taking glee in feeding time at the zoo, every viewer will be able to watch the architectural Jackson Pollocks swing their arms, violently throwing paint on a vast white canvas. Each architect, reluctantly placed on Magnar's soap box, will show off, or try to hide, their most intimate moments of how a creative mind gyrates.

No design competition has ever had such peculiar requirements, but Magnar, this believer in the arts without rules, obsessed over the participants and their processes, *his* participants. Through this bizarre stage for forced performances, the rules of the competition would create an exhibition of untapped vanity and necessary showmanship. The challenging venue will expose each candidate as a tenacious architect and assertive competitor. His board, the press, the Bay Area community, and the world might get much more than they anticipated, and perhaps more than they wished for.

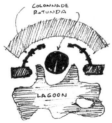

COLONNADE
ROTUNDA

LAGOON

PALACE OF FINE ARTS
BERNARD MAYBECK
1915

CORINTHIAN
COLUMN
-GREEK

CHAPTER 2

Museums: Vessels of Life or Death

N OT FAR FROM SFMOMA, the children feed the ducks, tossing scraps from their morning bread towards yearning beaks. Parents' watchful eyes monitor the kids as they negotiate the distance between land, lagoon, and quacks at the Palace of Fine Arts. This is the venue for Magnar Jones's public announcement.

From the global short list of "starchitects," Magnar Jones had hand-picked six architects to participate in his fantasy game of art and design. Seven, actually—one company is comprised of a husband-wife team.

The formal announcement is due today, another beautiful Northern California morning. Celadonna has chosen a beloved jewel of San Francisco as the backdrop for Magnar to publicize his scheme to transform the ramshackle Alcatraz Island into a world-class arts institution. As the grand presenter, he is eager to also unveil his list of the candidates who will vie for his project.

The Palace of Fine Arts, architect Bernard Maybeck's "temporary" monumental jewel of the 1915 World's Fair, still stands today, a century later, as a nostalgic icon of the city. Architects revel in how a fictional ruin expresses an enduring melancholy of lost civilizations. After the conclusion of the fair, the Panama-Pacific Exposition, the heroic palatial structure remained. Rebuilt in 1965 and again in 2009, the beloved Palace of Fine Arts is a popular venue for weddings and photo shoots, ranking high in the long list of tourist attractions.

Maybeck refuted the Modernists' grand idioms, "less is more," and "form follows function." This architect had more in keeping with the counter phrase from Postmodernist architect, Robert Venturi, "less is a bore." Quite the opposite from Magnar's slick contemporary art, the Palace of Fine Arts presents an abundance of Corinthian columns and pilasters. Lots of history.

This doesn't bother Magnar. Few things derail him. Magnar aims to draw the highest attendance for his performance, and where better than the beloved city monument with its foreground of a large reflecting pond—a location nestled amongst the affluent and elite, and the scenic Presidio? Celadonna likes the mix of the past and the future, as well as cloaking her boss and lover in the backdrop of great architecture. Much better than a hotel ballroom or convention center lobby.

A podium has been centered in the majestic rotunda standing over 100 feet high. Massive clusters of speakers are wired to Magnar's podium, also wired to his ego. He relishes this type of publicity event where he is the center of attention, where he can pontificate, exude influence and superiority. He is after all, a manipulator of his surroundings. This includes people.

For this press conference, his charcoal suit is paired with a bolo tie, as well as one of his favorite accents of panache: dark green western boots with inverted flame stitching in white. Against the backdrop of the typically sophisticated city dwellers, Magnar looks like either an out-of-place, self-absorbed individual or a western-themed clown.

He steps up to the podium, *his* podium. Over the past hour, a crowd has gathered—curious members of the general public who read online teasers, and the press stationed on the sidelines held back by taut red ropes between brass stanchions. There are also government officials, some who enjoy the political alliance to this developer, and others who hold only disdain for an arrogant son-of-a-bitch. Several hundred have gathered and counting—a growing crowd of onlookers who happen to come across this press conference turned social media spectacle.

Magnar clears his throat much too loudly but doesn't care for social graces. He leans into the microphone, *his* microphone. Magnar Jones smiles with proficient welcome, but it is accompanied by his obvious smirk of greed and agenda. Celadonna stands in the background supporting her man. She is ready to take the stage as rehearsed.

Magnar decides to open with an observation. He spurns having any kind of introduction to who or what he is—his ego deeming such information as self-evident. He offers no mere "hello," but instead launches into an attempt of an ice-breaker.

"It is said in jest and sometimes in truth, engineers know every-thing about nothing, and architects know nothing about everything."

Leaving air for a patter of chuckles in the room, he waits then continues.

"The engineer studies intense calculations resulting in the highest detail of this-and-that with some random coefficient to the 1/1000th of an industry classification. On the other hand, the architect has to design with all the clients' preferences in mind, as well as the proper number of fire sprinkler heads, light fixtures that meet energy-com-pliance codes, and so on."

Like an overly-confident stand-up comedian warming up his crowd who at this time are beginning to glaze over, the broad shouldered developer carries on, "so I repeat, the engineer knows 'everything about nothing,' and the architect knows 'nothing about everything'!

"And today, we are here to talk about architecture, and hopefully, our architects know a lot more than nothing." He waves his arms in the direction of the architects seated like kindergarten students awaiting roll call.

The audience members do not so much as roll in the aisles with laughter, but Magnar's ice breaker grabbed some attention. And he greatly appreciates the attention.

He then asks a question with a boom, almost like a threat, "What is a museum, people?!"

The well-suited Oklahoman enjoys answering his own question. Attempting to sound academic, he begins to preach. "Traditionally, museums are empty vessels that come to life when artwork is inserted, a neutral backdrop. Opposing this, architect Frank Gehry's 1997 Guggenheim Museum is a work of art in and of itself. Gehry created for the Spanish town of Bilbao, a design that counters the classical mute environment for art."

One audience member comments under his breath to his partner, "Is this a press conference? I didn't come here for a college lecture."

The architects look bored of all the pomp and circumstance. Instead, they're all ready to start the competition.

Magnar feels the energy course through him as he looks upon the faces of over 300 people. "In another example, when Frank Lloyd Wright completed his Guggenheim Museum for New York City in 1959, visitors were stunned. There were no defined galleries. Rather, a continuous sloping floor of exhibit areas spiraled up six stories. Complaints from curators were immediate."

Magnar offers a hand gesture indicating an upcoming side comment. "And I love this next part, people," he waits a moment, then adds, "when Wright was questioned about his museum design, he responded with indifference. The architect proclaimed that visitors have come to see art. And here, the art is *his* architecture, the building itself, not the negligible objects within!"

The audience is mildly amused but more importantly engaged, and Magnar is gripping them into his palms.

Finally, the museum developer stretches both arms out towards the crowd and boasts, "I am Magnar Jones, people! And I will deliver the greatest museum to the city of San Francisco, to the world!" He is nearly yelling, but no mention of Alcatraz, at least not yet. The bustling crowd finally make themselves heard with cheers and applause, and the man at the podium stands silently with his head down feigning modesty. In reality, Mr. Jones is soaking up as much attention as he can get, like a dry sponge in a kitchen sink full of water.

Magnar announces, "May I introduce to you the lovely Miss Celadonna Kimm, my Director of Marketing."

She approaches the podium wearing a Cerulean-blue cocktail dress more suited to an evening social event than this morning's assembly. Crisp air blows into the open rotunda from the Bay. Her bare shoulders are cold, freezing actually. But for Celadonna, one should not mind suffering when making a fashion statement. A gift from Magnar on their first date, her chunky necklace of hammered bronze keeps her neck warm, so she tells herself—which of course it doesn't.

He finally steps down from the podium but keeps one foot on the platform's edge, a territorial move. Celadonna speaks closely into the mic, almost intimately. Unlike her boyfriend, she begins with the requisite comments and welcoming soft smile.

"Thank you, Mr. Magnar Jones, for having me. My name is Celadonna Kimm, Marketing Director for the World Museum of Abstract Art. I am pleased to be here with all of you gracious citizens of the great city of San Francisco. The rumors are true: there *will* be a grand new museum, and I am thrilled to announce the six architects selected to compete for the opportunity to design this museum. And after I introduce our competitors, Mr. Jones will return to the podium to speak about the project itself. And we can't wait, can we?"

She superficially adjusts the mic for a dramatic pause.

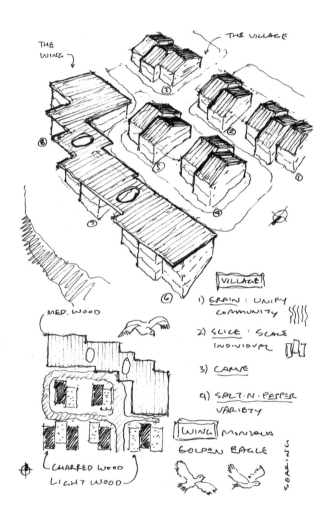

THE
WING

THE VILLAGE

MED. WOOD

VILLAGE

1) GRAIN : UNIFY COMMUNITY

2) SLICE : SCALE INDIVIDUAL

3) CARVE

4) SALT·N·PEPPER VARIETY

WING MONTANA
GOLDEN EAGLE

SOARING

(CHARRED WOOD)
LIGHT WOOD

CHAPTER 3

Meet the Competitors

"I AM EXCITED TO INTRODUCE our six world-famous architectural candidates. They have gathered here today, ready to begin their work." Another pause while she adjusts her necklace.

"First, meet the voice of Postmodernism, San Francisco's own, Parker A. Rand of PAR Designs," she says with a genial smile.

Parker and his fellow competitors now stand in front of their seats, as instructed. In his recently purchased black suit, Parker modestly raises his hand in acknowledgment of his name called, like a boy wanting his mom's acknowledgment. Well known locally, his home town roars in support. He smiles comfortably enough, but awkwardly.

"Next, I am proud to introduce the husband-wife, East Coast power couple, Chip Tooney and Ling Liang of the Boston architecture studio, ChipLing—rigorous believers in Modernism and the Bauhaus art movement." Chip is wearing a khaki suit and Ling a brown knit twin set with a predictable short string of freshwater pearls. The married couple stand hand-in-hand, more a gesture of professional solidarity than affection. They nod in unison.

"Next is the colorful Mid-Century Modernist master, Los Angeles-based, Maxwell Brand, from his company MCM Associates."

Less applause for the Southern California participant. Fashioned in his best 1960-themed attire, Maxwell Brand takes a few steps forward to separate him from the very straight line of architects and raises both arms as if already victorious.

Celadonna looks at the next contestant. "Here is British royalty, Dame Margo Hunters of the firm, Hunting Ground. With her courageous sculptural visions, she is the most established female architect in history."

Enshrouded in a dark green cape, Margo Hunters stands in the massive rotunda of the Palace of Fine Arts humbled more by the legacy of her predecessor and less so, by the empty introduction from someone in a cocktail dress. She mentally gives thanks to her fellow knighted Brit, Dame Zaha Hadid, the first female to be honored with the prestigious international Pritzker Prize, the equivalent of the Nobel Prize for architecture. Margo makes no gestures, her face unchanged.

Overall, Mr. Jones is pleased. Celadonna is doing well, using her fetching good looks and charm to hold the attention of the considerable gathering.

"And next is the internationally awarded museum expert, Johnny Furnsby, from the global corporation, General Architects, Inc."

Trying hard to look too-cool-for-school and clumsily failing, Johnny simply sort of salutes in acknowledgment. He looks like a corporate formula: a navy sport coat from a Nordstrom's sale, gray slacks, dress shirt with a striped gray and white tie.

Celadonna prepares her final introduction. "Last but not least is the world-acclaimed, uber-architect known as the Flying Dutchman, all the way from the Hague. Allow me to introduce from the design company, Office Studio, our final competitor, Lars von Meester!"

But there is no sixth architect in the line of big names and big egos. The audience look around, then at each other, then glare at Magnar for a response. Where is the final competitor?

As Celadonna looks over her frozen bare shoulder to Magnar, he's visibly pissed off. How dare someone not show for this occasion, *his* occasion? For some reason, he turns to look Parker's way.

The San Francisco architect leans his upper body forward, his expression apologetic, and speaks up to Magnar, "Lars never showed up for our breakfast meeting today. I had three cups of coffee while waiting for him."

Parker looks towards Celadonna and shrugs his shoulders. As she turns away with mild interest, he notices the top few buttons on the back of her dress are unbuttoned. Is this hasty dressing, buttons that Magnar is supposed to have fastened, or some kind of invitation? Celadonna notices that he is staring at her legs then shoulders, the exposed parts of her body. She brushes off his gaze throwing Parker a look of contempt, even as she relishes his attention.

She snaps back into presenter mode and addresses the crowd, "Sorry folks, Mr. von Meester is apparently unavailable at this time. I am sure he overslept due to the jet lag of a long flight"—a poor attempt at an excuse—"let me bring Magnar Jones back to the stand."

Ready to take the spotlight once again, Magnar says his first obligatory phrase, "Let's give a round of applause for our competitors," and the audience provides the necessary clapping. He revs himself up again with lots of energy and conceit.

"So y'all heard, right? I am going to build"—he waits a few seconds—"the World Museum of Abstract Art at *Alcatraz*! It will be the greatest museum of art in the world!" Magnar shouts.

A wave of reaction flows through the audience. They twitter and gasp as reporters jot notes and some whisper anxiously to each other. A woman in the back questions, "Did that guy just say Alcatraz, as in the dilapidated former prison on that small island?"

"The rumors are true? Alcatraz?" responds another bystander.

Without missing a beat, Magnar continues, "Most of you, locals especially, know the history of this nearby island—the federal prison, murderers and bank robbers, unknown fires, Indian occupation, tourist trap, and so on. What a transformation it would be for such a storied parcel of land to become a class-A art institution. With my personal collection of Abstract paintings and sculptures as the main ingredients, my new museum will indeed be home at the infamous Alcatraz Island. And the world will know this art institution as WoMA!"

Magnar beams, his head held high, as if at this moment, he is a rock star. He has everyone's attention. His hands are at his sides with his palms open towards the crowd, as if greeting all the attention, soaking in glory.

"And there is one big thing to point out: The six architects will work out of galleries within your SF Museum of Modern Art. Because I appreciate art, both the product and the process, the competing architects will work over four days in full public view. And people, if you choose,"—almost like a challenge—"you can watch every minute of the artistic process as it is unveiled in real time."

The amused smiles of the audience morph to perplexed stares. Some grimace as if creeped out. Comments filter through the crowd, now 400 people at least. Maybe more.

Someone utters, "Is this a professional process to find the most qualified architect, or is this a game show—or worse, a bad TV reality show?" Regardless, everyone is fascinated.

Magnar hasn't yet mentioned the hidden cameras.

He goes on to explain the logistics, "Yes, they will live at SFMOMA for four straight days. Food will be brought in from the museum restaurant, and accommodations will be provided, such as showers and beds"—makeshift beds behind the makeshift hospital-like curtain. "The architects will have full access to the 170,000-square-foot facility to be inspired by the more than 30,000 works of art.

"Four days, people." Magnar emphasizes.

"Day one: Transform your assigned gallery into your design studio. Research, due diligence, brainstorm.

"Day two: Visit Alcatraz, then sketch, come up with your Big Idea.

"Day three: Develop and refine. Test and test again.

"Day four: Finalize your work. Create your presentation. Race to the end.

"And the competition commences immediately after this press conference, when the architects arrive at SFMOMA. Everyone, thank you, and I am excited to see you all again in less than a week, where each architect will present their design to all of you. My board of directors and I will carefully judge each entry, and shortly after, announce the winning architect that will deliver to San Francisco, and the world stage, *my* new museum!"

Magnar quickly strides off, Celadonna dashing behind trying

to keep up. He never looks back to see if she is in tow. He takes no questions from the throng of hungry reporters—uninterested in anything anyone has to say. The audience is only there to hear his impressive voice.

As Celadonna chases after her man, form-fitting fashion now a liability, Parker takes a last yearning glance at her unfastened buttons revealing a soft glow.

The architects know each other, some personally, some by reputation. The handshakes are certainly the calm before the storm. They take their time to enjoy this brief moment before needing to rush over to SFMOMA. The contestants joke and jest, poke fun, even laugh as Johnny Furnsby questions, "Do you realize that with all the talent in this group, not one of us has the Pritzker Prize?"

Parker responds, "Winning this new museum could be the stepping-stone to such an accolade." The group of architects laugh nervously, because they know well, that the Pritzker is the singular top award in their business—an honor unobtainable for 99.99 percent of practicing architects.

The gestures conceal the nervousness amongst them all. Architects being sequestered? Like circus animals, being required to design in front of a large public audience? Four days—will they get any sleep or find time to eat?

The architects do their best to hide the discomfort that is slowly edging into their psyche—their professional postures crumpling as dread sets in. For this commission of their lives, these colleagues will soon transition from expert colleagues to shrewd competitors. The smiles and nods turn disingenuous, hiding one thought: Like Hollywood actors approaching their auditions, each of them would kill for the part.

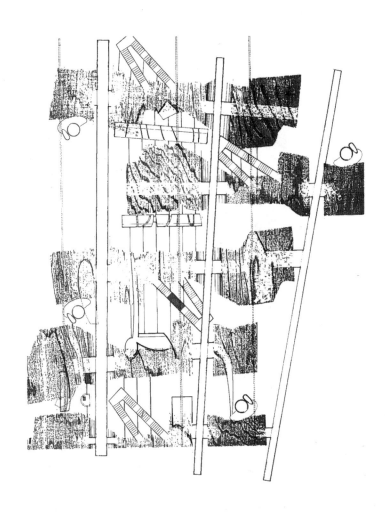

Death by Design at Alcatraz

CHAPTER 4

Sizing Up

T H E   N O O N   T I M E   S U N doesn't quite warm the brisk air from the bay waters—air that has begun to chill. The massive crowd of attendees slowly depart, while the architects stumble around awkwardly looking for an escape, or at least a repose. Some architects are momentarily frozen in place, brains overloaded with information delivered by Magnar Jones, their new client.

As Parker is about to leave the press event, he eyes his competitors, and wonders what they are thinking of this prestigious design contest—outrageous too. Opportunity and adventure vs. confrontation and exploitation? Only a short trek to SFMOMA to commence this competition, the architects mentally prepare to be sequestered for four days. Parker's shoulders tense and his eyes focus on subjects slowly coming into view.

Recently arriving from London to the San Francisco International Airport, Margo Hunters is armed with determination, the glory of more design awards than her competitors combined, and even more interesting, the knighthood from the Queen by Royal Victorian Order. Only a handful of architects have ever been knighted, and she prides herself, Dame Margo Hunters.

Parker knows of this woman by reputation, for better or worse. She has been called an irritating quasi-intellectual. In the middle of an interview once, Margo launched into a reading of an essay from the *Harvard Design* magazine. She spewed, "Unlike architecture that seeks to articulate understandings about the nature of things through expressive or metaphoric mimings, this remarkable building yields us actionable space." No one knew what the heck she was talking about, but her conviction was convincing.

Tall and imposing, Margo towers with presence. Her British stiffness might categorize her as sexually unattractive, but her classic features and white skin, that no sun had ever touched, does make her striking.

People call her "hard" as in a "tough cookie." What this meant is that no one would ever catch Margo petting a dog, holding a baby, or smelling flowers. Like her aversion to lipstick and eye shadow, this renowned architect has no interest in such saccharine antics.

She stands confident that she possesses the design chops to run circles around the two California architects standing nearby, Parker A. Rand and Maxwell Brand. She observes how both are stuck in the past—one with 1980s Postmodernism, and the other, 1950s Mid-Century Modernism. Margo finds the married couple, Chip Tooney and Ling Liang, irritating and fixated upon their righteous dogmatic Bauhaus teachings. And the corporate architect? Johnny Furnsby is formulaic—representing nothing new, nothing more than boring big firm design clichés.

She believes that her only competition is the Dutch genius, Lars von Meester, and she takes delight in hearing that the Flying Dutchman was a no-show. How convenient, she thinks, breathing a temporary sigh of relief. A sigh of guilt too.

Different than Margo's assessment, Parker wonders if Johnny Furnsby is the one to beat. This Chicago architect and his monstrous IBM-like company, General Architects, Inc., has completed more museums around the world than any other architect—within the WoMA competitors and beyond as well.

A company man, Johnny is the product of American corporate culture. Short and stout, he possesses a body type that is on the razor's edge between being adorably huggable vs. simply overweight. He tries to conceal his unfortunate belly by not tucking in his designer dress shirts, which ends up not youthful and hip, but sloppy and unprofessional.

Johnny doesn't just leave the event towards his parked car, but rather, sort of saunters, though with an unconvincing swagger. It is the kind of movement of someone trying too hard—trying to be "too cool for school."

Some critics have called Johnny's architectural ideas "passable" or "obvious and predictable based on the company's corporate success formulas." But Parker is more keen, aware that a lot of factors will play into winning Magnar's prized project. Johnny taps into the developer's business side who appreciates the proven methods of conventional construction and working "on time and on budget." Such selling points of expertise and experience, as banal as they might seem, resound in Magnar's ears of practicality. Johnny believes that for himself and the others, this competition will be untested ground, a struggle to design a complex building on a complex site, whereas Johnny handles similar challenges on a weekly basis.

His work though has been accused of repetition—of being "all the same." Parker has heard Johnny's defense several times, "Is sameness such a bad thing? Most of The Beatles songs sound similar—with those peppy lyrics and obvious chord progressions? So too does much of Stravinsky's music, with his mishmash of beauty and rage. Warhol, Picasso, all of them—each pursued a lifelong expression that resulted in a vision that one might wrongly dismiss as being all the same."

Johnny is sure footed with his resume, but to Parker's eyes, Johnny's stiff corporate-y demeanor laced with too much self-assurance makes him more of a jerk than a respected industry professional. Parker is not intimidated, but cautious.

Parker overhears husband-wife, Chip Tooney and Ling Lang, already launching into an intellectual debate, bubbling with cerebral delight. Chip references Magnar's opening line. "'What is a museum?' Magnar got it right. It's almost like a challenge, dear."

Ling responds only with a question, as is her way, "What is the inter-relationship between art, its expressive representation in current society and politics, and the human condition over time?"

Chip shrugs, opens his eyes wide, and asks, also in his way, "Can architecture portray the critical discourse between the art, the artist, and the audience, as well the aesthetic phenomenon of formalism vs. paradigmatic anti-essentialist theory?"

Parker cringes, chuckles a little too, at the pomposity of these two self-absorbed, Ivy League-trained architects. He grins as he notices the absence of physical affection between the married pair. Parker wonders if their academic debates and scholarly activities have supplanted the romance of marriage.

Chip and Ling approach all their work with rational and rigorous thought—possibly overly rational. Unlike the arbitrary and personal, yet stunning buildings of Los Angeles' Frank Gehry, historic work of Barcelona's Antoni Gaudi, or Alcatraz competitor Margo Hunters, the married couple's explorations are taut, reductive, and edited down for efficiency, as their Harvard education preached. Parker visualizes the impressive projects of Chip and Ling: spare rectilinear forms, large expanses of concrete and glass surfaces.

Ling states softly to Chip, "truth to materials," and Parker reacts, *So cliché, that prevailing tenet of hardcore Modernism.*

Ling stops Chip in stride and says, "Our approach has to conceptually clear, dear, and not fall into stylistic trappings of someone like that Parker A. Rand." Maybe they noticed that Parker is nonchalantly listening.

Slightly bothered by this slight, Parker's eyes squint as he tries to overhear the last bit, but their voices begin to drift away as they retreat towards the parking lot. Fading commentary, Ling says, "…remember our teachings…'Ornament is a crime'…" Parker knows this one: Adolf Loos, the Austrian architect of the early 1900s.

Last to leave to SFMOMA, Maxwell Brand gives a warm gesture to Parker—an arm stretched out vertically and waving vigorously side to side, as if conducting the landing of an airplane. Maxwell yells out, "Good luck to us Californians."

Wincing, Parker doesn't really see the two of them as colleagues from the same state. One state yes, but there is a severe divide between his Northern California and Maxwell's Southern California. Not just climate such as fog vs. sunshine, but culture too, lifestyle, tastes, etc.—and the cars. *Why the hell are there so many cars in Los Angeles? The traffic and the freeways, what the heck*, Parker wonders as he watches the remaining audience dissipate towards public transportation, their bikes and scooters, and even an intentional walk back to the office.

With bright whites, Maxwell Brand presents a constant wide smile to Parker. Maxwell's ruddy-brown wavy locks sweep across his forehead like an advertisement for the ocean he surfs every morning in Los Angeles. He doesn't believe that a "six-pack" abdomen is hereditary; so each day includes a mandatory gym visit—free weights, rowing machine, bench press, all of it. Maxwell's bright eyes soften the resulting broad shoulders and square jaw line. This may all sound superficial in his sunny town of superficiality, but for Maxwell, it is a lifestyle of existence. With a contagious cheeriness, he actually glides away across the lawn, not merely taking conventional footsteps.

Parker has heard Maxwell once say in an interview, "Looking good is part vanity and part feeling good about one's self," which is sort of the same thing.

Maxwell's trepidation around this upcoming contest is calmed by his easy-going attitude, one that draws calm from a common sentiment heard at the Academy Awards in Los Angeles. The Oscar-nominated actor claims as convincingly as he can, "I am just honored to be nominated." Desperate to beat the competition, the phrase is almost sarcasm.

Maxwell behaves similarly on the surface, one hand always casually draped into a pant pocket. But his graciousness doesn't bring him comfort. For all his success in renovating Mid-Century Modern masterpieces around the country, from homes to city halls, he knows the achievements are merely a design niche, though a profitable one. But a reputation of impeccable and historical taste and style can only propel an architect so far. What about intellectual capacity, original thinking, credentials, international honors? Or what about a curriculum vitae like Johnny Furnsby's?

Parker wonders, *How did Maxwell get here, invited to an exclusive competition with such prestigious colleagues? Well, how did I get here after all my shortcomings?*

With Maxwell's high energy level, the Los Angeles architect thinks little of working for four straight days and nights. He is up for the challenge, physical and psychological. But even so, the odds are certainly against him. Though in every challenge and opportunity, Maxwell Brand has been resourceful, sustained by a passive shrewdness that only a few have witnessed.

Parker unenthusiastically waves back a final farewell to his regional colleague. Parker awaits some warmth from the noon sun as it peacefully breaks through the lake mist and the skeletal branches of ancient trees. He realizes that Magnar has in mind the spirit of the famed ambitious school presentations, of which Parker is all too familiar: the *crits*.

Such presentations are made public—to fellow students, teachers, guests, and any and all members of the university community, invited or not. Crits include open judgment from a jury of academics and prestigious professionals, classmates too.

Parker teaches at the nearby university and for his students, as well as the WoMA competitors, these crits are guaranteed public spectacles. Stars are made in this venue, and others go down in flames, as if trapped in a burning building. This kind of presentation and review of one's work is an open forum of theatrics, melodrama, and catharsis. In preparation for her crit, the designer might not have slept for days, subsisting only on a diet of cigarettes, coffee, and sugar.

For design presentations, students and professionals alike begin with, "My project is about—." This "about" is the Big Idea, and this so-called Big Idea has to be intriguing, articulate, and convincing—and sometimes embellished with an air of highbrow bullshit. Young and old, beginners and veterans, know that not only is the Big Idea important, but it also has to lead to worthwhile design results. The teacher or client, in this case Magnar, might be heard judging and then proclaiming, "Your idea is excellent, but unfortunately your execution is underwhelming. Strong yet sad."

To his college students, professor Rand offers a warning, "Architects work in the eye of the public, the community at large. Your completed buildings could stand for decades, even generations. Your designs hopefully take in praise, but just in case, you must be able to deflect, as best you can, any criticism. Architects, beware: some criticism have cut careers short—stopped a professional rise in its track."

What he does not state is that such criticism, whether from colleagues, clients, or general members of the community, can—and does—wound even this articulate teacher. But judgment and disapproval aside, it is Parker's overwhelming ambition coupled with self-criticism that has scarred his spirit.

All the WoMA competitors are conscious of their schooling, crits, and juries. Such academics, or call it antics, prepared them for a life of being judged. There will always be a random critic that might argue, "Your design is only somewhat interesting."

Architecture takes not only tenacity and a very thick skin, but it requires courage. The architects invited to this big competition have come with bravery to face the unknown and the conviction to win.

Victory no matter the consequences.

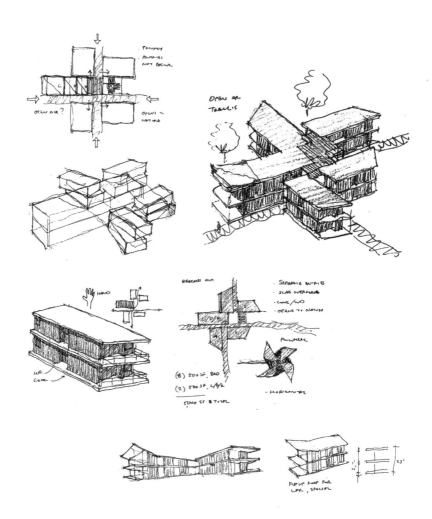

CHAPTER 5

Sign Here and Enter to Win

A S THE DRIVER SHUTS the car door for Magnar Jones and Celadonna Kimm, the contrast is stark. They leave behind the exterior of his black luxury car with black windows and black trim, no chrome, no other hues, and the self-satisfied couple now sit within the privacy of the automobile's stark white-leather interior. He enjoys hearing the click when the door closes firmly—a sound indicating that he can tune out the bothersome static of the outside world.

He convinces himself that it is only in private that he subtly pats himself on the back, stroking his immense ego. This is not true, something Celadonna wisely keeps to herself.

Magnar begins, "That was fantastic. I was fantastic, a booming success, even if I say so myself. Did you see, Cela? The crowd really loved me, my project, the competition, everything. I found the perfect spot for it: The Palace of Fine Arts. Such a gorgeous setting. Genius."

Celadonna says nothing.

He doesn't stop. "Did you see how the public welcomed me, en-joyed my ice-breaker, paid attention to my astute observations about museums, basked in my—" Of course, Magnar makes no mention of her participation, and continues to speak as if not even needing a breath, or even needing to have a listener next to him. His own voice amplified within the confines of a car fuels his vanity.

Celadonna knows her place, her role in this scenario. It is not today for her to upset the status quo. There are times she is actually entertained by hearing him speak endlessly and doesn't mind indulging his desperate need for glory. Other times, she simply holds an unblinking smirk and allows her mind to drift towards cursory items, i.e.: where to eat tonight, what to wear, wine selection, etc. She has also learned when and how to gently interrupt his upward spiral of narcissism.

"Mag, dear, why this design competition? Why not just hire the architect that you like best?" she asks sincerely, but also aware that she is edging him on. She finds it fun to do so.

With this interruption, only a second expires before his mouth is off and running again. "Good question, my sweet," he addresses her condescendingly. "Of course, I can hire any architect in the world. They would all kill to work on a 'Magnar Jones Production.'"

She doesn't blink. She has never heard that phrase before. He makes up self-centered labels all the time, and she doesn't care enough to comment.

He says, "For many architects, the design competition borders on ritualistic. One can enter such a contest as a budding professional with the hopes of winning big and jumpstarting a career—as Parker A. Rand did successfully right after college graduation with that library competition.

"Or, a seasoned architect can try his hand at a competition in later years hoping to advance a slow design business. But, my thinking here is that if you haven't broken through the riff raff of mediocrity after your first years of effort, you are probably destined to exist sadly in the margins."

Celadonna has no interest in interjecting that there are plenty of architects that blossomed late. I.M. Pei designed the world-famous glass pyramid at the Louvre Museum in Paris when he was 71.

Magnar continues, "For me as the client, the spirit of the competition, the hope of winning—desperation too—bring out the most stupendous of design ideas from which I can choose. Let me tell you, Cela darling, most architects are optimistic even naïve, too driven by determination. I don't mind tapping into that—fine, taking advantage of it. I enjoy establishing architectural competitions and watching the designers duke it out, vying for my attention."

"But you don't pay them anything to participate?" She finally finds an opportunity to chime in. Here, she does aim to learn—just not be his devoted follower. She has ambitions of her own though none she'd share with him. Her agenda remains mute for now.

"Lesser competition organizers will give a small monetary stipend for the architects to participate, but I don't have that need. It would be an honor for any architect to compete for my projects. I bet that some architects would even pay me for the opportunity. Besides, I am not forcing anyone to compete. If they don't want to play my game, if they don't want to submit free designs, that's fine by me. But then they have already lost, having walked away from winning one of my big commissions."

Shifting gears, he pontificates as he often does, "Most history fans know the improbable and inspirational story of Maya Lin." Celadonna has heard him tell this story numerous times. Yet, she allows him to perform once more, demonstrating his tokens of knowledge.

"At merely 21, a college senior at Yale University, Miss Lin beat out an expansive field of international architects to take home the Washington D.C. commission for the Vietnam Veterans Memorial. Can you believe she went from a nobody student to designing one of the most celebrated architectural monuments, which the American Institute of Architects has on their list of *America's Favorite Architecture?*"

She tries to shift Magnar's stream of consciousness. Having assembled the list of WoMA competitors, she comments, "You know, our Los Angeles architect, Maxwell Brand, once organized a local contest at UCLA."

"Oh yeah,"—Magnar barely feigns interest—"tell me about it, my dear."

"Brand's competition was really great. He asked any interested students to design a bird house in the style of their favorite building, like Frank Lloyd Wright's Falling Water or the Great Pyramid of Giza."

"Very cute. Open competitions or school contests are for fools. Architects like that Chicago-based Johnny Furnsby or our big talking Lars von Meester are so confident of their design swagger, but they were stupid to enter the open competition for the 9/11 Memorial in New York. Did you know that 14,000 hopeful designers yearned to be sole winner? This means there were 13,999 losers which included Furnsby and von Meester!"

She can't stop his outpour now, and he continues, "What I am doing is an exclusive invited competition, not open to just anyone. Also, my Alcatraz competition is not one of those silly 'idea competitions,' where some wannabe thought leader is looking to receive design concepts, but regrettably has no money, land, or support—no fortitude to bring the winning idea into reality.

"My WoMA funding is in hand, I possess the island, and I have community consensus. And for our six architects, I am generous: I have reduced their odds from 1 in 10,000 to a more favorable 1 in 6. This is the kind of event that architects beg to be invited to, the stage where architects want to perform—my great stage!"

He's on a roll. "And these architects are such characters, each and every one of them. Did you see Rand's cheap suit? And his shoes. Cheap. And he seems to have no backbone, slouching around at my big event."

She wants to defend this architect, arguing that the garment in question is of decent quality, but he continues to rant, "And the married architects—they look like a perfectly matching, creepy couple from the pages of a J. Crew catalogue. I admire their talent, but Chip and Ling are so predictably Ivy League, so Boston stuffy. Ever wonder what their blissful homelife is like? Probably ice-y intellectual arguments.

"Then there is Maxwell Brand who looks like he just walked off the set of *Mad Men*. I don't know whether this is supposed to be authentic or ironic. His plaid sport coat—applaud or laugh? His big grin makes me nervous too."

It appears that Magnar doesn't need to inhale any oxygen as he continues his stream of evaluations—his face flushing redder with each assessment.

"And Margo Hunters? Established and famous, yes, but why dress like a Halloween witch scaring the families at the Palace of Fine Arts? Does she carry a broom?

"Heeeere's Johnny! A corporate monkey who learned to put on a blazer and polish his wingtips. He reminds me of the high school nerds from the math team, that I happily enjoyed shoving into the lockers. His tie was so poorly knotted, a clip-on tie might have been a better choice. Such a stiff, probably needs to get laid..."

Celadonna wonders if her boyfriend will ever stop talking. But she holds that perfect Mona Lisa smirk.

She's already thinking about the contest logistics, social media, and even a possible producer for the whole affair. After all, it's almost like a made-for-TV reality show. This will be fun. Wicked fun. And her biggest gig to date. The competition could make her famous and launch the next stage of her career, with or without Magnar.

Her personal prestige aside for just a moment, she appreciates soaking up the vibes and energy of creative people. For her, Parker A. Rand exudes a quiet cool, and she's heard that Lars is quite the outrageous self-assured character. The other architects intrigue her, too: the brainy prowess of Chip and Ling, the colorful style of Maxwell, Margo's headstrong determination, even Johnny's dorkiness.

Arriving at his penthouse, Magnar's mind turns to the one blemish on his otherwise spectacular event today: Lars von Meester is missing.

Magnar's posture stands defiantly, his face knotting with anger—he demands of Celadonna, "Find out where that idiot Dutchman is. I want his head served to me on a platter."

A sunshiny morning, no longer lost to inexplicable fog. Earlier this day at the construction site of Lands End, mere hours before the start of the press conference, the crew was hustling, bustling even, but not on the project itself. At the edge of the cliff, electricians and carpenters took pictures of the waters 200 feet below. But inadequate photos resulted, as their limbs shook with fright. Even the machismo of construction workers could be pierced by a dreadful sight—a spectacle not typically associated with laying bricks and installing windows.

A dead body floated on the surface of the ocean. The limp corpse hovered like a superhero, sort of flying with its black three-quarter length jacket spread in a triangular shape, like a cape. The arms aimed forward—a crusader soaring. But this morning, there were no superheroes, just a deceased architect named Lars von Meester, the Flying Dutchman.

The construction crowd grew quickly at the end of the land. Workers pushed aggressively forward to get a glance at the departed. Voices yelled out, "Stop pushing! Stay back! Calm down!"

Such desperate requests were not out of respect for the lifeless European architect, but rather for the workers at the front peering over the edge of the cliff. They worried for their own safety as a large crowd shoved forward, some with toolbox in hand and others copper pipes and two by fours.

Breaking off from the construction herd, a small group of workers drove down the side road that wrapped the hillside arriving at the coastline, where the land's end met the ocean's beginning. The police already called, but this crew was eager, as if performing a critical rescue during a construction accident. Armed with cables and grappling hooks, they attempted to retrieve the body.

The scene was both morbid as it was surreal. Surreal because the workers looked like the fishermen of San Francisco's wharfs casting a net into the sea, hoping to catch something. Morbid because the workers didn't actually want to hook flesh.

Success finally, if you can call it that. Half a dozen men kitted out in construction gear nabbed their big fish. They pulled the prize to shore, brought the perished body in. One would think the 190-pound corpse would not be a challenge for the sturdy men. But the architect's clothing had soaked up a small portion of the ocean—his insides have as well. Seaweed and various forms of marine algae had wrapped themselves around the Flying Dutchman's limbs and neck, and disturbingly came out of his mouth—as if stopping a verbose architect from talking too much.

Glistening in the morning sun, the lifeless figure appeared to be coated in glossy black lacquer. One worker recognized the carcass. "We know this guy. Isn't this the architect, the dude from Amsterdam or Belgium or wherever? That's Lars von Meester."

"Didn't people called him the Flying Dutchman?" asked the electrician.

"Yeah, uuh, I guess he is no longer 'flying.' Should we refer to him as the Falling Dutchman?" Mostly silence, punctuated with a couple inappropriate snickers. Most of the guys were simply stunned, staring at an unnerving composition of a stiff white corpse, soaked black clothing, and seaweed. Lots of seaweed.

Unfortunately, the zealous worker tried one more time desperately for attention, which is doomed on delivery, "Let's just go with the Dead Dutchman."

More silence.

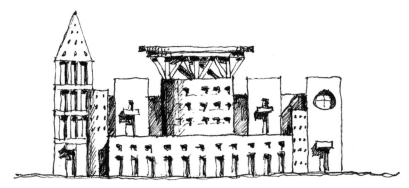

"PO-MO"
POST· MODERNISM

MICHAEL GRAVES
DENVER CENTRAL LIBRARY, 1996

CHAPTER 6

The Local Hero: Parker A. Rand

I T WAS A PREDICTABLE, tongue-in-cheek question. "Hey Parker, what does the "A" stand for in your name? Ayn, as in Ayn Rand?"

He is tired of hearing this question, and each time, the inquirer believed the comment was clever and original.

Parker A. Rand responded, "Oh, I don't know. Maybe architect, artist, author?"

His Hawaiian mother gave Parker the family name, Ano. But he felt that "Parker Ano Rand" was unpleasing to the ear. Also, a straightforward "Parker Rand" didn't work for him either, because of his interests with the multi-layered names of famous architects: Frank Lloyd Wright of course, Robert A.M. Stern, Eric Owen Moss, I.M. Pei, Mies Van der Rohe, Charles-Édouard Jeanneret, or even Leonardo da Vinci. And so this San Francisco architect constructed "Parker A. Rand."

Aware of references to author Ayn Rand, he was no disciple of the seminal book, *The Fountainhead.* In this 1943 architectural novel, the author presented the fictional Howard Roark, an individualistic architect whose extraordinary modern designs were never accepted by society. With uncompromising spirit, Roark lived an epic tortured existence of righteousness, sex, and conflict. A must-read for students of architecture, the story served as both inspiration and disdain—activist philosophy and campy pop culture.

Though entrepreneurial and keenly intelligent, Parker A. Rand constantly questioned the purpose of his talents and even his existence, *Will I succeed as an architect?*

Yet he already has several award-winning projects under his belt. He was not absent of ego and pride though. His mom attributed both his healthy confidence and severe anxieties to having read *The Fountainhead* as a child.

Parker knew something was not right—that he was not comfortable in his own skin. His boyish good looks entices friends to joke that he resembled actor Keanu Reeves who played an architect in the 2006 film, *The Lake House*. Parker brushed off such absurd comments, not even offering a conciliatory chuckle.

A sensitive-thinker always carrying a personable smile, he attended the University of California Berkeley, one of the few West Coast architecture schools that rivals the East Coast elite. He obtained an integrated education as was the institution's intent: architecture, art, history, and philosophy. To this ambitious list, he added an additional passion: piano. A proficient pianist in his college days, Parker composed cheesy love ballads to woo one fellow classmate. His first attempt at song writing resulted in a sweet but corny, Barry Manilow-influenced tune, which he meekly performed for his college crush, Adrienne Veley.

Adrienne walked on air. She had an ease about her as if her life would always be great. She likened her short red hair to a metropolitan 1920s flapper style. Though rock band T-shirts and needed-to-be-laundered sweatpants were the college norm, her staple was long gray designer dresses, afforded by the spoils of her international banking father. Money got her not just what she needed, but what she desired.

Unfortunately, Parker's cooing melody won no romantic dates with Adrienne. But the endeavor was not entirely disappointing, and the two started a dialogue of a hypothetical future to be called, *Rand Veley Architects.* This short-lived discussion was more a fantasy of a wishful young man than a serious business plan of two soon-to-be professionals.

After graduation, college dreams faded quickly, and they lost touch. Parker launched his solo career path in downtown San Francisco, and

Adrienne was last rumored to be engaged to an ironic jazz musician who called himself, Diles Mavis.

In the bustling South of Market district, a young Parker opened a boutique studio, named PAR Designs—signing a lease for a warehouse space off an alley, off another alley. Feeling at home in a gritty loft not unlike the bare bones studios at Berkeley's Wurster Hall, he appreciated his exposed brick walls, wood bow string trusses, and polished concrete floors. He filled the office with the obligatory drafting tables, lamps, and stools, as well as computer monitors. The industrial space full of rolls of drawings and large-scale cardboard models possessed a romanticized feel of artistic cool. His neighbors provided the city vibe: liquor store, tattoo parlor, and tire shop. The nearby wine and cheese store signaled impending gentrification.

The local media always loved Parker, due partly to his affable nature, but mostly to his eagerness to make himself available for interviews. He was often asked, as are many architects, "What is your style?" The press attempted to capture one's design philosophy in a sound bite.

Parker responded, "Many interior designers have packaged meaningless responses, like 'eclectic,' 'warm and welcoming,' or 'contemporary yet timeless.' But style should not be an elevator pitch. Some of my colleagues have invented clever labels for their work, but I question that too. For example, Steven Ehrlich, based in Los Angeles, calls his work 'Regional Modernism.' New Mexico architect Predock is a self-described 'Cosmic Modernist.' Herzog & de Meuron of Switzerland have been coined, 'Elemental Reductivists.' From New York, Steven Holl's work involves 'typology, phenomenology and existentialism.' The list of fancy taglines are endless, even to include our city's prominent developer, Magnar Jones, who loves the work of the 'Post War Abstract Expressionist' or 'Nonrepresentational Nonobjective' artists."

Parker continues, "When I think of style, I think more of process than product. For example, why not apply jazz concepts, like spontaneity and improvisation, to the architectural process?

"I also love wit, puns, irony, and humor." He thought of how his name is synonymous with the great jazz saxophonist, Charlie Parker.

As university faculty at Berkeley, professor Rand applied the script of one of his lectures to the interviewer's question. "Historians refer to the art movement of the 1970s and 80s as Postmodernism. This movement posits the notion that good architecture should provide human scale, harmony and beauty. Sounds obvious, right? If so, why do cities contain so many cold, white, boxy buildings that lack life and any sense of community?

"Through the teachings of Postmodern architects, we understand that one approach to making a building inviting is applying classical architecture, such as a Greek column or a Renaissance arch—but in a new and fresh way.

"We call it Po-Mo, and such practitioners go even a step further by infusing joy and charm. I personally love to add vibrant colors to my buildings, make columns extra tall or extra fat, or even re-interpret a classical pediment as a simple triangle. Postmodernists love to inject clever metaphors and visual cues to make one smile when seeing a building."

Parker enjoyed architecture as something energetic, colorful, and friendly, not icy steel and glass structures. Whether he called his style Postmodern or not, he tried to avoid labeling his stylistic interests. Truth be told, he dodged labels for fear of being proven wrong. A failure to one's manifesto.

He was thrilled to be invited to Magnar's competition, though apprehensions plagued him. He ponders, *Am I ready to compete for such an opportunity? What if I fail?*

This self-doubting architect challenged himself to envision a friendly Postmodern building that would refute the grave tales of Alcatraz Island. But he had an additional worry, a burden actually.

As a California architect, he could not ignore the fact that significant museums in his state had been designed by out-of-state architects. Parker was disgusted by a growing list: SFMOMA and the

DeYoung Museum designed by Swiss architects; LACMA, The Broad, Getty Center, and the Peterson Automotive Museum, all by New York companies; MOCA by Japanese Isozaki; Academy Museum of Motion Pictures and the California Academy of Sciences, both buildings by Italy's Renzo Piano; and the Pavilion for Japanese Art by Oklahoman Bruce Goff. No major Californian museums are from California architects, or even the West Coast.

Parker was determined that a regional architect should design this new museum. He was cursed with the righteous and territorial belief that he represented something far greater than his own wish to further his career.

For this anxious man, proving the values of Postmodernism or advocating local architects were only two of the many crusades on his daily to-do lists. His thoughts cycled often and ridiculously so, like a cyclist frantically pedaling up Nob Hill in first gear. Despite the fast rotations of pedals and gears, the bike barely moved forward at all. Battling his demons, he wondered each day if he is going silently insane. *Is every artistic mind and creative soul haunted?*

Author Rand described her philosophy of Objectivism as "the concept of man as a heroic being…with productive achievement as his noblest activity, and reason as his only absolute."

Perhaps, the ghost of Howard Roark, Ayn Rand's fictional hero, influenced Parker more than he knows, and the ends could justify the means. Succeed at all costs

For Parker A. Rand, architecture was for those that believe it was still an honorable field, that the design of a community center could enliven a neighborhood, a great office building could make citizens more productive, and a new museum could grace the world with the beauty of art. But at what cost to one's character and soul? What was the price paid, not in dollars, but in the currency of sanity?

LANDS END
POINT LOBOS, GOLDEN GATE

CHAPTER 7

Day One of Four: Master of the Universe

O UT OF OVERWHELMING BOREDOM, Magnar Jones walks out of one his perfunctory board meetings. Having delivered Celadonna to his penthouse after the press conference, he arrives at his headquarters in the city's Financial District. The usual course of action for Magnar: conduct executive business by making his staff feel small. As he views it, he was forced to assemble a group of useless—mindless actually—individuals, only to comply with business regulations and articles of incorporation.

"You have to form a board of directors…you need a group of advisors…like-minded…fiscal responsibility…" harped Magnar's legal advisors and colleagues.

He couldn't care less, but he conforms mostly for his entertainment—to have an audience for his onslaught of commentary about the failures of big business in America. Magnar leaves behind his board-of-whatevers in his walnut and marble conference room situated on the top floor of the Salesforce Tower. As the tallest building in the city standing over 1,000 feet high, he delights in knowing that whenever he gets impatient with corporate escapades, he is only one flight of stairs from his helipad above—a convenient escape for a man easily bored by his surroundings, an escape into the limitless skies.

A no-name assistant races up to Magnar—no name because he makes no effort to learn the names of any employees. The young man in a wrinkled dress shirt and overworn tie, out of breath, pale in the face, says, "Mr. Jones, boss, sir…"

"What?" he snaps, forehead clearly perturbed.

"Well, I just heard…" the assistant starts to shrink, visibly trembles, quivers even.

"Spit it out, man!"

"Lars von Meester is…is dead." This messenger is not shot.

Magnar storms away to find seclusion in the privacy of his office suite. He shouts a silent scream at the panels of tempered glass that separate him from the panoramic view of a city surrounded by the water, as well as a dramatic fall 61 floors down. How could this man die now, when all eyes should be on Magnar's museum competition?

He is not saddened or even taken aback by the news. As narcissism extinguishes any empathy, Magnar only thinks of himself and the increased publicity for his architectural contest. He worries that he might lose some of the spotlight but realizes it would be only temporary. The news of this architect's passing on the heels of his press conference may overshadow the launch of Magnar's project, but he appears more focused on his next chess move, than any remote form of mourning. The competition gets a black eye before it even begins, but he doesn't see it that way.

Grabbing the remote control, he urgently turns on his television, and six wall-mounted monitors, three stacked on three, illuminate at once—a practical installation of technology for a man needing to be in touch with data and information from around the globe. After irritably surfing a few channels, he finds a local station reporting the unfortunate turn of events.

The assistant is correct. The information is true: one dead architect.

The news displays images of police at Lands End, trying to instill order to a scene of chaos and tragedy. Detectives and coroners are arriving, and the police commissioner is preparing to make a brief statement while the news reporter vamps.

Like an infant to a shiny object, Magnar is briefly distracted by the upper right monitor flashing stock exchange updates in bright colors and pulsating lights.

Back to the local news. With the endless horizon of the Pacific Ocean as his backdrop, the commissioner speaks, yet Magnar's distracted attention only hears snippets, "...the discovered body identified as Lars von Meester, having arrived this morning from Europe...we don't know much yet...small rips at the tails of von Meester's jacket... coroners are on their way to examine compact bruises on the chest, maybe from jabs or kicks, scratches to the face as well..."

"Oh, c'mon, man!" Magnar screams at his monitors, as if awaiting the TV to speak back. Shaking his fists in frustration, he continues his one-way dialogue, "The reporter just mentioned that my architect fell a sheer drop over 150 feet into the ocean from the rocky cliff above. Straight into the water? Could the body have bounced off rocks on the way down causing some injuries?"

His haphazard deduction is cut short as the commissioner continues his not-so-definitive statement. "We are studying the footprints in the dirt and construction debris. At this time, we cannot state how the death occurred, accident or homicide. There are signs of a brawl, but that is as much as we can hypothesize this afternoon."

The reporter, clearly overwhelmed as she shakes in the afternoon breeze, trying to arrive at a professional appearing stance, returns on screen to introduce one of the coroners.

This official states with a stern professional look in his eyes, "We can't make any final conclusions right now. A report will be provided to the commissioner as soon as we can. The face of the corpse"—he says "corpse" so matter of fact—"appears to have been scratched in a multidirectional pattern. It is unlikely to be from the rocks, ocean waves, or algae. More like the paw of a large cat, but I can't really say any more at this point."

Bent over his executive desk in frustration, arms supporting his upper body, Magnar inexplicably blurts out to the faces on television—the commissioner, police, coroner, reporter, "The footprints should say a lot—the bruises, scratches, torn clothing. I think this unfortunate man was pushed to his death!" And again, this time as a lingering whisper, "Pushed to his death."

Magnar pretends that his conclusion reverberates through the surrounding crowd of construction workers, police, media, and growing nearby bystanders. The phrase sounds through Magnar's head, where it can't be unheard.

He flips through a few stations to obtain additional pieces of information, desperately grasping at the straws that will inform his next maneuver. The local newscasters are not conclusive, nor was the statement from the police commissioner, but it is enough for Magnar—enough for him to stroll calmly out of his office looking upwards. As if with X-ray vision, he gazes through the ceiling a glimpse of his helicopter escape, standing by to take him away.

Yellow crime scene tape cordons off a perimeter at the cliff's edge. The highlighter yellow contrasts with the gray hues of concrete, nails, and trash. One investigator finishes the safety border anchoring one end of the tape around a temporary power pole. To ensure all is secure, he pulls the rope-like tape tightly around the pole, like the seaweed wrapping around the neck of a dead Lars von Meester.

ALCATRAZ ISLAND

1850-1934 MILITARY PRISON AND
           CIVIL WAR FORTRESS
1934-1963 FEDERAL PENITENIARY
1964-1969 BIRD SANCTUARY
1969-1971 AMERICAN INDIAN OCCUPATION

CHAPTER 8

Alcatraz Island:
Battle Ground

T H E MEETING WAS BRIEF, but crucial. Months prior to Magnar Jones's event at the Palace of the Fine Arts, he invited Parker A. Rand to coffee. In part, he was being auditioned, but the developer also wanted valuable insights from a local architect.

Though the setting was non-descript, some Starbucks in the Financial District, the developer arrived meticulously dressed as if greeting Wall Street power brokers. Celadonna in tow.

Immediately, Parker disliked the superficial charisma of this loud, fast-talking Oklahoman. The architect thought of novelist and architectural critic, Thomas Wolfe, and his "Masters of the Universe"—a satirical persona that represented influence and self-importance. But Parker did not laugh at this caricature in front of him. Instead, he presented a professional and gracious face appropriate for a potential client.

Parker was well aware of the importance of this meeting, aware that a cup of coffee could be an opportunity for great things. He told himself this over and over, so to not be distracted by the captivating woman who had seated herself near him—perhaps too closely near him.

With no cordial greeting or handshake, Magnar started as if already in mid-sentence: "—this city, full of tourist attractions: Golden Gate Bridge, Coit Tower, Chinatown, Fort Point, Fishermen's Wharf, the Cannery, Lombard Street, and so on. The list is endless for such a small town surrounded on three sides by water."

"Interesting observation, Mr. Jones," Parkers responded plainly, shifting his weight uncomfortably. "Where are you going with this?" feeling his home town slighted. Parker was proud of his San Francisco. To this native, the city was much more than a collection of tourist attractions.

"Fishermen's Wharf used to be an actual operating dock and is now a tourist attraction of shops and food. The cable cars used to be an actual means of commuting. Now a tourist attraction moving up and down the steep hills. Fort Point used to be an actual military base. Now a tourist attraction with guided tours at the hour on the hour. The Cannery used to actually have canning operations. Now a tourist attraction of, well—you get my point."

"Sort of, but not really."

"This city of yours used to be a place of greatness, of heritage."

"Still is."

"No!"

"Again, Mr. Jones, respectfully, what are you getting at?" Parker questioned impatiently, defensively, arms twitching.

"Here's my point, Parker: San Francisco used to be an actual city. Now it is just a massive tourist attraction—a theme park called 'The City'!"

Parker doesn't care where this diatribe was going. He noticed that the woman, during this entire banter, has remained still like a translucent wax figure. The glint in her eyes indicated she appreciated her man's bold declarations, wrong or right. The half-smile she offered Parker suggested that he was not much more than a newly adopted puppy for this powerful promoter.

Magnar said, "As you may have heard through the grapevine, I am seeking an architect to design a new museum for this town. I want it to be magnificent—like nothing ever built before in the world. I want this new arts campus to be a beacon of evolution, of transformation—a project that breaks from the pattern of yet another empty-headed tourist trap."

"Exciting. I am thrilled," was all Parker could muster at the moment. Deep down, he was already envisioning the prestige of personally designing such a museum.

"But here's the thing: where?" Magnar enquired. "Where in this precious city do I place my museum? What location in this ironically beautiful town would be unexpected—a catalyst maybe, literally earth-shattering?"

Parker realized the significance of this question. He pondered, *Where indeed? Should a museum be an iconic structure on top of a hill or a stimulus for downtown development? Is the location to be near a university or in a rundown neighborhood as urban renewal? What can I say to impress this potential client? I don't know. What am I doing here? Who is she?*

"Tell me, Mr. Parker A. Rand"—Magnar addressed him for the first time directly, not just as audience—"you are supposedly an expert of this city. I ask, where?"

Pausing to think, and for the first time controlling the pace of this coffee meeting, Parker reached a remarkable conclusion. He squared his shoulders and jerked his back upright. One word, "Alcatraz!"

"Alcatraz, as in Alcatraz Island?" Celadonna finally chimed in, slowly raising her chin.

"Yes, that Alcatraz," Parker repeated, but this time with more conviction. He knew the gravitas and thrill of this unconventional recommendation.

Magnar tested, "What the hell are y'all talking about, my man? The abandoned island in the middle of the bay?!"

"Let me tell you a few stories, sir." Parker thought back to high school field trips to what is The Rock. "Roughly a mile off the shores of our idyllic town, this 22-acre mass of land was originally a military fortification, then a federal prison. As a developer, Mr. Jones, think about completing these fortress-like buildings. It would be no small feat of construction logistics across ocean waves." He knew that this description would attract Magnar's interest, as he loved a challenge.

"Go on, Mr. Architect, you have my ear." That doesn't happen often.

"Yes, please continue. Don't stop," she said softly with too much breath in the words, sounding too intimate.

"In 1934, the first group of inmates arrived: 137 prisoners in total—bank robbers, violent criminals, and notorious murderers. It was known then as the Island of the Pelicans." Parker knew such details, not just because of field trips, but he recently gave such a lecture in his architectural history class.

"Over the next three decades, a total of 36 inmates attempted to escape off the island"—

he was now telling the story not simply as fact, but reeling in his client with salesmanship, drawing in Celadonna, too—"not simply breaking out of the concrete cells and evading the guards, then finding a way out of the military-grade facilities, but also swimming through the freezing waters of the San Francisco Bay!"

"This is fantastic," was all Magnar spoke at this moment, engrossed in the storytelling. He is leaning forward attentively.

Parker relaxed his shoulders, leaned back, slouched comfortably in his chair. "Some reports claimed that no escape plans were successful—that the prisoners drowned in their futile attempts. But,"—a dramatic pause accompanied by direct eye contact with Magnar—"other investigations listed five escapees as missing. There are rumors that two inmates, both found guilty of murder, made it to the city's shore, and live within the San Francisco community, right now, this very moment!"

"What the?"

"And urban legends speak of the ghosts of the drowned prisoners returning home to haunt the island, only to be confronted by the distraught spirits of their murdered victims."

"My God, man, I asked you a single question, and you give me an evolution and transformation. To be direct, Mr. Rand, your answer hasn't disappointed."

On a roll, Parker continued, "Speaking of evolution, after the maximum security penitentiary closed in 1963, another chapter transformed Alcatraz into the stage for Native American occupation. Calling themselves the United Indians of All Tribes, they demanded social awareness of broken treaties and reparations. During the occupation, several prison buildings were destroyed in a mysterious fire. Was it the protestors or the government, and for what purpose?"

As was needed when Parker presented a design to a client, story sells an idea. "In 1976, the island joined the National Register of Historic Places, and became a part of the Golden Gate National Recreation Area in 1986, accompanying Lands End"—dropping his professional demeanor and loosening his shirt collar with a crooked index finger—"where you, Mr. Jones, are building yet another over-stuffed shopping center." Parker bravely tossed out a disapproving tone, in defense against Magnar's disparaging commentary on tourism.

Before the developer could interject, the architect continued calmly, "As to your statements of irony and tourism, Alcatraz Island received the designation as a National Historic Landmark, and currently, two million tourists visit by ferry each year."

"Stop. No more discussion is necessary. I have made up my mind. There is no doubt that Alcatraz Island will be the site of my new museum. I already had it high on my list of options."

Celadonna knew this was not true.

She then considered the marketing value of this audacious proposal. Slowly she stated, unexpectedly and articulately, "The Rock is spoken of with such reverence. This will help attract patrons to the museum. Alcatraz possesses many strata and layers of legacy, infamy, scandal—the Civil War fortress turned prison, then gave rise to the Red Power movement."

Parker saw that she was good with words, and joined in sync, "Also has the first ever constructed lighthouse on the West Coast, a source of hope and illumination on a tragic island."

"From an army facility—" she said, edging closer towards him.

"—to a sanctuary for seabirds, and even a community garden. All true," he responded.

"What about popular culture?"

"Alcatraz Island made its way into movies, television, books, video games, and even an animated children's program. Most recently, Ai Weiwei, the prominent Chinese artist, created a full-scale installation on the island that questioned human rights and freedom of expression."

Magnar found this ping-pong irritating but didn't stop the momentum between his lover and his architect.

She beamed, "A haunted island once a jail becomes a new haven for ideas, a pop-culture reference, and a political statement!"

Magnar was convinced and determined. He did not fear the complications of building an entire arts institution on an island, nor the costs or politics. In fact, it all intrigued him, dared him to try.

Magnar proclaimed, "People, Alcatraz is my new canvas. And there will be stories to tell, new lessons to teach, and messages to heed. The tales of curiosity and infamy will be transformed by the Abstract art housed in my museum. The very structure and location will acknowledge history but move forward with new rules and ideas—inspire new artists to create even greater masterpieces!"

Parkers was taken aback, but not entirely surprised, by the abrupt change of posture for Magnar—chest puffed up; arms holding triumphant fists. He acted as if the Alcatraz idea struck him and him alone, like lightning on starving kindle. It was dramatic and delusional.

Magnar asked, "What could be more exciting and even rebellious than *my* idea to redesign the abandoned prison in the Bay?"

He declared this as if he authored the entire story, as if Celadonna and Parker had not been promoting, gushing even, about the location for the past ten minutes. Magnar, like many ego-maniacal buffoons, claimed the ideas of others as his own self-absorbed creation.

Regardless, Celadonna and Parker nodded together. She tossed a sly smile his way. At this moment, he wasn't sure if it was reality vs. adrenalin—that her hand unsuccessfully reached for his knee.

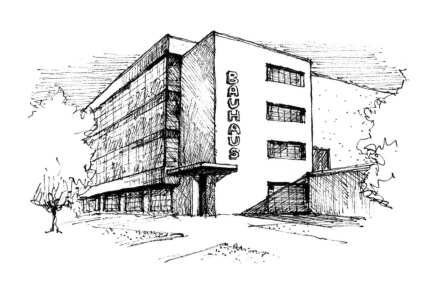

CHAPTER 9

Day One of Four:
The East Coast Power Couple:
Ling Liang and Chip Tooney

T HE ELECTRICITY IN THE AIR within the brick clad SFMOMA is both that of exhilaration and tension. Shortly after the press conference, the architects have been delivered to their destination, their purpose—and now sequestered. No word of Lars von Meester's death has reached the group. Not yet. But the timbre in the room between the ambitious competitors is uncomfortable enough as is.

Parker A. Rand tires to relax his clenched jaw, while Maxwell Brand readily smiles glancing from competitor to competitor. With hands wringing, Margo Hunters is anxious to get to work, but understands the protocol of comradery. An edgy look between Chip Tooney and partner Ling Liang passes between them.

The contestants are seated for lunch on this first day of Magnar's WoMA competition.

Johnny Furnsby twitches with uneasy energy. Wise cracking as usual, he points an impolite finger in the direction of Chip and Ling, and jests, "I label your social genre with an original acronym, WHAW. It stands for White-Husband-Asian-Wife. Chip, Ling, what do you think? WHAW: a predominant pattern in architecture businesses."

Chip Tooney and Ling Liang were not yet the power duo when they first met at the empowered Harvard University. The prestige of their Graduate School of Design was a result of a few things: having the most notable architects in the world teach there; only admitting in students presented as "the best of the best;" number one on every ranking system year after year; and of course, the school's legacy that began in the 1600s.

The legendary Walter Gropius was appointed Chair of Harvard's architecture department in 1938, and with him came the revolutionary teachings of the German Bauhaus school. And with that came the long shadow of intellectual dogma that still influences every professor and student at the school today. The game-changing presence of Gropius, this pioneer of Modernism, and of the generations of followers, were not lost on competition organizer, Magnar Jones. He possessed a fanatical, almost devout, respect for the Bauhaus' claim that history is mute, and one creates his own destiny. It was rumored that Gropius reinforced his beliefs by brazenly discarding all the books in the Harvard design library and donating them to Columbia University.

One superficial lesson Magnar learned from this tale was that he should demonstrate audacity for the sake of being audacious.

For Harvard's Graduate School of Design, commonly called the GSD, it adds to such near-mythical tales the actual faculty presence of Pritzker Prize architects like Rem Koolhaas, Tadao Ando, Rafael Moneo, Alvaro Siza, and Peter Zumthor roaming the halls, sketching with students at their desks.

The Pritzker Prize was the world's highest honor in architecture. Annually, the Pritzker family supported a jury "to honor a living architect or architects whose built work demonstrates a combination of those qualities of talent, vision and commitment, which has produced consistent and significant contributions to humanity and the built environment through the art of architecture." And the GSD faculty had collected the highest number of recipients.

Well bred, Chip Tooney was of good East Coast stock. As the heir apparent to enormous wealth stemming from the family's beginnings in the cotton industry and later investment banking, he rarely used his prestigious last name. He chooses to simply go by "Chip," because that folksy utterance actually implies Hampton privilege. His symmetrical features, messy short brown locks, and lean height made him the prototypical perfect Ivy League student.

In tall black boots, her white knit top nearly covered her entire small frame—the young Ling Liang assuredly approached her handsome GSD classmate. Chip had no idea that an attractive female was making conversation, attempting to flirt. In fact, he was often unaware that his stars were so lucky, that young women and men alike wanted to say hello out of the blue.

His New York elitism was never off putting because of his likeable steadiness. He carried his station in life not as exclusivity, not as good fortune, but simply as the way the universe was supposed to be. Harvard was not the school he hoped to get into by beating out thousands of ambitious applicants. No, it was merely the next logical step in his life, as simple as dinner follows lunch.

Contrasting the easygoing Chip Tooney, Ling Liang was a force with which to be reckoned. The small package of her physical body contained a determination and intellect that implied she was in control of her destiny, and maybe others' as well.

Long black straight hair, a smoker mostly for style and rebellion—she claimed herself as "not visually challenging," but in truth was plenty attractive. Though one year behind Chip in school, she was years ahead relentlessly manufacturing her future life and career path. His too. In their blossoming relationship, Ling was the front man, and Chip, the bass player quietly and happily complementing the action at the front of the stage.

Years after graduation, Chip Tooney and Ling Liang launched their Boston architecture company under the moniker, ChipLing. The now married couple work side by side proving their status as the "East Coast Power Couple," as colleagues teased.

With corresponding skills and personalities, her go-getter risk-taking approach was accompanied by his meticulous thinking and relaxed patience. The architectural couple believed themselves to be heirs to the Bauhaus agenda and the ghosts of Walter Gropius and Mies van der Rohe. "The devil is in the details," argued the latter—a profound statement that reached all levels of conversation.

As in many industries, many architecture practices are run by husband-wife teams. But out of curiosity or perhaps some loose form of anthropological research, Chicago architect, Johnny Furnsby, bracketed a trend: WHAW.

Chip and Ling twist a little uneasy in their seats. Their colleague has little concern for political correctness. To the pair, he is simply a joker, a fool.

Johnny has no qualms stomping on society's graces. "My evidence of architecture companies led by a Caucasian male and an Asian female includes so many, just off the top of my head…" He stands promptly and proceeds to bore them by naming more than a dozen such couples in the profession, each reputable and successful. He concludes, "…just to name a few, my friends," standing there smugly.

The observations entertain Chip and Ling, and they encourage him, perhaps hoping Johnny will put his foot further in his mouth further. "Go on, court jester."

Johnny looks around the room at his competitors, each with amused faces and tickled interests. Maxwell simply says, "Go on, Johnny. There's more, right?"

"Here is my thinking regarding our clients. The WHAW combination has strong marketing value. Some clients may see the W-H half, the White-Husband, as the expected norm: safe, reliable, white male professional. And the A-W half, the Asian-Wife, brings the exciting exotic side that delivers a worldly and experimental edge. Am I correct, friends?"

Johnny doesn't stop and scans his colleagues for consensus that does not surface. He is on a roll of unfortunate momentum. "I am not saying this is 100 percent accurate, but our clients probably believe the W-H person best understands architecture as a muscular structure, an engineered space shaped by iron and concrete. Whereas the A-W person is viewed as the sensitive stylish designer best suited for the selection of details, furniture, and light fixtures."

This corporate-y architect finally ceases his diatribe. A car that should have run out of gas miles back.

Ling Liang and Chip Tooney care little for their colleague's critique. Accurate or not, their focus remains on their Bauhaus teachings, starting their work from "Ground Zero" where "form follows function" and "less is more," and with the "devil in the details." Like warriors bracing for confrontation, they are determined to prove their dogma. These teachings are not just slogans, but the moral foundation from which civilization should be built. So they believe.

Death by Design at Alcatraz

CHAPTER 10

Banter on a Glass Bridge

C ELADONNA ENTERS the dining area abruptly as the architects are leaving towards the lobby. "Lars von Meester is dead!"

Stopped in their tracks, the architects say nothing, not knowing how to respond. Is this another part of Magnar's game?

A saddened soft voice from Celadonna, "I am sorry to tell you all, but Mr. von Meester's body was found an hour ago in the ocean, having fallen at Lands End…probably happened right before the press conference…I don't know, it's on the news, no one knows anything yet…" She makes little sense to her attentive audience. Her typical poise gives way to dropped shoulders and a trembling lower lip.

"I apologize, I have to go. Mr. Jones wanted to send someone else to tell you, but I felt that I…" and she leaves as suddenly as she arrived. Then there is only an ominous quiet.

"What in the world?!" says Johnny, breaking an uncomfortable silence. The discovery of a dead Lars von Meester unravels the architects, six competitors now down to the remaining five.

Dread moves quickly through the San Francisco Museum of Modern Art, where the architects are stationed, impounded actually. Immediately following the press conference, they have already become prisoners of some twisted architectural challenge.

This elite group finds itself having congregated on the glass bridge perched five levels up within the massive cylindrical lobby. Through the transparent floor of the bridge, one can see the dramatic fall to a gray marble ground floor below. Scary enough, and only one-third the distance that Lars fell to his demise. The architects gather but not to console. They are already sizing each other up, posturing and posing.

As it happened at the Palace of Fine Arts, the group stare at Parker, and he tries to avert the attention. He questions, "Why don't we know more?" his shoulders shrugging, throwing his hands up. "Was he pushed or did he fall by accident? An architect doesn't just slip during a construction tour and fall off a cliff, right? Architects and construction workers are sure footed, trampling over uneven conditions all the time, like a tightrope walker balancing on a steel-roof truss."

"Don't be naïve, Parker. I am sure that the news will tell us soon that Lar was murdered!" Johnny Furnsby argues. He stands there defiantly like he knows something.

Chip Tooney asks calmly, "Parker, you knew him. Didn't you see Lars last? This morning?"

"I have no idea who saw him last."

"When you did see him, what did he say? Did he talk about the competition? Did he say anything strange or alarming?"

"Not that I recall, sorry." Parker tries to diffuse an escalating situation.

Maxwell Brand chimes in, "This is unbelievable. Such a tragic accident. Such unfortunate timing. I mean, Lars von Meester was a great architect—"

Ling Liang interrupts him, "Looks like we have to get used to saying, 'was a great architect'? And Johnny is probably right. Can it truly be an accident?"

London architect, Margo Hunters, coolly asks, "Accident or murder? Murder or accident?" That's all.

Ling, fiddling with her phone, panics, "Why is the Wi-Fi so bad? Did Magnar cut out the service? How are we supposed to get any information locked in here?"

Johnny downshifts his gears, "I didn't know Lars. I do know his work. Impressive shit. But I have to bring this up: Do you think Mr. Jones is going to cancel the competition?"

Nothing more is said for the moment. The competitive minds have already considered Johnny's question. Will there be some kind of announcement to puncture the vacuum in which the architects stand right now?

Death looms like a black cloud over their heads. The stakes are high, and the question sits in the room like an elephant on a glass bridge. Not the question of accident vs. murder, but the status of the contest. They avoid eye contact, as they are all aware that one contestant, one who had great odds to win, has been eliminated.

Maxwell breaks the competitive reticence, "Maybe it wasn't an accident or a murder. Maybe some kind of suicide, some kind of grand artistic gesture?"

The group reacts with an onslaught of commentary.

"What's wrong with you, Brand?" questions Margo in a sedated voice.

"Don't even—to speak of a colleague in such a way," demands Johnny.

"How did you jump to that conclusion!?" asks Ling.

"Is that what design schools in Southern California teach? Has the West Coast sun fried your brain? Idiot!" quips Chip.

Flabbergasted, Maxwell steps back from the outbreak, and attempts to justify his thought, "It was just a hypothetical, guys. Creatives souls are extreme. Historically, artists *have* killed themselves for their art—sometimes as a dramatic statement or sometimes being mentally unstable. Or both."

The chaotic discussion resumes reaching a point of exasperation for all except Margo. She has not said much, at least not yet. She does well hiding her thoughts about the changes in odds: from one in six, to one in five.

Agitated, Ling leaps to conclusions, "Who would push a guy off a cliff—the body breaking against the rocky hillside on the way down, then drowning in the sea, or did he fall straight into the water because of a strong shove?"

"That's a pretty horrible way to phrase it, dear. We don't know how it exactly happened, or what happened at all," her husband tries to reel her in.

But she continues to speculate. "Was it one of the construction workers? You know how it gets at construction sites with the pushing and shoving, the yelling and insults—the macho egos. Framers hate carpenters, flooring installers hate painters, electricians and plumbers are always on top of each other. And they all hate us architects. Maybe Lars got pushed by—I don't know. Forget it. Sorry." Ling retracts a few steps back from the conversation.

But the discussion continues like a wagon losing its wheels. Johnny loses his stiff company-man demeanor and starts to gesticulate. "No doubt there is a lot of physical activity at project sites, shouting matches and put downs, even a few wrestling matches. But c'mon guys, why would a construction person push an architect into the Pacific Ocean?"

Maxwell adds, "Listen, I know a colleague who was such a pretentious prick of an architect that the construction crew beat him up, then locked him in the portable toilet for four hours. They despised how the architect would show up in his fancy clothes and point out construction flaws. This colleague, and I won't name names, was a pompous ass."

Chip's face crunches up and says, "Fine, fights and insults and all, but it never escalates to murder." He pauses. "Does it?"

Margo Hunters finally joins in all the chatter. She has been preparing. For the most part, she has stood in the background leaning on the handrail of the glass bridge waiting for the right moment. Her colleagues are all too familiar with her pseudo-intellectual phrasing.

Margo says in a flat voice, "Our socio-political circumstances as a privileged faction of enterprising architects are not ideal for the stages of this construct, an existential detachment from the norms of one's fleeting day-to-day human condition. But I ask this: Wouldn't anyone of us covet this non-representational state of affairs, and survey your own competitive advancement when a worthy opponent is purged? I desire the opportunity to nab this Post-Structuralist museum project, ala Foucault and Barthes, probably more than any of you second-rate architects."

Second-rate!? reacts Parker, internally.

Chip responds, "What in the hell are you trying to say, you pretentious—" he doesn't finish.

Margo glares at each of them one by one with no concern that she just slapped them all in the face. "I posit this: I was situated within this critical universe, destined to design the museum at Alcatraz, and create other Deconstructivist, Fem-Lit-Crit museums."

"It's not about you, lady," says Johnny. He couldn't wait to jump in.

Her arrogance loses some steam, and her Thesaurus-driven language weakens. "This is not some trivial shopping mall or an inconsequential high school gymnasium that litter your unfortunate portfolios of projects. WoMA is out of your league, and when I win—" Margo's mind wanders, as she throws her hands up thinking her audience doesn't deserve another word.

Parker appreciates that the group's spotlight is not on him, but he can't help not diving in, not defending. "You are such an obnoxious... so insufferable, yes, offensive—" voice trails off for a second, until he can start back up with more certainty. "We all want this contract. I am sure we think each one of us is better than the next. I admit it, yes, I think I have a good shot of winning. And sure, I would have a better chance if there were less competitors. But who in this group would ever kill a colleague—even think it, even say it—murder a competitor to better the chances of winning?" Parker avoids eye contact. The stares and silence are too long for comfort.

"Hold your horses, man," says Johnny.

"Who said anything about architects killing architects?" asked Chip and Ling in surprising unison.

"How did you arrive at such thinking, Parker? You kind of went from zero to sixty there, didn't you, buddy?" asks Maxwell.

Parker tries to respond, "I...I certainly didn't mean to say that there is a murderer amongst us—"

"Fuck off, Parker! You are ridiculous. And insane!" says Johnny.

The banter is both maddening and entertaining for Margo, as she randomly chants, "Improvisation, impromptu, rhapsodic, and obscuring. Good."

"What the fuck are you muttering about, Margo?" demands Johnny.

"We might have an executioner amongst our exalted ranks. Afterall, we all have the same motive: to win."

Reaching the end of his stamina, Parker states, "I don't find any of this talk useful or meaningful. Let's stop discussing falling, dying, accidents, killing, murder—" his voice tapers off. He feels the pull of a downward spiral, something he has dealt with all his life. And he knows for the next four days, the spiral has a lot further down to go.

Chip comments, "Like we said, Parker, you were probably the last to see him. And I think you might be hiding something."

"Get out much? Love those ocean views, right?" Johnny adds sarcastically.

CHAPTER 11

Downward Spiral

N OW A WEARY MAN, Parker points his finger at no one in particular, "No, no. Leave me alone." Though only a few words of dialogue, he feels like a boxer getting pounded in the corner of the ring unable to stop the jabs and hooks.

He panics, "Let's calm down, okay? Standing on this bridge many floors in the air is worrisome enough. We are wasting valuable design time having this kind of argument. We are all getting worked up. We are all upset about Lars. Some of us knew him personally, and all of us respected the heck out of this guy."

He glances at Margo who clearly has no respect for any of them, then Parker requests, "Please, let it all go for now."

In addition to the already present tension, anxiety and impatience builds as the group of architects know that soon the public will be arriving as per Magnar's instructions. They huddle in a circle of confusion, misdirection, and unconvincing accusations. Parker feels the glare of a spotlight because of his scheduled appointment with Lars this past morning. Chip and Ling want answers, and Maxwell's warm smile has faded. As Margo, so certain of her talents, is determined to start her design work now, Johnny loses interest in the banter.

He says, "Okay Parker, whatever you say, boss. You were the last in contact with Lars von Meester, right? You said that you were supposed to have some early meeting, and you said that he never showed up. That's what you mumbled at the press conference when Magnar stared you down. Sounds like there is more to your story. Right, everyone?"

"For the record, I did not murder Lars!" Parker can't take it any further. "Sorry, but I am getting off this bridge, leaving you all. I don't know what you are talking about." He runs off.

As in movies, this last line sounds more like a suspicious clue than a denial.

In Magnar's rules of confinement, with the architects sequestered in this building for the next four days, Parker doesn't get far. He wanders toward his temporary workspace. A sleek sign hangs at the entry: "PAR Designs, San Francisco," sans-serif font in silver on a glowing translucent panel of glass. Exhausted from the exchange with his colleagues, he tries to appreciate the sign, tries to smile proudly. He remembers opening his office 20 years ago, when he literally hung a wood shingle in the window. It stated, "On PAR." He thought it was clever.

Each WoMA competitor has been provided a similar translucent panel. A sign over what was to be Lars's workspace is visible to Parker's immediate left, leaving more doubts and questions that accompany his already crowded thoughts.

An obsessive over-thinker, he leans sloppily against his studio wall, not certain whether to stand upright or slump to the floor. He runs circles in his mind, *I am an architect, an artist, not a killer. But who am I really? What am I supposed to be?*

Notions of murder aside, one thing lingers. Parker struggles with Margo's insult about his "second-rate" body of work.

He wishes his gallery space had a door that could give him privacy, shut out the world for a few moments. But the galleries, as per Magnar's design, are left entirely open on one end, nothing to separate from the lobby save draping black velvet rope—recalling night clubs of the '80s that separated the social elite vs. everyone else. For this WoMA competition, the public is prohibited from entering the architects' work areas. But the visitors can stand, point, and gawk at the animals, whenever and for as long as they want over the several days.

This San Francisco architect's mind starts an uncontrollable descent. *I know I am meant for bigger things. If I know I can do better, then why don't I? Who has created me and why? This pounding echo in my head—is it a symptom? Of what?*

He blankly stares at one of the white walls of his assigned studio, imagining a panoramic view of something peaceful, something of nature perhaps. *Can I truly create greatness from my bare hands? But I haven't yet done great things yet, have I? My colleagues' successes torture me as they design and design, one project after another, each one more spectacular than the last. I want to shut down the circus, this festival of my insecurities? How can I get rid of the ghosts that are behind me, in front of me?*

This kind of mantra reoccurs inside Parker A. Rand's head every night. If he is being kind to himself, he labels it, *a self-reflection on ambition* or *a chemical imbalance.* But if he is being critical, *absolute psychosis.*

Awkwardly pacing in his studio all alone, his three Magnar-allowed employees not having arrived, Parker confesses to himself what everyone probably already knows, and what he believes anyone would do to advance his career: *Architects are driven by too much ego and ambition, too much vanity—an aspiration to have a lasting legacy.*

Lars von Meester, the Flying Dutchman, was the shoe-in winner. His designs have reshaped entire cities. Infatuated and star struck, the media labels him the "architect of architects," and his persona is bigger than life. Articles, websites, TED Talks, university lectures, etc.—whatever/whoever can't get enough of Lars, as he hatches up more and more exciting ideas: a town under a blue glass dome, hotel made out of discarded airplane parts, or an underwater seafood restaurant.

Parker has a difficult time stopping his mind when it starts down probing paths. *And what a stupid company name: Office Studio. Really, Lars?* he says under his breath. *Gimme a break. As if it wasn't pretentious enough, you use the short acronym,* "os." Parker is not talking to anyone; the audience are the demons in his head. He finds himself no longer wandering in circles but hunched over his Magnar-provided desk.

I hate all those generic company names like Lars's, so pretentiously unpretentious. When I find out what the acronym stands for, I am even more disappointed: OMA *for Office for Metropolitan Architecture,* ARO *for Architecture Research Office, or* FOA *for Foreign Office Architects. It's all absurd!*

He drives himself mad and cannot stop. Parker is as if giving an unflinching lecture to his students, but there is no one paying attention to this frantic man about company names. He starts to list them like a litany of obscenities. *Profoundly plain names like: ArchitectureFirm, Word, or General Architects. Or overly complex like: SHoP,* SPF:a, *wHY, or No.mad. How does a receptionist answer the phone?*

Parker's thoughts coil darker, as he starts to pound his fists on the desktop. The voice in his head rings sinister even. *We all envy Lars von Meester. Are we jealous?*

He answers himself without hesitation, *Yes.*

But, do we hate him? Yes. But, do we hate him that much? Yes, I despise him. I admit that he is more talented than I, than the rest of us. Yesterday, I was nothing in comparison, simply nothing. But today, am I still nothing? For me, for anyone of us to have a shot at winning this project, Lars von Meester would have to be gone.

And now he is.

The skeletons hiding in Parker A. Rand's brain dance the early afternoon. This architect doesn't know whether to let them or to stop them.

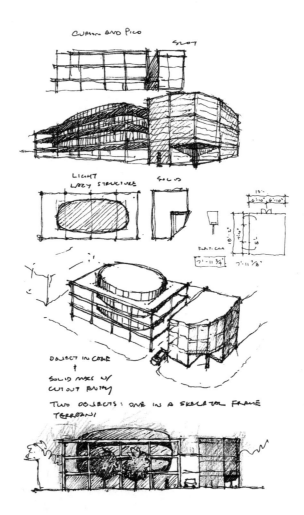

CHAPTER 12

The Corporate Man: Johnny Furnsby

H E WAS IRRITATINGLY pretentious and unbearably pompous. Architect Johnathan Furnsby preferred Johnny because he believed it gave him endearing charm. But with Furnsby's colleagues, "Johnny" resulted more in ridicule than camaraderie.

Johnny Furnsby was well traveled and cultured—and a bother. He believed he has the chops to argue anything, to provide intellectual discourse on nearly any topic—Apple vs. Amazon, the technical specs of an electric car or that of an espresso machine, and the latest documentary on documentaries. But in truth, he just tried too hard, and ended up being nothing more than tedious.

Johnny wanted to be cool and nonchalant but failed horribly. He was one of those insecure men that desperately wanted to be popular but fell short when trying to participate in mainstream conversations, like the Super Bowl, pop music, or celebrity couples.

Not Ivy League-bred like his East Coast competitors Chip Tooney and Ling Liang, Johnny's training was by no means below par. Originally from windy Chicago, his undergraduate degree came from the West Coast, California Polytechnic State University San Luis Obispo College, just Cal Poly for short. In contrast to Chip and Ling's praised Harvard and Parker's commendable Berkeley, Johnny's schooling at Cal Poly's College of Architecture and Environmental Design was more technical than design-oriented, more pragmatic than artistic. Graduates from other programs looked down at Cal Poly as merely a trade school—a curriculum to teach computer drafting and technical detailing, but never the poetry of design.

Aware of the limits of his first degree, Johnny obtained a second degree, Master of Science at the elite Manhattan institution, Cooper Union, fully known as The Cooper Union for the Advancement of Science and Art. To the few accepted into the Italianate brownstone building in New York's East Village, the school's methodology combines art, engineering, and science.

He was proud to boast to his friends, "My practical Cal Poly education of tectonics and materiality complements my Cooper Union's soul-searching artistry." With two well-known degrees in hand, the young graduate printed business cards and attempted to launch his entrepreneurial career, as did all the Alcatraz competitors upon graduation.

As hard as Johnny tried, his newly-formed, one-man company operating out of his tiny Chicago apartment did not succeed. In architecture school, professors provided students with hypothetical projects to design. Example: "For this semester, design a sports arena at Hong Kong's waterfront." But here was the thing: How does an architect, such as an insecure Johnny Furnsby, land such a project in reality?

Having left the comforts of school, he pondered such challenging questions over and over again. Regardless of trying so hard, he had no clients. No sports arena or university building. Not even a kitchen addition for a random uncle.

All students graduated with the hopes of being a giant of architecture like the impresario Frank Lloyd Wright or the mighty Le Corbusier. In Johnny's case, it simply wasn't in the cards. So he eventually did what many failing entrepreneurs reluctantly do as part of survival and growing up: Get a job at a company.

He envisioned the steady salary, health insurance, collaboration, and big clients that come with being employed at a large corporation. As a company man, he could design within the safe confines of the firm, work slowly up the ladder of promotions and titles, serve prestigious clients, and someday obtain company stocks and profit sharing.

Johnny's WoMA competitors rejected this much-despised corporate route. Maybe it was ego that had the others stay on their entrepreneurial path, having the name on the front door, and being one's own boss. But for this clever man, Johnny viewed his career choice as "not selling out, but buying in."

With good intentions, he joined the Chicago-based, IBM-like company known as General Architects, Inc., an international conglomerate of over 5,000 architects with global offices in 50 cities. The name itself, like General Electric, suggested a faceless empire. Regardless, such an architectural corporation reeked a reputation of financial success and stability. General Architects prided themselves on, "projects done on time and on budget," and unfortunately with little creative vision or soul.

Within this anonymous machine, Johnny flourished. Many of his co-workers attended schools like Cal Poly, training to be part of a team, a productive gear in the system. But Johnny's Cooper Union studies made him stand high above the rest. In this company of mediocrity and formulaic designs, his unique background earned him the executive position of CDO, as in Chief Design Officer.

At this international company, Johnny's rise resulted in being named within the industry as the international expert for designing museums. His department of a hundred architects, called Arts and Culture, produced some of the most sure-footed museums in the world. Despite the Alcatraz competitor's judgments, Johnny and his corporate sidekicks defended themselves with, "We are the go-to architects when a client embarks on a wholly new museum, an addition of several wings, or an intensive building renovation. We know the ins and outs of a museum's program, dimensions and specifications, and technical requirements of lighting and climate-control systems."

This Chief Design Officer capitalized on the company's digital library of stock design details, fixtures, and furniture. With a few lazy clicks of a computer mouse, Johnny pulled up template drawings for stainless-steel cylindrical column covers, specifications for Carnelian-red granite, and a catalog of items from the ubiquitous Design Within Reach. No, it wasn't difficult to succeed in this plug-n-play design setting at General Architects. CDO Johnny Furnsby had been given the keys to the empire and with them, the associated library of answers. Such resources were the giant's shoulders on which Johnny stood high.

Smart if not inspired, hardworking if not gifted, this Chicago architect did create slews of significant buildings, more than his competitors combined. Maxwell, Chip, all of them—even Margo—feared the weight of an international company that buttressed Johnny, providing him every resource to bring home the prized museum project. He approached Magnar's architectural contest as sport, as a Sun Tzu warrior of corporate stealth and strategy.

And there was that literal army of a thousand architects at Johnny Furnsby's side.

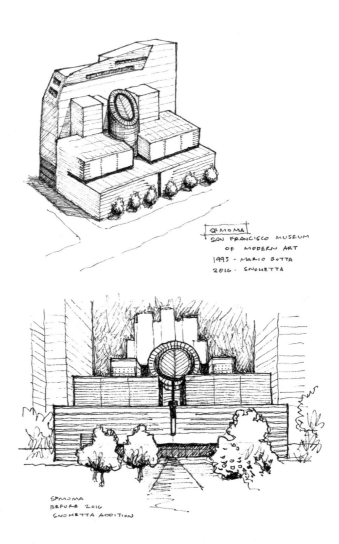

SF MOMA
SAN FRANCISCO MUSEUM
OF MODERN ART
1995 - MARIO BOTTA
2016 - SNOHETTA

SFMOMA
BEFORE 2016
SNOHETTA ADDITION

CHAPTER 13

Blank Canvases Await

A KIN TO BLANK CANVASES, the studio walls demand attention. The blank gallery surfaces of SFMOMA surround each architect—whiteness awaiting inspiration, confronting them. The remaining candidates—Parker A. Rand, Chip Tooney/Ling Liang, Johnny Furnsby, Maxwell Brand, and Margo Hunters—mourn von Meester's passing, but only as much is needed to satisfy appropriate professional respect. As when a cup of coffee is finished, when the break is over, the architects simply move on with their day. This early afternoon, on the first of four days, informs each competitor that much more is to come, reminds them to expect a roller coaster.

The architects set up their designated work areas, transforming assigned vacant galleries into their design studios. Each studio has three expansive white walls, 20 feet wide by 20 feet tall. The fourth wall opens to a central area that is directly off the building's lobby. Magnar has set up such a configuration so the arriving visitors can watch, from one stationary position, nearly each architect working within the studio—a wanting white cube of space: 20 feet by 20 feet by 20 feet.

In part, the design of the panopticon inspired Magnar's arrangement of the studios. This 18th-century architectural idea comprised a prison design, a system of control, and a disciplinary concept.

"Panopticon. Perfect," Magnar once said to Celadonna.

From the conclusion of the morning's press conference, a few groups of spectators have already found their way to this competition venue already in gear. Only the graceful sweep of the velvet rope at each studio opening separates the public's staring gazes and pointing fingers, from the architects trying so hard to focus. These creative minds try to tune out the relentless and growing public crowd—Magnar Jones's contrived audience of curiosity—sometimes intimidation and judgment.

He arrives to the central area, panning a view into each architect's studio. Magnar patiently waits for the opportune moment, studying the positions and reactions from members of the public.

"That's the guy, Magnar Jones, the billionaire developer from the press conference," says a bystander.

"Looks like he is going to make a statement or something," says another.

This is exactly what Magnar is waiting for, not just to be acknowledged, but to be recognized—to have an audience form around him. Fawn around him. As murmurs buzz from the crowd, he waits and waits until it is right.

"What's he doing here?"

"Probably checking in on his architects."

"Hush, he is about to say something."

Magnar clears his throat, no need for his microphone in this setting. As usual, he doesn't feel there is a need to introduce himself or offer any kind of formal primer. He faces into the studios and requests, "My architects, please stop what you are doing and join me here." That is all he says, and each architect reluctantly steps over the rope to gather near their client.

"Geez, what's this all about?" asks Johnny Furnsby.

For some architects who have already been deep in their artistic stupor, buried in ideas, and already scrawling out museum designs, they are stunned when finally noticing the scene of bystanders. 50 viewers already, 75 or maybe more—the public crowd keeps growing like bees to honey.

To the architects crowded together, Magnar raises both arms and announces for all to hear, "So be it. The show shall go on. *My* show shall go on." He makes no mention of Lars von Meester, though everyone from architects to the general public has heard the news by now.

"There is no need to regurgitate the news or speculate about a death at my construction site. There is an ongoing design competition, and I am not stopping or delaying it for any reason—not for a national holiday, medical emergency, death in the family, or even the murder of an architect. Got it, people?" He speaks to the architects but is well aware of all the ears listening.

"Murder?" trembles through the crowd.

The public starts to understand their role in this Magnar tournament. Oddly, glee takes over confusion, as the crowd settles into their position as onlookers to a spectacle. They feel like one of those elated audiences that have waited in a long line for the opportunity to watch the filming of a TV sitcom—typically presented on a stage set of three walls. Yet this is no comedy, there are no explicit cue cards asking the audience to "laugh" or "moan," and no one yells "cut" to end the scene.

Back in their work areas, each architect continues setting up, transforming empty galleries into stages for design. They all understand Magnar's demands: In addition to standing out as the best candidate for his museum, he wants a show. Magnar wants theater—a dramatic performance centered around architecture.

For the next three and a half days, Mr. Jones, this Puppet Master of sorts, has made the building open to the public all day, all night. He is obsessed with putting the architects and their work on view in real time. Magnar tells a reporter, "I want to capture every minutiae of the design process, the experiments and risks, debates and disagreements—every breath taken."

The agenda is both fascinating and cruel: to capture then exhibit the minds of artists to a lay public.

For the contest, Magnar instructed each architect to bring their three most trusted employees from the ranks: a project manager for quality control, job captain for technical development, and young designer to provide drafting.

For each studio, the teams are diverse, but the associates follow the mold of each lead architect. Parker brings his team of eager self-starters—introverts mostly. Chip and Ling arrive with their Ivy-league-trained employees in Boston preppy attire. Johnny doesn't miss a beat with his corporate-suited white males, looking more like accountants than creatives. Maxwell's cast of characters include well-put-together gay men outfitted in Mid-Century-inspired fashions. And Margo's comrades comprise international young women with an air of intimidating intellect.

As developer of complex projects, Magnar knows well that any famed architect is supported by a team. Yet, the media enjoys heralding individual genius, posting easily digestible headlines like, "Architect Peter Zumthor Unveils His Design for LACMA," or "Falling Water: Master Work by Frank Lloyd Wright." But architecture is rarely created by a solo act or a single burst of brilliance.

Professor Parker A. Rand addressed this, often using music as a metaphor for his Berkeley students. In his seminar, *The Profession: Practicalities of Practice*, he instructed, "Consider an orchestra. Each musician possesses great talent on their selected instruments. As a team of creative souls— as a collective whole—incredible music results from the ensemble's synchronicity. To direct the Big Picture, the symphony conductor helms the ship, but there is no music without the band—no progress without the ship. Know this: Most architectural projects are created in a similar manner. To deliver the buildings that make up our cities, from office towers to university buildings, from hospitals to train stations, celebrated architects may be these conductors, but they need their orchestra.

"Until you guys get into the professional world, you can't even begin to imagine the number of people needed to execute a single structure. Just to name a few, there are the technical leads researching acoustic insulation, computer designers detailing the weld for a steel post, managers of building codes, experts of fabrication, and well, I think you all get the idea."

Each and every time, Parker enjoyed delivering his final line, "It takes a village to raise a building." A big smirk and with an outstretch of neck from the college podium, he looked for reaction.

Days earlier, the gallery walls were stripped clean of the usual paintings that hang in SFMOMA. The emptiness of the rooms—these exciting canvases—were a haunting beginning, until now. The teams have gone to work attacking the bare surfaces with zeal. They are not yet designing a building in any detail, but rather composing their space—curating a backdrop of inspiring material.

Waving his arms frantically, Parker directs his team to plaster their gallery with images of projects from their favorite architects. A standard approach—to examine case studies from history. The architects of PAR Designs wallpaper the room with 11"x 17"prints of museums from around the world, like I.M. Pei's steel and glass pyramid at the Louvre Museum, the world's largest arts institution.

Parker addresses his employees with his professorial tone, "Pei's addition came 200 hundred years after the original 1793 structure. Contemporary meets classical. In the context of the original French Renaissance buildings, Pei's modern work is a jarring structure yet works beautifully. Maybe we keep parts of the Alcatraz prison buildings, and add modern glass structures?"

The public bystanders, gawking from the studio's wide doorway, watch in respectful silence. The only response is the music that buzzes in the background: Thelonious Monk, a jazz master that inspires Parker to be more spontaneous, take more risks, and not fear the consequences of hitting a wrong note.

In another studio, Los Angeles architect Maxwell Brand highlights a different precedent, "As inspiration, let's examine the Sydney Opera House by Jørn Utzon. The iconic shell-like building gracefully floats in the harbor. It's definitely a starting point for us."

From ChipLing, music of abstract minimalist John Adams plays loudly—an appropriate sonic background for the married couple to stay true to their Bauhaus roots of starting with a clean slate. They ignore the adjacent Johnny yelling, "Such pretentious music, guys!"

Instead of gathering up reference materials of other architects' projects—remember, Ground Zero—Ling simply asks her teammates, "What is the purpose of a museum?"

Her husband responds, "Honey, please don't continue that absurd speech from Magnar Jones." Chip tries to imitate the booming voice of the Oklahoman developer, "What is a museum, people?!"

She states him down. "Be serious, Chip. Should a museum be an empty vessel for art vs. a building as a work of art itself? Also, is a museum only for the bourgeois elite?"

Chip knows this practiced routine from school. He is only to answer questions with more questions, to open up possibilities and free the mind. "Ling, should our design be an homage to the roots of this savage island?"

"What about designing a smaller project, then proposing some of the construction dollars go towards addressing the shortage of affordable housing? Or providing social services for the homeless?"

"Is Alcatraz, a deserted island, truly the best location for a new museum, or should we suggest a site that is not only in an active part of the city, such as the Embarcadero or Mission Dolores, but will result in urban development, city revenue that can benefit the citizens—"

"—and easy access, not requiring a boat?" Ling completes his thought.

Chip asks, "Who came up with the insane idea of Alcatraz anyway? It's fascinating, but ridiculous. And imagine the construction logistics." The viewing audience enjoys this tennis match of questions upon questions which continue throughout the day.

Nearby, the gallery walls of Johnny Furnsby and General Architects, Inc. include a multitude of large photographs and floor plans of, not the work of historical architects, but their own museums. Self-congratulatory, the images display how Johnny has completed over a dozen museums in ten countries. Not only do these poster-size pictures boost the team's confidence, as well as provide extensive technical reference, the display is an intimidating tactic to the other contestants—as well as bragging rights to the viewing public.

Then without warning, the corporate architects display their confidence and complacency, and launch into a company tradition, bellowing the lyrics they know too well from Bohemian Rhapsody.

Mamaaa,
Just killed a man.
Put a gun against his head.
Pulled my trigger, now he's dead.

The audience starts to sing along to this popular anthem, but some realize the inappropriateness of the words. The empty studio with the sign for Lars von Meester still hangs.

The walls remain untouched with Margo Hunter and her company, Hunting Ground. Instead, these architects have curiously gathered a small pile of famous poems and images of Abstract art. Next to this small heap are large material samples of terrazzo, sandblasted glass, and weathered steel. The team arranges the collected artifacts in the center on the gallery, composed like an art installation.

The other architects peer in and can't make sense of this set up. After he takes a look, Parker returns to his team, "Is it poetry and genius, or a stupid attempt to mystify their process?"

At the velvet rope, Chip yells to Margo directly, "What the heck do you call that background music of yours, if you can even call it music. All I hear are senseless sounds and textures.

"This auditory narrative was engendered by an algorithm I created that applies sounds of my kitchen. The concretized premise exploits the captivity of women and society's operational obligation to have us cook meals."

"Oh, uh huh," Chip cautiously moves away, like walking backwards from a rattlesnake coiled to pounce.

In the midst of this, minimal furniture is being delivered to the studios, some small cots, desks, chairs, etc.—the bare necessities not of home, but for an austere existence of several days. Magnar's staff set up computers and model building stations. For those architects interested in the archaic tools of the trade, there are even vintage drafting tables with T-squares. The vast arrangement of equipment and supplies looks like the stage set from the Kitchen Stadium of *Iron Chef*, television's cooking contest.

Theater, thinks Magnar. Theater.

Unknown to the architects, hidden cameras were installed earlier. Magnar told his AV handymen that the equipment is for the "security of the architects and their work, as well as the valuable art within the museum."

For Magnar, the competitors, and the public audience, the overall mood is tense and foreboding, but indeed stimulating. These architects are generals with soldiers organizing for combat, ready to wage war. Like a football coach with his X's, O's, and squiggly lines on a green chalk board, each principal scribbles architectural sketches, their battle plans.

Anticipation hovers in the air, because in a few short days, the architects will present their ideas and one architect, only one, will be selected for the so-called "commission of the century"—a game changer for the winner's career. And the others will have to accept defeat, swallowing both the heartache and the money and time wasted, going home as a failure.

Not just tension, but fear cuts through the atmosphere—not only because there will be losers. Rather, for each architect, there exists the pressure to produce something that will amaze, something sublime and eloquent—something that will rattle the coffins of legendary architects in history. And do all this in only a mere couple of days. Accomplishing such an act, while having the public witness every move, is no small feat. And so, desperate measures set in.

Back at Magnar's hilltop penthouse, Celadonna questions cautiously, "Aren't the hidden cameras a little much, an invasion of privacy? I don't know, maybe even a tad illegal?"

But she is brushed aside like one would a mosquito. She stands her ground, and the questions linger long enough to demand a response.

He wants to say, "Don't worry your pretty little head, my darling." But doesn't. Even he knows better.

Instead Magnar says, "I set the rules of my game," and he taps an app on his phone, connecting his tiny screen to cameras that are 1.5 miles away within the SFMOMA building. He is impressed with himself. "Yes, I can now watch the architects at my leisure." In his sordid mind, the surveillance is perfectly appropriate.

Not to be dismissed as merely an accessory, she says, "Mag, this is very perverse actually—a blend of an Orwellian Big Brother with a Peeping Tom at a sex club. You actually don't see anything wrong with this twisted set up? It might be exciting, but is it right?"

Celadonna Kimm receives no answer. She believes that during most of Magnar's life, he wishes he was an architect, wishes he could create—not just hire people to create for him. Wishes he could paint just one of the spellbinding paintings in his collection.

She ponders, *My lover is only enjoying the design process vicariously. He is experiencing as much as he can soak up, take, or steal, yet he can't truly participate. He is a critic not a creator. A master not a maker.*

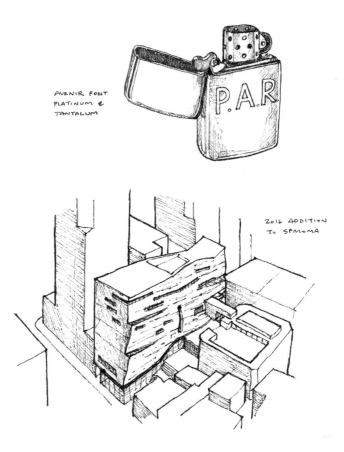

AVENIR FONT
PLATINUM &
TANTALUM

2016 ADDITION
TO SFMOMA

Death by Design at Alcatraz

CHAPTER 14

Ignition

T H E ARCHITECTS DART BACK and forth in their museum galleries transforming them into impressive working design studios. In the central space out front each studio, stands Magnar Jones and what appears to be his crowd, his disciples. Magnar speaks, pontificates, smiles, grandstands, and relishes the spot light. The architects care little and just want to work. They don't mind having the attention of the large growing public, over a 150 bystanders, off of them for the moment.

Maxwell Brand eyes this arrogant developer standing in the midst of his assembled public audience. Maxwell says to his employees, "Not much more here than a second-rate cult figure."

Glancing in the direction of PAR Designs, Magnar notices a missing competitor. Magnar frowns that his full ensemble isn't in attendance. Scanning all the architects quickly, left to right, right to left, he questions, "Where is that darn Parker? Find him. Tell that man that I require his presence in his studio with his associates working at all times. My audience deserves a full cast giving it their best."

The group didn't even notice Celadonna Kimm present, until Magnar stomped away like a tempestuous child—his large figure revealing the petite frame behind him. Taking a few steps of action, she responds, "I will go look for Mr. Rand," but Magnar is no longer in earshot. She pauses then softly says to no one in particular, "Good luck to you all." She awkwardly adds with the pretense of checking in, "Um, does anyone need anything?"

It's no secret. The architects know her relationship to their client. They also know that she is not the person to whom they should place requests such as, "Can I get more thumbtacks? And a glass of water?"

Parker's teammates speak to each other quietly, "What's the big deal? Our boss was just here. Maybe he just had to get some fresh air?"

"Yes, and to get away from all the hot air," says the junior associate.

"Or maybe, just sick and tired of these antics. Parker just wants to do good architecture, not be part of any of this absurdity," says the third.

Celadonna circles a few museum floors in search of Parker, only to round the corner back at his studio. She finds him, no difficult task. Parker is already back at work with his colleagues. Was he away merely to use the restroom, or perhaps another brief interlude, more of an internal meltdown—again debating in his head the names of architecture companies, *Office dA, llLab,* or *Coop Himmelb(l)au. Who in the world is going to learn how to type these names?*

Unnoticed, she observes this busybody architect bouncing around in his studio. She likes what she is studying: deeply introspective, attention to detail, vigor and intensity, and wild waving of his lanky limbs. Unaware of the observer, Parker appears as if conducting an invisible orchestra, gesticulating with his arms, facial expressions directed at photos pinned to the walls.

Celadonna is compelled to know more of him and has wanted to ever since the playful back and forth at Starbucks. This titillating repartee was followed by the unusual exchange of subtleties at the press conference. Both of them are aware that some subtleties can carry tones of both desire and invasion.

Parker is busy pinning up sketches upon sketches, layering stacks of incoherent scribbles to the walls. To her dismay, he doesn't even notice her a few feet away.

She chooses not to interrupt his actions with, "Nice to see you again." No, too common. In such circumstances, she is known to only need speak a few words. Men typically come to her, are drawn to her.

Celadonna stands there, leaning stiffly against the side of the gallery entry, wanting to be acknowledged. But Parker is engulfed, obsessed even, with his design process. He does not notice this striking woman beckoning like Alcatraz's historic lighthouse.

No, the local architect has his head in his sketchbook, then his laptop, then back in his sketchbook. Parker hasn't come up for air yet. He doesn't lift his eyes to mind his surroundings.

Celadonna is taken aback. Not to be embarrassed any further, and hoping no one saw her fail for his attention, she marches out of the area. She has never felt this kind of frustration before—not just being unwanted but being overlooked.

An hour later as the dusk sunlight showers the building, Parker steps out onto the upper terrace taking in the city skyline, a silhouette of manmade structures set on rolling hills. Only three paces behind, Celadonna follows and abruptly asks, "Do you have a light?"—a routine question. She holds a slender cigarette towards her pursed lips.

Startled, his forehead crinkles a little, he is able to reply, "Uh, hi. I actually do." He reaches for the balcony handrail, seeking something, anything to steady himself. "I have this cigarette lighter…a college graduation gift from my dad…but I rarely smoke. I carry it with me for good luck…the lighter makes me feel good about myself…" Parker's nervousness causes him to ramble. He kicks himself, *What the heck is wrong with you? Just be normal, damn it! Calm down.*

Out of his jacket pocket, his shaking hand presents a glistening platinum lighter, with the inscription, P.A.R. As he shows it to her, he finds himself both proud and embarrassed.

When Parker's father saw his son smoke in college, he was never disapproving, because he knew smoking would be a passing fad. Regardless, the dad thought an exquisite piece of craft and function would be an ideal gift for his graduating son, a budding architect. After leaving the Berkeley campus, smoking became a fading memory for Parker—no need to fit in with the late-night, smoke-infused crowd of design students.

These days, the San Francisco architect uses the lighter only here and there for a social drag, but this afternoon, he has this one opportunity to justify its existence. On a breezy upper-level patio, the cigarette lighter has a purpose, even an agenda.

Anxiously, Parker reaches forward with one hand igniting a tiny flame, and the other shielding it from the soft wind. Celadonna welcomes his hands, pulling them closer to her face. In turn, his body is drawn closer to hers. His clammy hands feel equal heat from the small flame ignited within his palms and the warmth of her small hands cupping his.

He jumps back distraught, like an anxious teen near a woman for the first time. Without warning or apology, he dashes back into the building, leaving a disregarded Celadonna Kimm and her unlit cigarette.

As he rushes towards the refuge of his studio, his messy drawings, and stacks of books, Parker tells himself, *I left her to smoke in peace.* He is breathing heavy.

But for Celadonna, she feels once again unnoticed. She wonders, "Who is this peculiar individual that finds little interest in me, not wanting to spend even a few minutes in conversation?"

As Parker nears his work area, his employees gawk, pointing at him. No, not at him, but pointing behind him.

Four police officers in daunting shades of blue and black, geared up with guns and batons, briskly approach the architect from behind. Parker, confused and lost in thought, is unaware of the law enforcement on his heels.

An officer shouts with such commanding authority that the sound waves are physical not just aural. "Mr. Rand. You there, Mr. Parker Rand. Stop!"

Alarmed by the force of the roar, he turns around to see a sight he never would have expected from his quiet, piano-lesson upbringing: a formidable police force reaching forward to grab him by the shoulders and arms. He stops frozen in his tracks.

"Parker A. Rand, come with us for questioning," the imposing tone continues.

Having seen the march of officers, the other architects scurry over near Parker's workspace. They are shocked, and none of them turn away. This episode is like coming upon a car crash. You want to look away, but instead hope to see a dismembered limb. And some imagine yet another competitor gone, increasing their odds to win.

The police officer demands, "Come with us to the station."

Parker can barely speak. "But…what have I done?"

The officer states with clarity for the architect to hear—for all the architects to hear—"You are a person-of-interest in the murder of a Lars von Meester."

Within the swarm of four officers, Parker A. Rand is pushed forward and out of the building. At least no handcuffs.

MID-CENTURY MODERN HOUSE
WILLIAM KRISEL
1953, PALM SPRINGS

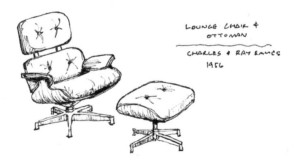

LOUNGE CHAIR &
OTTOMAN

CHARLES & RAY EAMES
1956

CHAPTER 15

The Peacock: Maxwell Brand

F LAMBOYANT ARCHITECT, Maxwell Brand, was wildly successful with his clients. Growing up in Los Angeles, California, he was popular, wildly popular. He had charisma, that magnetic appeal that attracted everyone into his world. When he entered a room, people quickly gathered around him, happily shoving their way forward to get one of the first handshakes from this Southern California designer.

Everyone wanted to be Maxwell. Women wanted him—men too. And he courted the latter. Never missing a beat, he did not stumble on his way out of his high school closet.

When not working, he dressed as many Angelenos do, in recreational wear. Beach fashion was not just for comfort, but allowed one to, at any moment, go for a hike or jog. Even when wearing a nicely pressed dress shirt for a business meeting, more of the shirt buttons were left undone than considered appropriate.

His father an attorney, his mother a doctor, but Maxwell was no beach bum. Maybe it was growing up in a Richard Neutra-designed house perched on the cliffs of Palos Verdes, or maybe it was the interior designs of the celebrity-studded hotel bars he frequented, Maxwell loved design, details, and decor. He enjoyed fabrics and textures, stone finishes and antique accessories. He loved studying how the L.A. sun bathed a space, "objets d'art" casting their long shadows.

He attended the Southern California Institute of Architecture, known by the confusing capitalization as sci-Arc.

Parker once thought, SCI-*Arc? What the heck? Why not Sci-*ARC, *Sciarc, or scI:arC? Who makes this crap up?*

Long established universities, such as Parker's Berkeley or Chip and Ling's Harvard, viewed SCI-Arc as a struggling institution. Ling once called it, "the warehouse-inhabiting, scrappy program—the step-child of fancy architecture schools."

Looking at SCI-Arc's patchy origins, director Eric Owen Moss once said, even boasted in jest, "We used to be considered one step ahead of the IRS, one step ahead of creditors." Unlike the founding of Harvard University in the 17th century, SCI-Arc was indeed young, founded only in 1972. But make no mistake: the school's pedigree ranked high, and this "scrappy program" commanded an exorbitant tuition no different than the Ivy's.

Exciting and experimental, the student work at SCI-Arc was often described with the overused adjective "edgy" or worse, "avant-garde." Students of local USC or UCLA poked fun at what they didn't understand, "Those SCI-Arc graduates will never be real architects. But they might make their riches designing graphic T-shirts!"

At a local flea market, recent graduate Maxwell found himself drawn to a signed photograph of Case Study House No. 22 in the Hollywood Hills, by architect Pierre Koenig. The black and white image was magnificent: a glass house hovering over a shimmering Los Angeles below—two women socializing, dressed in period-appropriate gowns with their hair perfectly bobbed. One female was situated in the transparent corner of the room, and with the floor cantilevering off the hillside, she looked like an angel perched over the city fabric of infinite lights.

Later, Maxwell discovered that he had unearthed a vintage photo from Julius Schulman, one of the most well-known architectural photographers of all time. In addition, Maxwell's new purchase was considered, by nearly everyone in the business, as one of the single most important pictures of architecture. *Time* magazine called it, "the most successful real estate image ever taken." And *Architizer* argued, "widely credited for bringing modernism into the mainstream."

As if possessing an original Picasso, this one Schulman photograph was the catalyst for Maxwell's abrupt turn from SCI-Arc's "cutting edge" curriculum. He fell back in love with his designer-y early years—his easy enjoyment of patterns, textiles, furniture, and the Open Plan. This single Schulman image inspired the young architect to focus a business entirely around the ideas of Mid-Century Modernism. His mission was a loaded premise, since Southern California clients were already obsessed with this revival style.

Maxwell explained to his new employees, "Abbreviated as MCM, Mid-Century Modernism encompasses all aspects of design and lifestyle: architecture and interiors, furniture and graphics, even ceramics, fashion, and fine art. Though stemming from Bauhaus teachings, I enjoy how the MCM approach is less fussy, not as strict and dogmatic—not so intimidating or threatening as the teachings from Gropius at Harvard. It is important to acknowledge that this style of the '50s had a social agenda too, to bring affordable homes to post-war American suburbs."

Always affable, he spoke proudly and strutted around like a peacock, "Back then, new engineering techniques allowed for large expanses of glass and the now famous post-and-beam configuration. The signature ceiling of large beams with tongue-in-groove planks invited the eye to follow the lines of structure and gravity. Our work will honor the substantial mid-century catalog of American pioneers such as Neutra, Eames, Frey, Ellwood, Krisel, Lautner, and of course, Pierre Koenig."

He joyfully preached to all his clients, "This architectural descriptor, the most powerful of design concepts—the Open Plan—eliminates enclosed rooms to have a large flexible space. Rather than the compartmentalized functions of your old house, such as the hidden kitchen and formal dining room, the Open Plan provides a composition of rooms without walls. I believe the result promotes social interaction instead of division, highlights spaces instead of walls, and provides natural light and fresh air instead of dank areas."

Maxwell branded his architecture practice, MCM Associates. Accompanying his irresistible flair, he switched out his athletic wear for brightly patterned sport coats, with a tailored silhouette exactly as if from the '50s. He enjoyed being both an intriguing period piece and promoter of the MCM revival, as well as having a profitable business riding the wave of an enormously popular design trend.

Upon meeting his WoMA competitors that first day in SFMOMA, the reception for Maxwell Brand was not as anticipated. No, not gracious at all. The announcement of Lars von Meester's death had not yet been delivered, and the debate and insults amongst the competitors energized each other.

Johnny Furnsby's opening comment caught Maxwell by surprise. "There he is, Mr. Mid-Century Theme Park—here to play with his nostalgic collection of stale clichés."

Ling Liang was more critical. "Maxwell, your Mid-Century Modernism waters down our Bauhaus roots of Modernism. Your ideas have already faded away like drive-in theaters, saddle shoes, and doing The Twist to Doris Day. At Palm Springs' annual Modernism Week, you zealots arrive in '50s-themed attire and antics—like Trekkies parading their geekdom at Comic-Con, dressed as Kirk, Spock, and Klingons!"

Chip Tooney supported his wife and added, "You seem like a decent guy, Brand, but as an architect, are you inventing anything new? You are merely embalming a style of a gone generation. And your approach is basically paint-by-numbers, the creation of historical replicas."

Margo joked, "MCM should stand for Mid-Century Mausoleum."

The colorful Maxwell stood unflinching at his colleagues' unwelcome. He produced a sizable natural smile and thought about how he laughs his way to the bank and on to the covers of *Dwell* and *Atomic Ranch* magazines.

Months ago, Celadonna and Magnar were at dinner discussing their potential candidates for the WoMA competition.

She asked, "Isn't it fascinating to see how this Maxwell Brand guy not only relives the past, but explicitly promotes it to his clients?"

Magnar knew of Maxwell's obsessions, and couldn't wait to see what he would create for his Alcatraz project. He raises his glass. "How will the Los Angeles designer insert the optimistic Mid-Century themes and fetishes into the old federal penitentiary for murderers?"

With delight, Celadonna added a tidbit, "Did you know that Maxwell is also Feng Shui-certified?" As WoMA's Director of Marketing, her mind raced with the PR potential of a Feng Shui architect for San Francisco, a city with a quarter of a million Asian citizens.

Magnar slams his palm down on the dining table. He didn't believe in the philosophy of Feng Shui which dates back to 4000 BC. "Is it art, science, philosophy, or superstition?"

But it doesn't matter, a good story was good publicity. And good publicity enhances this developer's legacy and swells his ego.

If Maxwell's competitors weren't already rolling in ridicule, Feng Shui was the final straw.

Ling, "Hocus-pocus."

Chip, "Smoke and mirrors."

Margo, "Hippie astrology for the Kerouac-infused, Beat '60s of the Bay Area."

Always positive, Maxwell sounded off, "Feng Shui is the Chinese art of placement that brings harmony and balance, even love, fame and health, to one's existence."

He stopped there, aware of deaf ears. No need to educate or convert. Maxwell had no concerns for this chit chat. This competition was not a war of words, but a tournament of design skills. Maxwell Brand brushed off the catty insults and prepared himself for architectural warfare.

And the spoils will go to the last man standing. The last architect breathing.

THE SECOND (OF FOUR)
CLIFF HOUSE
1896

Death by Design at Alcatraz

CHAPTER 16

Drinking Three Cups of Coffee

PARKER A. RAND LIED. He wants to come clean but hasn't figured out how. He did see Lars von Meester.

The morning Lars's body was discovered floating in the ocean, a few early risers saw the two architects at the nearby Cliff House restaurant. It was evident that Parker did not have "three cups of coffee waiting for him," as he claimed during the Magnar's press conference and later argued that he never met this Flying Dutchman.

The lead detective asks, "What's the story here, Mr. Rand? Shed some light on the situation for us." His name is O'Booker, a cranky, stout, and astute detective—his facial features too small for the size of his large head.

The four police from SFMOMA ushered Parker to the Mission District police station, where he and detective O'Booker are seated at a steel table this evening. Within the interrogation room, with aging memos stapled on the dingy walls, Parker tries to distract himself from focusing on the topic at hand. Mind wandering, he observes that their table is no mere piece of furniture. He thinks, *This vintage metal table is a striking collector's item, a 1945 Tanker Desk from McDowell Craig manufacturers.*

A second detective, Mr. Shenng, stands behind Parker, making him uneasy with odd bodily noises of grunts and clicks. Shenng is tall and fit. His features are too fine, too pretty to be a detective. Maybe that is why he stands behind, his noises more intimidating than his baby face would be.

Concluding his assessment of the steel table, Parker begins to panic. He is flustered, not knowing what to do with his nervous hands.

With an intimidating tone, O'Booker says, "Mr. Fancy Architect, why lie? At the Palace of Fine Arts, you withheld information, didn't you? You said that you waited for Lars von Meester at the restaurant. You said after drinking 'three cups of coffee,' he still did not show. But we have witnesses that identify you with Lars the morning of his death."

"I don't know what you are talking about." As before, this response from Parker is unconvincing. In fact, he knows exactly what the detectives are talking about, but his nervousness has yet to come to terms with that early morning at Lands End.

Literally breathing down Parker's tense neck, Detective Shenng chimes in, "Tell us why you were a few hundred feet from the crime scene, and"—he tries another approach—"why all you architects are such pencil-neck daisies?"

"Should I have a lawyer or someone?" Parker shrugs. He doesn't know the protocols and procedures, other than watching cop dramas on TV.

O'Booker leans forward realizing his partner's bullying was ineffective. "Sure, you could lawyer up. Wouldn't that make you sound guilty? We just have a few questions, pal. Up to you, Rand." O'Booker looks too comfortable in his seat.

A few questions, the architect thinks, but O'Booker's attempt to disarm the situation only leaves Parker feeling more defensive. Regardless, *I didn't do anything wrong*. "No, let's just get this over with. I have a lot of work to do and need to get back to my team."

Shenng broadens his shoulders from behind Parker and begins, "A few buddies of yours from this design contest, or whatever, passed on some interesting talk. They reported that you didn't seem to mind if this Lars fellow was gone. Your buddies also mentioned how in general, you have a chip on your shoulder—something against big-name European architects stealing your clients."

O'Booker jumps in, "Sounds like you have some beef with Lars."

Parker finds some strength to speak up, even as he shakes in distress. Most of the torture is internal for this architect, not arising out of the interrogation. Parker can't help himself as he blurts out, "Do you think being a competitive professional is motive for killing a colleague?"

He shrivels on delivery. Parker doesn't know why he said this, and notices that he has infuriated the two detectives. O'Booker looks over to Shenng, both ignoring the awkward architect, "Look here, the architect who colors with pretty crayons knows the term 'motive.'"

To Parker's red face, Shenng says, "Don't be a smug smart ass."

Parker is aware of his natural tendency to be conceited when nervous. He tries to be more congenial, but witnessing his own unraveling, he feels anxious, keeping whatever internal skeletons at bay.

O'Booker says, "Your colleagues mentioned that things got heated when you heard about Lars's death. You also felt similar heat at the press event, right? Most of the others only knew of Lars by reputation. But apparently, you followed him at a lecture, wanting to get close."

Before the detective could use the word, "stalked," Parker says, "No, nothing like that. I simply attended Lars's TED Talk at Stanford University. I joined the reception afterwards to introduce myself and compliment him on a great presentation." Parker feels self-consciously sycophantic over a colleague.

The investigators stay silent waiting for him to boil over.

And Parker finally does. As if the architect walked face first through a glass door sending broken glass to his feet, he begins with pain then embarrassment. "Fine, okay, I did meet with Lars that morning at the restaurant, but please know this: I didn't murder Lars von Meester. After meeting briefly over coffee, I watched him walk out of the restaurant, not dead at all, to his construction site at the adjacent Lands End."

To keep him talking, Shenng attempts a calm posture, trying to offer the comfort of a casual conversation. "Listen, we don't actually think a talented architect like yourself, a person of your respected reputation, would actually be a killer." Sheng's disingenuous phrase, "your respected reputation," echoes nicely inside Parker's head.

The tone works as Parker's pulse slows, the praise a balm to his fractured self-image. He thinks briefly of Adrienne Veley and how she crushed his school-boy dreams of romance. Since that unfortunate day at the piano, he is still looking for repairs to his sureness. *I should have been more assertive*, his mind wanders, but then is rudely interrupted.

O'Booker keeps up the charade. "We pushed you to see why you were lying. But it just didn't add up. Why not tell the truth from the start, to us, to your colleagues?"

"Please allow me." To the surprise of the detectives, Parker's tone is now more a client presentation or university lecture, than that of a murder interrogation. "About a month ago, I got a peculiar email from a Ms. Celadonna Kimm. I had no idea why she was reaching out. Later, I did meet her and developer, Magnar Jones, briefly for the first time at a coffee shop. Today, she has been wandering around our design studios at SFMOMA. Seems like a nice lady. Yes, very, ummm, striking woman." He takes a quiet second and visualizes this attractive person.

"Her mysterious email included a list of architects that were to be invited to design a new museum. And there was some info about us architects competing in public, like sport or something. Without knowing who this Celadonna was, without any other information, I was intrigued, eager to find out more."

"Keep talking."

"The list had names of the best architects in the world—some I knew personally and some through their work. I was pleasantly surprised to see my name. A single architect stood out though, Mr. Lars von Meester. At the time, I'd never met him, but I knew a lot about him, his very prolific career. Preparing for the competition, I wanted to learn more about his company, Office Studio, so I attended his talk at Stanford. After hearing his presentation on his projects, there was no question in my mind, that Lars would be the guy to beat. I have to admit. I was intimidated by this guy."

With his pace accelerating, Parker sits up straight, and finally and apprehensively provides his thesis to the detectives. "I had this idea, a Big Idea. If I could have a conversation with this Lars architect face to face, if I could convince this man to join forces with me, then together we would unbeatable. As a joint venture, Lars would bring his international reputation and the resources of a big design company. I would bring my regional expertise and local connections."

He quickly adds, "And I would bring *my* list of talents, awards, and honors too."

Only mildly interested, O'Booker says, "Go on," not wanting to stop the flow of information.

Parker carries on, now with a dash of enthusiasm. "By teaming with him, not only would this be a strategic partnership, but I would also have eliminated my biggest competitor.

"I have to tell you guys that I was nervous to meet him at the Cliff House. At the TED Talk, it was just a passing hello. At the restaurant, it was a serious sit-down meeting of competitors."

Parker starts to reveal the incessant roller coaster of thoughts that had preceded the meeting. "If I propose this joint venture idea, am I admitting that I can't win the competition on my own, that I don't stand a chance against Lars? Though I didn't even know specifics of the project, I was already unsure of myself. I was already falling on my sword, already pumping the brakes before getting my car out of the garage. Would my proposal of combining businesses constitute admitting that I was second-rate?"

Shenng sighs audibly and rolls his eyes at Parker's bluster. The detective just wants the CliffsNotes version of what transpired at the Cliff House. He responds, "Got it, you had a big business proposition. So what? Let's get to the meeting at the restaurant. Why did you withhold that information, up until now?"

Parker unwinds himself when he should instead be building up defenses. "I was hesitant to meet. You see, when two architects meet for the first time, there is typically a kind of measuring contest—as in who is better, who has more built projects, more awards, more press, and so on."

O'Booker jests, "Yeah, we get it: Who has the bigger dick?"

Parker doesn't respond, not because it isn't funny or accurate, but because it is embarrassingly so.

He says, "The breakfast encounter was far from what I had in mind. I envisioned two intelligent minds making plans for not just winning a big commission, but an ongoing collaborative partnership. But when Lars arrived at the restaurant, he walked right past me. When I stopped Lars to greet him, he barely recognized me. He had no recollection of meeting me at Stanford. When I stood up from the table to be more recognizable, to offer a handshake, I received a cold shoulder."

The next part was a big blow to the San Francisco architect. "After I re-introduced myself as Parker A. Rand, he called me, 'Peter' Rand."

His body contorts as he recalls how Lars disregarded him. "This von Meester character was an arrogant ass. His charm was so fake, and his rock-star-persona was a total poser thing. Lars was self-important, so into himself. And he spoke loudly and impatiently. Yeah, I guess our world was too slow for him, providing him no more than boredom.

"He then said, 'Get to the point, and do it quickly. Let's get this over with, son. Why are we meeting?' I was so disappointed with this narcissistic man."

The two detectives stay silent and immobile. They do not want to curb Parker's confession turned rant. But confession of what exactly?

"I tried anyway. I mentioned to Lars this mysterious female, her email, a list of invited architects, and an upcoming design competition for a new museum. Then I proposed to Lars the joint venture idea. I said it was a win-win: design, profits, working across the globe together, designing over meals and wine, and so on. But I was so naive."

Parker's composure demonstrates his defeat, his body slumping in his seat like an inflated balloon slowly losing air. "I sat there waiting for Lars's acknowledgment of my proposition. I didn't know if he was considering my idea or just bored. And here's where it gets really bad. Lars didn't even have the nerve to respond!

"He just got up and started to leave—leave me dangling with my mouth open in shock. He got up from the table, and not even bothering to look at me, commented that the idea of a partnership was desperate and ridiculous. He said that he didn't need a partner to win, that a 'small-town architect' like me brings nothing. As the restaurant door shut behind him, he was stammering about me in a bothered tone."

Lars's exit was quick that morning. The blow to Parker's ego quicker still.

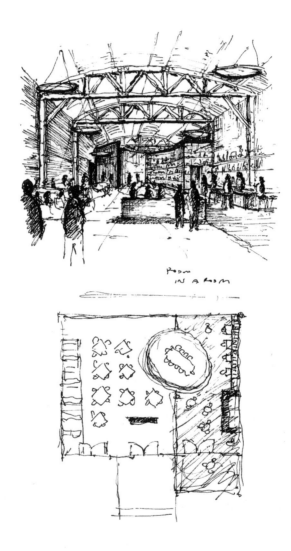

Death by Design at Alcatraz

CHAPTER 17

Confession and Concession

T HE DETECTIVES HAVE LITTLE CONCERN for professional antics, other than hoping a motive might surface. Now they may have one: a wounded ego.

Parker confesses but a very different kind of confession. "I was embarrassed, mortified. I had approached a colleague with a good idea. Afterwards, I was humiliated. Lars didn't care enough to give me more than two minutes of his time, didn't even know my name. He was so eager to disregard my proposal—disregard me also."

Parker pauses for a brief moment, his brain downwardly ascending, shame coloring his face, eating at his spirit. He tries to conclude. "As quickly as the encounter occurred, as quickly as my idea was found absurd, as quickly as I was dismissed, I tried to forget what happened. I had to because I couldn't come to admit what had transpired. It was so insulting. I couldn't talk about the meeting with my WoMA colleagues. I was humiliated. I would be ridiculed not just for being foolish, but probably for being underhanded too, for seeming to go behind everyone's back."

He takes a deep breath. "I lied to myself to protect my sanity."

O'Booker and Shenng have no idea where any of this is going. The detectives listen, but with little sympathy. O'Booker is on the edge of his seat, but not due to the suspense of Parker's story. This detective has been waiting to pounce, like a cat ready to play with a new toy.

He interrupts, "I think I got it. You were a sad architect who lost his little red balloon. So, Mr. Rand,"—long pause—"what about the witness who was delivering cabinets to Lands End?"

"I don't know who that is."

"He saw you with Lars at the construction site. And you just said that Lars left you alone at the restaurant, and you never saw him again. This worker recognized both of you and overheard a heated argument. You two were going at it, getting into some kind of scuffle—"

Parker is caught off guard, and once again tries, "I don't know what you are talking about." He shrugs his shoulders unconvincingly. For this third time, the statement has become stale.

Detective Shenng leans in, his face in Parker's. No longer breathing down the architect's back, Shenng has now moved to sit across the table, front and center, staring at the tangled architect. The detective repeats what his colleague stated, but more aggressively, "A construction worker saw you with Lars von Meester at Lands End, even though you say you never saw him again. You two weren't exchanging niceties. You, Mr. Famous Architect, were seen getting into a fight with Lars."

Similarly to before, the confused Parker focuses more on being called "famous," than being caught in a lie, being seen with the victim just before his death. It keeps getting worse for Parker and this forlorn architect gives up finally, entirely.

"Okay. After Lars slighted me, after he rudely left me sitting there at the restaurant, I followed him. I knew my joint venture business proposal was dead, but I felt the conversation was not over. I don't know why I followed him. Maybe I followed him out of the restaurant, because I wanted some respect, some kind of acknowledgement that I mattered. I won't be disregarded again and again." His "agains" reference other demons beyond the scope of the interrogation.

Parker carries on, "Lars walked quickly into a dense fog at Lands End, denser than usual for the coastline. I had a hard time chasing him down. It was eerie. Some of the construction materials, like sacks of concrete and plumbing parts, looked like people staring at us.

"I startled him. What came next was stupid of me: I actually asked him for an apology. Demanded, actually. This man with the ridiculous nickname of the Flying Dutchman, with a sort-of-short, sort-of-long black coat, just scowled at me. And get this: He had no idea what he was supposed to apologize for. And this next part infuriated me further. He acted like he never spoke to me, never met me before. Damn it, we just spoke five minutes ago face to face!"

His body visibly shaking, Parker starts to sound guilty of something. "We got into a bit of an argument. I called him pompous and other colorful words, saying that there was no reason to be disrespectful to a colleague. He was shouting that he didn't care, that I am small to him, that no one even knows who I am.

"Yes, detectives, there was shoving. But that was it. And we weren't anywhere near the edge of the cliff."

After a few schoolyard pushes, flaring of nostrils, and exchanged insults, Lars walked away from Parker totally bored. Again, so bored. Then he disappeared into the ominous shroud, the infamous fog.

"For a minute or two, I stood there feeling very foolish. Then I walked off the property, got into my car, drove off. That's it. I swear. That's the whole story. I didn't know anything about Lars being missing or murdered until later. As much of a jerk that he was, I am saddened by his death. No one deserves to die, definitely not like that."

Having now exposed his insecurities, Parker's disposition starts to relax a tiny bit. He unfortunately keeps mental record of all his failures, *The hopeful idea of partnering with a great architect; rejection of the business idea; dismissal as a worthy competitor; wanting an apology; quarreling and insults; and a short skirmish.*

Drained, he says, "I know this looks bad."

For some reason, O'Booker says, "Believe it or not, but I believe you. I do." Was this a trick to provide the local architect a false sense of security?

Shenng adds, "But we believe you only for now, only for today. Got that?"

Maybe an investigative tactic, or maybe they feel sorry for a broken architect. When investigating this murder case, the detectives do not concern themselves with bruised egos from an architectural competition.

Shenng and O'Booker cannot imagine that this delicate man could physically overtake a larger Lars von Meester, ultimately pushing him over a cliff. They don't believe that Parker has such twisted darkness in him to kill someone. The detectives recall how the report identified numerous cuts and abrasions on Lars's face, such as from fingernails. Would Parker attempt to scratch Lars's face instead of customary fisticuffs—throwing a decent right hook?

The two detectives signal to each other like a pitcher and catcher passing the most covert of baseball hand signs. To Parker's astonishment, the interrogation ends abruptly, just like that. He can't figure out if such a speedy conclusion is a good thing or a bad thing.

Last request from O'Booker, "Parker A. Rand, you are free to go, but I warn you: Don't go far."

He does not question this hasty ending. He doesn't know how to react other than so say, "You know I can't really go anywhere, right? All of us architects are locked up in a downtown building for four days as part of the competition rules. Like laboratory rats."

Shenng responds, "Whatever, I really don't care. Just stick around. I am sure the three of us will be meeting again soon."

Parkers doesn't like the foreboding tone that hangs in the air as he walks out of the room. The San Franciscan architect, innocent so it seems for today, leaves the police station exhausted. He needs to return to SFMOMA quickly to continue work. Though he should be thinking about his WoMA design and how much valuable time he has lost, he is more consumed with his confession of self-doubt and shame.

He tries to rise from the interrogation chair quickly, but his exhausted body weighs him down. As he stands brittlely, a dark cloud has temporarily lifted, but only briefly. He reminds himself of the detective's words, *talented architect* and *respected reputation*. But such hollow compliments settle dank and morbid into the recesses of his mind. Knowing such adjectives are only catchphrases, Parker questions, *When is it my turn? When will I be famous?*

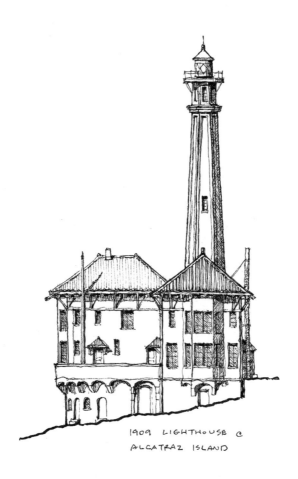

1909 LIGHTHOUSE @
ALCATRAZ ISLAND

Death by Design at Alcatraz

CHAPTER 18

Day Two of Four: Stomping the Rock

N OT MUCH SLEEP FOR THE COMPETITORS, as many of them toiled into the night with their design ideas—minds active even during their uneasy slumber.

All the architects, teammates included, have been summoned by Magnar Jones, through the graces of Celadonna, to gather in the lobby on the ground floor. A Blue Bottle Coffee stand in the background, the weary-eyed architects are thrilled to, for once, not have to wait in an hour-long line for the single origin bean beverage. Though eyeing a few token pastries, something more substantial would have been appreciated.

"Is starving us part of the billionaire-tyrant's game?" whispers Johnny to his giddy employees.

"Good morning, architects," Celadonna calls out to the meandering group. "I was thrilled to see the progress yesterday, of how you staged your creative spaces, what inspires you, the research, and more importantly, the early sketches and explorations."

"Young lady, who cares what you think?" Margo states in a slow and low hush ensuring that only her teammates hear.

Celadonna continues, "Please wait here, and relax for a few minutes. We will soon be taking a bus to the wharf and from there, take the ferry for a tour of the site itself." She stands even more upright, and her voice grows with excitement. "Yes, Alcatraz Island." A short pause, "*The* Rock!"

The group of architects attempt to stay calm and professional, as if this was just another typical site visit, yet this is Alcatraz—not your usual piece of property.

Into the bright morning sun, Celadonna leaves quickly through the lobby front doors. And the competitors stay behind and wait—and are forced to mingle. But this is not a social event nor a networking function. It is a cut throat competition for the greatest prize in the industry today, and the architects face each other with competitive apprehension.

The last time everyone saw Parker A. Rand, he was being dragged away by four persuasive police officers. He arrived back in SFMOMA late last night with little fanfare to his colleagues, all too busy—consumed with the launch of their exploratory processes.

This morning, fellow competitors acknowledge Parker's return, but no one knows what to think, what to ask exactly. There is both suspicion and sympathy. On this second day of Magnar Jones's contest, the air within the SFMOMA is taut. Launching the first day by setting up their studios while being watched by a crowd of strangers provided exhilaration. But the pomp is over. Anticipation and friction remain.

Leave it to Johnny Furnsby to toss out, "So, is the murderous architect joining us today? Did you use the candlestick, lead pipe, or revolver?"

No one is amused.

Maxwell Brand interjects, "Seems like the fun and games are over. Everyone, let's just get to work, okay?" A logistical bond exists between Maxwell and Parker, since both are California architects. Though one is from the north and the other the south, there is certainly regional comradery against the competitors from Chicago, Boston, and London. And previously, the Hague.

Ling Liang says, taking an unexpected aggressive posture, "Face it, everyone. We are all aware that the kid gloves are coming off—"

Chip Tooney predictably finishes his wife's thought, "—and this is a battle for a big prize. This tournament is not a casual social gathering. With the press conference over, moving into the galleries done, and conceptual design underway, I think collegiality is a far second place to winning."

"Of course there is inherent hostility, inimical enmity, and systematic rivalry, because there can be only one victor," comments Margo Hunters, walking in a small circle, as if on a TED Talk stage. "A tremendous amount of vivacity, resources, and time will be invested and advanced—emotions and reputation too. Add to this: Our competition is ensuing in this uncanny public arena. Strange visitors are already arriving to survey us, heed our words. As each of our ideas is deliberated upon, as each drawing is being conceived, then erased, then drawn again, all progress or lack thereof will be on show for the entire public."

"It's a groundbreaking idea, but I find it unsettling. We will be judged in more ways than one," Parker comments as he thinks back to the police station, his body wincing.

There isn't much more interest in talking further. The architects have on their game faces, a skill mastered in school, where one's sheer focus can be in itself more intimidating than the actual design work. The morning's brief conversation concludes with a silent routine of sizing each other up, as was done at the conclusion of the press conference. For the so-called "commission of the century," there can only be one triumphant architect.

As Magnar stated to Celadonna prior, "One winner and half a dozen losers."

Day two of the competition launches with a scheduled tour of Alcatraz Island. Familiar with the Rock, Parker visited the attraction often touring his out-of-town relatives. But the other architects only know of the island by reputation—the legends, myths, horror stories, escape attempts, and acts of destruction. With its diverse history, there is no doubt that such a site, such a canvas, fascinates each architect. Eager to arrive on site, they want to feel the heart and soul of Alcatraz, its humanity or lack thereof.

With the competitors briefly held captive on the ferry boat bouncing up and down on the bay waters, Magnar does not squander his opportunity to speak to an audience. "The California Gold Rush of the mid-1800s fetched many visitors to the area—visitors not familiar with the treacherous waters of the West Coast. To assist lost ships, a lighthouse was constructed on Alcatraz. Did any of you know this was the first lighthouse ever built on this coast?" He's not really asking for an answer. "A modest 50 feet in height, the structure was erected in 1853 for only $15,000." Showing off knowledge.

Celadonna watches her lover beam. She is moderately entertained, and wonders if her nausea is from the bumpy boat ride, or Magnar's trivial storytelling.

Pleased with himself, he continues. "After the lighthouse was compromised by the 1906 earthquake, a taller and sturdier lighthouse was built in 1909, standing 85 feet tall. Refuting the overly cute East Coast Cape Cod style of the earlier design, this new and still-standing lighthouse was constructed in reinforced concrete, unadorned and severe even—similar to the power of Abstract art refuting a trivial painting of a bowl of fruit."

Mostly ignoring the developer's verbose history lesson and feigning enough interest necessary to show a client respect, the architects look outwards to the island coming into focus. They consider both the glory and infamy of this land mass. Already, design ideas travel back and forth in each designer's mind, cycling from one thought to the next, to another and another.

Wanting to break into Magnar's droning, Chip engages his assistants, "Should we honor the current buildings and create additions that respect the existing style of architecture—a seamless blend of old and new?"

"Or"—Ling perfectly in rhythm—"should we update some of the facilities, and design new buildings that acknowledge the past—"

"—but forge a totally different architectural character?" Chip finishes.

Margo waves her arms in the ocean wind. Her thinking is more aggressive. To her team, "I want to demolish all the existing Alcatraz buildings, and view my site as a blank slate for my genius? The decrepit buildings should be desecrated."

Johnny overhears and feels compelled to comment what everyone is thinking, "Margo, you speak of *my* site and *my* genius. A lot of 'my's.' When are you ever going to let up?"

Most architects, from students to these industry veterans, look to the project site for initial inspiration. The word "site" is not just a reference to the existing physical conditions, but also to the project's situation, as in all circumstances—from physical, social, economic, to even metaphysical.

With the competing teams impatiently awaiting to dock, each principal architect addresses his or her three employees asking them to brainstorm, share research, and pose critical questions. They have organized themselves for this visit bringing sketchbooks, measuring tapes, cameras. Most of all, they bring their imagination, deductive reasoning, and problem-solving skills.

Parker commands to his teammates, "Let's look at the basic construct of the site, such as the solar orientation, primary direction of the wind, views from the property, infrastructure like roads, sewer line, and so on."

With similar sentiments, Johnny engages his people, "SWOT stands for strengths, weaknesses, opportunities, and threats." He references a corporate cliché, and his associates are actually impressed. "The topography plays a major role in our analysis: slopes, terrain, access. The city also has parameters, from property lines to setbacks and floor-area-ratios." He thinks like a competent architect attuned to budget, schedule, and practicalities, but not yet to poetry.

Harvard training has taught the husband-wife team to think abstractly. Ling leads the group discussion, "What is the character of the site? Is there a soul to acknowledge? Are there emotional forces that inspire us?"

Chip adds, "Each site presents itself with some kind of identity—a personality, a spirit. Roman mythology calls this *genius loci*.

This concept suggests that a deity is present, that there is a sense of place. The genius loci of Alcatraz is intense, spirits may be present, and the sense of place is both bright as a sunny day and bleak like our worst nightmares."

As their ferry closes in on the island, the choppy waters become more violent. Waves crash against the side of the ferry and are more threatening against the rocky formations at the island's edge. The sounds are guttural, as if from an unwelcoming island god. All the architects stand in anticipation, as their adrenalin pumps through their bodies—hands and arms grabbing tight any piece of the ferry for stability against the rolling waves.

Standing on the hardened dirt of Alcatraz, Magnar gathers his tribe of architects. They take in the evocative setting, both magnificent and sinister. The museum developer and his lover are decked out in clothing more suited for the city's popular Black & White Ball, than to trudge around a wet, dusty, concrete vessel that once housed criminals. With the crashing roar of the bay waters behind him, Magnar stands proud, as if preparing to greet fans, as if having conquered the land.

He gives instructions—challenges his architects. "People, what does it mean to transform a federal prison into my house of art? How big, how tall do you want to build? Should your scheme sit sympathetically low in the topography or bold as a towering structure? My friends, I have hand-picked each of you to tell me your answers—to impress me. Show me why you deserve to be part of my legacy."

The setting of Alcatraz is both solemn and beguiling. Surrounding the group sits remnants of old buildings, storied concrete carcasses. Cracks on the island's tough surface show the arcs of beginnings and ends, both life and death. One fissure hiding under broken glass welcomes a tiny struggling patch of grass, a flourishing survivor in a vast surface of ruined asphalt and compacted dirt. Standing guard, the remnants of the taller buildings peer down upon the visitors and demand that the island is respected. Twisted corroded iron bars protrude from beaten stone walls, as if a child's cow lick that won't lay flat regardless of the amount of saliva. The counter balance to these disparate elements is the surrounding icy-cold waters that extend until unseen within a silky veil of fog, which on a luminous enough day, provides a cryptic silhouette of the city docks.

Magnar has provided four hours for the architects' site analysis, having delayed the usual barrage of tourist. Upon his concluding remarks, the band of designers scatter across the island like ants on spilled sugar. The architects point, take photos, and calculate. And, as architects enjoy doing, pontificate and theorize.

Two hours expire, and from afar, shouts and screams are heard. The lighthouse is ablaze like a powerful torch in the hands of a giant.

Being shaped like a chimney flue, the structure is quickly engulfed in flames. The enormous concrete tower gathers heat releasing it at the very top, flames blasting upwards to the sky followed by entrails of smoke and ash. All the architects run towards this spectacle to witness the demise of the iconic landmark.

Margo is heard whispering to her employees in an almost threatening tone, "When architecture burns, we architects feel pieces of our souls incinerate alongside."

The lighthouse being scorched right before witnessing eyes recalls the catastrophic fires during that Native American Occupation of the island. No cause was ever found back then, and three buildings were lost to the menacing flames and soot.

This lighthouse once stood to guide lost travelers to shore and safety. It has even been said that the lighthouse guided lost souls to redemption. Today, the structure's only lesson has little to do with direction or salvation, but rather, evokes sadness for a building of historic significance.

The mumbling amongst the architects turns to shrieks as several point to the pinnacle of the lighthouse. A hazy silhouette of a man stands at the top, his screams lost to the sound of fire dominant over architecture. There is nowhere to go, to escape. This individual holds tightly the black iron guardrail as flames rise higher towards him, surrounding him—and the heat of the guardrail singes the man's grip.

Horror on their faces, the young architects from MCM Associates point and exclaim, "Oh my god, that's Mr. Brand up there!!" They recognize their employer, their leader.

Maxwell Brand is trapped in a scene of black and red against a crisp blue sky—a composition of fire, smoke, and horizon—and impending death. The group of visitors stands isolated on a 22-acre island surrounded by freezing waters and rocky terrain. Calls to 911 are urgently placed, but there is nothing to be done for the doomed Los Angeles architect. There is no diligent bystander to pull a nearby fire alarm, and no fleet of firetrucks with choreographed firemen coming to the rescue.

All the architects can do is watch in terror. Magnar loses his usual executive composure, as Celadonna grabs his arm with a tight clutch, nails piercing his suit. She yells, "Do something!"

But Magnar can't do a thing. Despite his business successes and influence, there is nothing he can do. For once, the powerful man has no words to speak and no actions to take.

Gathering dangerously close, the crowd witnesses flames and smoke finally swallowing whole the lighthouse and Maxwell atop. Keeping the structure from collapsing, the reinforced concrete bones serve the flames upward to an unfortunate victim.

Maxwell is no longer visible in the plume of dark smoke trailing upward, spirals dancing tragically in the sky. The once majestic lighthouse, a structure that looked upon the many chapters of Alcatraz, is now a tower of mortality. The successful Southern Californian architect, Maxwell Brand, is now a scorched body, looking like the subject of a figure-drawing class—a shape captured in strokes of the blackest charcoal.

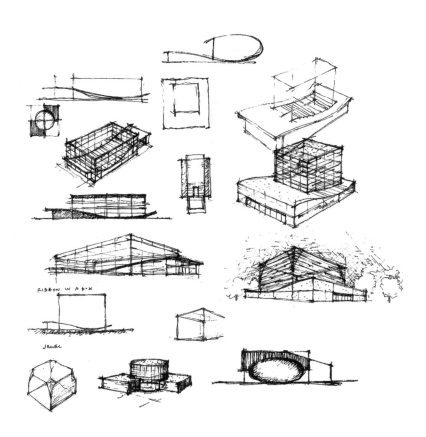

RIBBON IN A BOX

JEWEL

CHAPTER 19

The Mover and Shaker: Margo Hunters

S INCE INCEPTION, she had a sterling silver spoon in her mouth. The trust-fund daughter of the British family, the Hunters, Dame Margo was royalty, knighted by the Queen for "contributions to society."

Contrasting her pale complexion and blonde-hair ponytail, Margo Hunters often wore a short black cape—actually a capelet inspired by Frank Lloyd Wright's attire. Though Margo's male counterparts typically dressed in all black, as is the common uniform, most clients preferred to see their female architects in the traditional ideas of pretty pastels and delicate femininity. But most women architects, Margo especially, avoided matchy-matchy outfits, glittery jewelry, and high heels. She left such sexist fashion statements to fellow interior designers and decorators.

Similarly, accessories were rare for Margo, but the curated accent item might have existed from time to time—a handcrafted wristband or vintage fountain pen. Her favorite item—black round rimmed glasses—started with notable predecessors. Originator Le Corbusier wore such glasses in the late 1800s, of which Philip Johnson had Cartier make a replica in 1934. I.M. Pei continued this specific eyewear throughout his career.

Though Margo is married to an architect, she finds no interest in the adorable husband-wife duos like Ling Liang and Chip Tooney. Margo's professional work is her true husband. Margo runs her international empire of loyal architects by herself. Solo. And her spouse? Though a skilled architect himself, Margo requires that he minds the store as Director of Logistics and Operations, a fancy title for token duties.

As she devised since a young age, Margo attended the notable Architectural Association School of Architecture in London. Simply called, The AA, this independent school was the oldest of the private architecture schools. She loved gliding through the halls that call two Starchitects, Rem Koolhaas and Zaha Hadid, as graduates. Both Pritzker award winners.

More like a radical sci-Arc, and less like a structured Harvard, the AA was an open-ended introspective course of study intentionally without overarching doctrines. Perfect for Margo to chart her own path to greatness and originality.

Funded by parental wealth, she created in no time her company, Hunting Ground. Margo's affluent upbringing provided her the means to seek clients that specifically supported her vision, and not be bothered with "common clients," as she calls them. Margo's father owned her office building on Oxford Street, and her affluence compensated any architect who chose to slave away in Dame Margo's search for greatness.

Her first commission was not a mere house or restaurant, but an entirely new airport in China, which was indeed radical in many ways. An airport as a first project upon graduation at age 28 was astounding enough, but the design—yes, the design. The sweeping concourse floors fluidly warped up becoming the walls, and in turn, became compound curve ceilings—an amazing feat of engineering. The novel design of organic forms broke new ground, literally, and forged a revolutionary new chapter for the industry engaging computer-aided design and modeling.

Her work was revered by the press as "sculptural and curvaceous," but critics and envious competitors, mostly men, call the gorgeous shapes, "predictable female forms." Such words had no impact on Margo

Instead, she promoted what she labeled, "Noisy Architecture." Noise in this case was not acoustic, not about sound. The bold architect sought brash buildings that displayed a high level of risk and aggression—a visual and experiential clamor. She wanted her work to scream for attention, be controversial and outrageous. No, never ignored.

The team of Hunting Ground explored an additional and intriguing counterpoint to their philosophy. Years ago, Margo informally spoke to her office colleagues. Interestingly, when not boasting to peers, she speaks more plainly, less pretentiously.

She said, "Everyone has a favorite pair of jeans or maybe the old leather jacket. Isn't there beauty in a surface worn, faded, perfectly broken in—even cracking a little, almost poetically?

"No one wants a car that has been distressed, with a shattered windshield and scratches on the sides. No, cars want to be immaculate, like new. And unfortunately many think of architecture like a polished car. Buildings are constantly being renovated, trying to restore their original sheen.

"But, why don't we embrace a building as comfortably worn, like our favorite pair of jeans? Consider the gleaming white temples of Antiquity. Think of how they look today: tired, covered in soot and scaffolding. Most buildings unfortunately can't look the same as they did on the first day. And they shouldn't. Embrace building materials that age with inherent beauty. Allow architecture to breathe, express its age and soul."

She also quoted fellow AA classmate, Mohsen Mostafavi. "An approach to patina and weathering illustrates the complex nature of the architectural project by taking into account its temporality. The final state of the construction is actually indefinite, challenging the conventional notion of a building's completeness."

In a rare moment of being personable, she presented to the staff the small tag that came with her latest pair of jeans, "Variations and changes in color and surface are not defects of the material but considered to be part of the fabric's natural beauty."

Margo's largest commission to date, a 90-floor office tower in London, applied her, "designing with patina." A sensually twisting skyscraper tapering as it reached to heaven was entirely wrapped in copper panels. The aging metal was intended to weather over time, transforming from a shiny penny finish to a dark, reddish brown, ultimately reaching its most amazing state, a bright lime green.

At the ribbon cutting, Margo proclaimed, "My work at Hunting Ground counters my male competitors. Every year, these men generate yet another obvious steel-and-glass office tower—phallic structures trying to look virile and strong. Yes, these projects do glisten, but unfortunately the structures merely look like a freshly waxed sports car, a symptom of a man's midlife crisis."

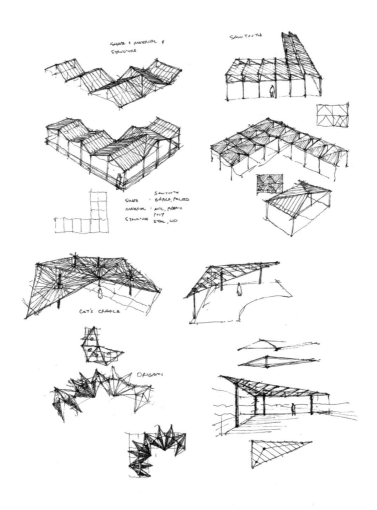

Death by Design at Alcatraz

CHAPTER 20

Karma and Dogma

T HE TENOR AT SFMOMA has become dismal. A tragically thick mood grows, almost a visible haze of gloom. Upon returning from Alcatraz Island, the architects confront the dramatic loss of their colleague, Maxwell Brand. The remaining four teams are confounded not knowing what to do next. The architects pace back and forth, back and forth, their stomachs turning. Some sprawl out on the cold gallery floor—bodies outlined by melancholy. They are all immobilized by the misfortune of not one, but two inexplicable deaths.

The death of a Californian associate devastates Parker. But he also thinks what others are likely thinking—but cannot, will not, speak. *The odds of winning went from* 1 *in* 6, *to* 1 *in* 5. *Now,* 1 *in* 4.

Everyone notices the eerily luminous sign that reads, "MCM Associates," hanging over Maxwell's studio entrance. Once an announcement of a successful professional, now this placard haunts like a cemetery headstone. Within the studio, Brand's employees are already carefully taking down drawings, dismantling both the design progress and their ambitions. They do so judiciously like anthropologists archiving objects, or morticians embalming a design idea. Maxwell's trusted workers empty their gallery—and their hearts as well.

The remaining architects do what many do in challenging times: Keep busy, one step in front of the next. Throughout, there is little noise, a few faint conversations only, until Magnar Jones arrives.

He feigns sympathy trying to soften his features and hands, but the result is unconvincing. Unaffected by the lighthouse catastrophe, he greets his architects as if he is a VIP executive receiving congratulatory compliments at his own promotion party. Sauntering behind is Celadonna Kimm, who teeters between her usual suggestive poise and a disquieting nervousness. Celadonna looks for a glance from Parker, though she has no idea why this particular individual from across the room would provide her any sanctuary. She is inexplicably drawn to him, and his lack of acknowledgment leaves her agitated and wanting.

With a bang, Magnar announces, "We are all thunderstruck by the tragic accident. The police are currently on the island. Unfortunately, some of you may need to be interviewed as witnesses."

Though nothing explicit, Parker feels that Magnar glared at him when he said, "Some of you." Perhaps, the architect is still reeling from his clash with O'Booker and Shenng.

Magnar carries on, "Apparently, Maxwell Brand entered the lighthouse to survey the island from an advantageous position at the very top. I appreciate the site research that Mr. Brand was hoping for, to grasp the *genius loci* of the Rock." Even now, Magnar tries to show off with his one phrase of Latin.

"My confusion is twofold, people. First, as the island administrators instructed, the lighthouse was to be restricted, closed to everyone. Celadonna here double checked that it was locked, and a warning sign clearly displayed, "Entry Prohibited." So how did Maxwell happen to stroll into the lighthouse?"

The architects exchange expressions of confusion and concern. Discomfort fills the room, as architects avert each other's scrutiny, staring at the floor avoiding eye contact.

Magnar continues, "Second, and more importantly, how did a fire start? Once the flames started to climb inside the building's shaft, there was nothing to prevent the structure from going up in flames in mere minutes." Calmly, he tosses out an off handed accusation, "Not pointing fingers, but if this fire was simply a terrible accident, then so be it."

The group of architects is perplexed, somewhat outraged actually.

"What?" Parker responds in a near-silent whisper. He thinks to himself, *Did our client just suggest in a roundabout phrase that Maxwell's death may not have been an accident. What does Magnar mean by 'not pointing fingers'?*

Parker harkens back to his snide remark to the pair of detectives, *Do you think being a competitive professional is motive for murdering a colleague?*

How many times has someone said, 'I would kill for such-and-such'? How literal is such a statement? With the perseverance required to be an acclaimed architect, ambition has few limits. Shrewdness and ego-driven resourcefulness are required in this business. From one in six, to one in five.

Now, one in four.

Magnar continues his non-consoling pronouncement. "There is too much at stake. Despite what has transpired,"—again, he puts on a false display of concern—"and it is indeed terrible, I deem that my competition will continue. I have gathered much talent from around the world right here on the fifth floor."

It's always about "I" when Magnar speaks.

"I am not going to release you, sending y'all home just because of two mishaps."

Mishaps?

"What would be the point in that kind of condolence—such a disappointing conclusion to a path that we've barely started? Maxwell Brand would want you all to continue."

Magnar revs up, "I have the funding for construction, agencies have granted me stewardship of the island, and I have invited y'all to show me your most impressive ideas, your design dogma. The competition continues, damn it, and you are my final four!"

Not only is his branding of the remaining competitors off putting, but the basketball reference strikes no chord with the architects. And the use of "dogma" is ridiculous.

"Let's all get back to work. Celadonna and I have examined the staging, research, and early drawings within your galleries, and we are thrilled with the progress. So too is your public. They are watching. Now, impress us and them further. Excite me with your big ideas. I am eager to see each *design parti* by the end of the day."

Johnny leans over to Parker whispering, "C'mon, really? First, he's dropping Latin like 'genius loci.' Now he uses the French phrase 'design parti.' He can't even begin to grasp the history and depth of such phrases."

As the royal couple begin to leave, Parker, seated on the floor, looks up from his labored thoughts hoping to catch a glimpse of Celadonna. Though only lasting mere seconds, he catches her looking intently back at him. She glowers with the pretense of a casual glance, as well as the gravitas of a plea.

Parker A. Rand battled internal demons his whole life—mostly in murky passages that housed his insecurities. He appreciated his childhood talents for art and music, now architecture, but he worried, *What will my legacy be? What infliction will befall me if my ambitions are too ambitious to achieve?*

His weekly psychiatrist, a feeble therapist in a posh office that looked down on Union Square and the associated consumerism, once stated, "Parker, your bucket has a leak." This life coach of sorts recited this at every session thinking it was a psychoanalytical breakthrough. But it was nothing more than a lukewarm metaphor.

The therapist suggested, "Water represents your accomplishments, and no matter how much water there is in your bucket, there is a small leak at the bottom. You never seem to enjoy how full your bucket is. You don't appreciate your gifts and successes. You only focus on the drops of water dripping out of the bucket. It's like anorexia, but instead of body dysmorphia, you have a distorted perception of your accomplishments."

Though not much of a religious person, Parker recalled one of his few mandatory Bible study classes as a young child. This memorable session examined the *Parable of the Talents*, from the Book of Matthew.

According to the scriptures, the master within the story provided his servants with goods to invest, called "talents." If a servant invested well, the master rewarded him with more goods—more talents—to enjoy and invest further. If a servant failed as a steward of the investments, all his goods were taken away.

Undiscerning as an adolescent student, Parker not only viewed the biblical "talents" as his literal artistic talents, but he also viewed the parable as a menace to his existence. He carried with him this cautionary tale, that if he squandered his talents, bad karma would come his way and take away all that he had. Tormented but determined to press on, he viewed the Bible as a threat to his rise to fame.

And the recent deaths as warnings, they plagued his mind. *Murder or accident?*

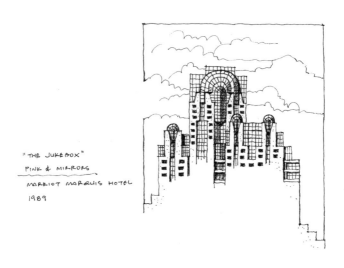

"THE JUKEBOX"
PINK & MIRRORS
MARRIOT MARQUIS HOTEL
1989

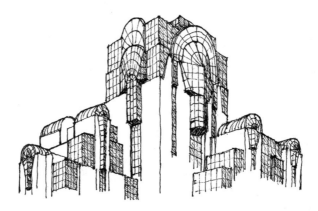

CHAPTER 21

What is a Design Parti?

W ITH HER PROJECT COMPLETED for presentation, a student
stood in front of the judging faculty, fellow students, and
general audience. "For this semester's project, my design is about—"

The word "about" weighed heavily. An architect's project, whether
as a student or later as a professional, had to be *about* something.

Two dozen of Parker A. Rand's Berkeley students surrounded him—
some on the floor, others squatted on stools, a few seated at the edge
of their drafting tables.

Comfortably at the center of attention, Professor Rand insisted,
"You can't simply present a project and say, for example, 'This house
has four bedrooms.' No, that is merely descriptive. Also, do not tell
me that you placed the hotel's swimming pool where there is the
most sun, or that the restaurant's dining room faces the view. Such
design moves are obvious."

The teacher's pet, Doogley, a fresh-faced sophomore with bright
red cheeks, spoke up, "Got it, Professor. Such presentation remarks
are mere facts, rudimentary design ideas, right?"

"Correct. They don't speak to the bigger picture. All of you, as
my current students and soon future distinguished architects, must
voice visionary notions. For example—and this is just off the top of
my head—my house design is *about* how a technological organism
can address an advanced domestic existence. Or, try this one on for

size: I was influenced by a reading of Tolstoy, and my design process is *about* his epic moral dilemmas."

Young Doogley squirmed his way to the front of the class, and said, "So a design must have a Big Idea, and ensuring that a swimming pool has an abundance of natural light is not a very big idea."

A fidgeting Parker expressed the awkwardness, but still he responded affirmatively though reluctantly, "Right again." He was not impressed with the parroting student, but the teacher remained encouraging.

"Ideas have to be intentional, meaning consciously with intent. Function and practicality are merely prerequisites. What we are talking about here is sometimes called the *design parti*. Without a design parti, the development of a project can fall into a trap of being arbitrary."

Other students braced themselves as they know Doogley will chime in here, "Parti? Isn't that French, sir?" He sought validation, while the other students groaned "Ugh" at Doogley's desperation.

Professor Rand leaned back in his seat—hands placed behind his head in a conceited manner, and explained, "Parti, short for parti pris, is the organizing thinking behind every move you make in the design process. From 15th-century French, parti translates to: the decision taken. Call it design principles, personal philosophy, or ideological tenets—a design parti exists to guide every decision you make, from how a floor plan is arranged to the building's exterior expression, from the finish of the metal to the detail of a light switch. Without the rules of your parti, you are only drafting random lines on paper—at best only meeting the basic functions of the project."

Simultaneously ignoring Doogley and waving his index finger at no particular student, Parker wrapped up his lesson with what sounded like a warning, "Look for the soul in each of your designs, but know this: Your ideas, whether here in the comforts of academia or out there in the real world, will be appreciated or judged. Praised or ridiculed. Sometimes, all four at once."

Parker's tone turns aggressive, as he leans forward slightly with hands intensely gripping the sides of his seat. "For most architects, the good ones at least, the design parti becomes a sacred moral stance, because it is the source from which all design life springs forth. Right now, you students are merely presenting a hypothetical project. But as a professional, you will be designing a real football stadium or a performing arts theater that you have worked on for years, even a decade. And upon completion"—Parker's message becomes ominous—"such a completed building is out there for a generation or more, in the public's glaring eye.

"Wonderful acclaim if you are lucky. Harsh criticism if you are unlucky. And sometimes, if you fail"—long pause, silence befalls the students—"mockery."

Months ago, on an empty evening planning the competition, Celadonna and Magnar found themselves wandering around his uber-luxurious condo. He cleared his throat, and the signal was heard clearly, yet half-heartedly. Regardless, Celadonna beamed as attentively as she could—wearing no make-up, hair messy, night gown offering just enough temptation.

Magnar started in on one of his discourses, "In 1989, the hospitality company, Marriot, erected a 39-story hotel in the heart of San Francisco."

She didn't know where this intro was headed, but she flirted back just enough to placate him.

One would think that smoking jackets and suede slippers disappeared generations ago, but Magnar's after dinner fashion was credible. He continued, "This story is intriguing, Cela, and infamous. Please pay attention." He was so patronizing. "I am thinking about it all, because our soon-to-be invited architects will be working hard to impress me, to win this WoMA competition we are planning. And I hope they don't fail the way the Marriott did."

"Marriott?"

He walked near her and grabbed her waist with one hand. City lights glittered for their late night backdrop. Magnar started in dramatically, pompously actually, as he always did, whether for an audience of one or one hundred. Releasing her, he sat down slowly in a crackled black leather lounge chair, and gestured Celadonna to sit across from him on the sofa.

Waiting for her full attention, he said, "Disapproval of the completed Marriott hotel in downtown San Francisco was fast, relentless, and without mercy. This skyscraper was ridiculed as the "Jukebox." With its pinkish exterior panels, abundant mirrored-glass walls, and a clumsy collision of rectilinear and circular forms—"

"Ooh, pink and mirrors could be so fancy looking," trying to sound both cute and intrigued.

He didn't approve of this interruption. "No, the color pink could never work for a 436-foot-tall building. The resulting composition was so ugly that citizens made their disdain known for years after its completion. A local reporter even published a 2004 article with the headline, 'The Jukebox Marriott and the Other Ugly Edifices We Hate to Love.'"

"That's sad for the architect. I feel horrible for him." She winked focusing more on Magnar than this unknown hotel architect.

He said, "It was rumored that the architect wrote an apology letter to the entire city, regretting how he ruined the beautiful skyline. But I ask this: Was the design parti wrong from the start, or was the execution weak?"

Celadonna found Magnar's zeal fascinating but did not respond or perhaps didn't care that much.

He didn't push for an answer. He often posed abstract questions such as this only to hear his voice resound through his penthouse— exquisitely staged with abstract sculptures spot lit against dark-walnut wall paneling.

Then, he simply assumed that her tempting outline against the city lights beckoned him to their private quarters.

Death by Design at Alcatraz

CHAPTER 22

The Theater of Architecture

W EIGHED DOWN BY THE DEMISE of a Maxwell Brand, some of the remaining architects are reluctant to reignite their design activities. But Magnar Jones has made his decree, and time is loudly ticking forward towards an impending deadline. Despite the unfortunate circumstances, unwinding and introspection are not options. Instead, urgency sets in for the competitors.

In front of each of the architects' studio, random visitors have swelled. Two deaths surely have added curiosity for the busybodies and intrigue for the morbid. Is all this just a contest to find the best person for the job, or is it more? Magnar wanted theater and spectacle, and in his eyes, both have pleasantly arrived.

At the onset yesterday, only a handful of spectators showed up, then a few more, eventually growing to dozens of nameless faceless individuals crowding to watch the architects work. On the afternoon of this second day, the crowds have increased to hundreds—several dozen at the front of each studio. The architects have become like zoo animals in captivity where children point and giggle, trying to get a reaction from the caged captee. One imagines tossing morsels of food even.

Leaning over his desk, Parker's head is buried in sketches from his teammates. He tries not to—he doesn't want to see. But his forces compel him to tilt his head barely to one side—to take a look at his audience. He tries not to make any eye contact, but he does catch a few familiar faces swallowed by hordes of unrecognizable smiles and jeers, squinting eyes and frowns—a host of enigmatic expressions that irk him.

Do I have to have an audience for my failures? Even these crowds of fans and bystanders appear to disregard me. They haunt me, remind me of my inadequacies and disappointments, missed opportunities, even lost friends and colleagues from distant pasts.

The mass of visitors shifts and shuffles along. If this audience is only to ridicule and judge, he rejects them all. This public crowd—a voyeuristic mob—is by Magnar's design. All aspects of the competition process have been, since the start, for viewing 24/7—a thrilling idea for some, divisive for others. From the increasing group, some viewers have coincidentally dropped by after visiting the museum's permanent collection, and others, self-proclaimed design fanatics, have planned their time in advance. Held back by only the velvet ropes, the public of San Francisco observes the architects' processes, with stares, gossip, discernment, and incessant memes for social media. The hashtag of #strugglingarchitects becomes a thing, and soon becomes viral.

Commentary ripples through the spectators.

"What are the competitors speculating, theorizing?"

"Is that particular drawing testing a large idea or examining a detail?"

"His preliminary ideas look crazy. What are they up to in that studio?"

"How does a concept become a building?"

And so on. What books, magazines, and websites are being researched—then deconstructed? Even, how are the architects dressed, fashion forward or predictably all black?

The fishbowl that the Puppet Master created is in full effect, and as he so cunningly envisioned. Without care for the architect's privacy or comfort, Magnar not only wants to share his love of art, he presents his enjoyment of watching artists struggle to create.

The design teams propel themselves into their artistic journey, postulating hypotheses that might steer their course. As taught decades ago, they all contemplate the same queries.

"What is our design parti?" Or "What is the project about? What is the Big Idea?"

Pacing back and forth in her studio, Margo Hunters calls out to no employee in particular, "What is our design narrative, team?" Aware of the contrived nature of this venue, she commences her quasi-performance by shouting, only partly to her associates of Hunting Ground, and more into the air above. Actually, for the onlookers, for theater.

Always ready with an absurd pun, Johnny Furnsby jests to his team, "How about: Your kar-ma ran over my dog-ma?" referencing Magnar's pretentious mention of dogma. Johnny side steps and seems to be enjoying himself, doing an awkward jig of enthusiasm. "Get it, car and dog?" This is his idea of leadership and coaching. His employees are ever so supportive and provide a fair amount of laughter. The audience watching General Architects is not too amused. A few disapproving groans are heard.

Hand on his shoulder, Ling quietly complains to her husband, "This whole public staging thing aside, Magnar is ridiculous with his appropriation of our teachings, i.e.: dogma, design parti, genius loci, and so on. He thinks he knows everything, from Latin to French to how an architect thinks. This client of ours is pathetic—wishes he was an architect. He is trying to own us, possess us."

"He is obsessed with us," Chip adds.

Though this is a demonstration of architects working, Magnar cannot resist showing up to grab some attention for himself. He stands at the one central point in the large area that connects to the entry to each studio. From this vantage point, he can see into every architect's gallery and the action within. More importantly, from this position, he can hold the attention of the entire public that has amassed this afternoon.

"Gather around everyone. Please, everyone." Knowing well who he is at this point, the spectators quickly form as his attentive audience. It doesn't take more than a few seconds for this developer to shift into his highest level of narcissism.

He carefully examines the room to ensure that he has everyone's full attention. Then clearing his throat, his impromptu address begins, though pre-rehearsed a few times recently, "People, the often-forgotten origins of the Eiffel Tower remind my architects to be courageous, to not fear new ideas."

Plenty of nods of acknowledgment from the public. Magnar nods in return as if endorsing the approval from the audience.

"When the Eiffel Tower was completed in 1889, it was unfortunately criticized as a dreadful work of architecture, a horrific nightmare for Paris. Even prior to the completion of Gustave Eiffel's iconic tower—politicians, intellectuals, architects, and citizens banded together condemning the design. The called themselves the Artists against the Eiffel Tower.

"And they proclaimed"—Magnar has practiced this lengthy quote often and generally gets it correct—"'We protest with all our strength, with all our indignation in the name of slighted French taste, against the erection of this useless and monstrous Eiffel Tower, a giddy, ridiculous tower dominating Paris like a gigantic black smokestack, crushing under its barbaric bulk, all of our humiliated monuments will disappear in this ghastly dream, like a blot of ink—the hateful shadow of the hateful column of bolted sheet metal.'" Close enough.

He looks out to the crowd, arms reaching forward like Moses. "Can you believe this, my people?" Magnar has not-so-subtly shifted his usual tag of "people" to a presumptuous "*my* people."

He continues his mini-lecture, now rant, "Those who fear progress and individuals lacking imagination—all such members of the narrow-minded population stood ready to say no to Eiffel. They feared the newness of new ideas. They embraced a naive motto: If it looks different, it must not be good." He appears to be pounding his chest. His determination for great design, no longer presented as a personal passion, becomes foreboding. "And so, my people—"

Unrehearsed, Celadonna jumps in to temper his sermon. Though surprised, Magnar welcomes her participation. She changes the tone of this speech and offers a kind voice, "These days, my friends, the beloved Eiffel Tower represents the pride of France, undisputed as one of the world's most recognizable monuments, a marvel of engineering, and a landmark of architectural beauty!"

The audience provides a round of applause and eager cheers of excitement.

Magnar and Celadonna stride off. Leaning in, he asks her as if a side comment, but not really so. He doesn't mind that the public might overhear. "From Gothic cathedrals to Chinese temples, heroic skyscrapers to contemporary museums—I give thanks to visionary thinking, like mine, that ignores the weak and stupid, the small and negligible. In my world, it is this kind of visionary thinking, my kind of fortitude, that moves the needle of progress forward."

A shrewd tyrant, he has faith that his hand-picked contestants will meet the challenge, will push themselves beyond their human limits, will capitalize on their egos that believe an architect can change the face of society.

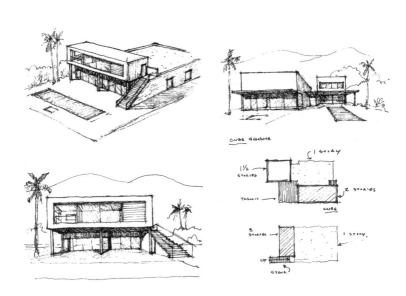

CHAPTER 23

Day Three of Four: I'll Take Two

A CCOMPANIED BY FAMILIAR FACES—familiar but not friend-ly—Parker finds himself once again losing valuable time. Unfortunately for him, this third day of the contest offers a familiar setting at the Mission District police station. Detectives O'Booker and Shenng are interviewing the local architect for a second time. Interrogating actually.

Take two: O'Booker starts, "Lucky you, Mr. Rand, we have brought you in again. Why? Because you were seen hanging around at the lighthouse."

Parker sits there, tense in the same chair, body in knots. O'Booker has both hands on the steel table and is leaning in too close.

Parker mumbles, "Lighthouse?"

"C'mon, Mr. Architect. The lighthouse on Alcatraz Island. You were there."

Shenng interjects calmly, "And it was right before the fire."

With an easy answer and avoiding eye contact, Parker responds, "We were all hanging around there. It's our job to understand the island. When designing a project, we have to study the site, the situation, the sense of identity..." his voice trails off, realizing the detectives don't care much about genius loci.

Parker's resolve only lasts a few seconds before he recalls the anx-iety and embarrassment at the previous meeting. That interrogation started in a panic, then disintegrated into a tormented downward spiral, concluding in shame.

But I am no killer, he told himself then, and tells himself this morning, after once again being extracted from his design studio at SFMOMA.

Shenng jumps in. He is circling the table, muscles flexing. "One of your colleagues stated that you were trying to break in—"

"I was trying the lighthouse door, not breaking in. I wanted to see if I could get to the top to get a good view. But the entry was locked, and a placard stated, 'Entry Prohibited.'" Parker starts to simmer; his head begins to shake a little side to side.

"Maybe you removed the sign, jimmied the door, and walked away innocently, which then invited your curious buddy, Maxwell Brand, to enter."

With a sagging posture on a vintage steel chair, Parker wonders about the word, "jimmied." Straightening his back, he finds just enough strength to refute the oncoming persecution. "Even if I messed with the lock, which I didn't, and left the door open, which I didn't—even if I did these things, and even if Maxwell entered later, how would I set a lighthouse ablaze? And why would I?"

"Do you smoke?" asks O'Booker abruptly.

"What? A little, only a little. Decades ago, maybe. But no, I don't smoke much these days."

Stunning Parker, Shenng slaps his hand firmly on the steel table, and an alarming metallic bang sounds through the room. He states, "At the lighthouse, the police found this very nice cigarette lighter with the engraving, P.A.R."

"Do you recognize it, Mr. Rand?" O'Booker with a rhetorical tone.

Shimmering under the spotlight of an interrogation, a platinum lighter has been placed in front of the architect, and though tiny, it sits there like a kitchen appliance. The inscription clearly spells out Parker's initials, intimidating him as if a vanity mirror. The luminous surface reflects a tiny irritating beam of light piercing into Parker's squinting eyes.

At this moment, his head spins, descends into a sorrowful state. He certainly recognizes the lighter.

With the two detectives awaiting an admission of guilt, he can only think of the *Parable of the Talents*. He saw his father as the master in the Biblical tale, and himself, the servant who was given talents. In his cruel mind, *I am burdened to impress upon my master that I am a good steward, that the investments of a college education and piano lessons paid off. This situation is not one where the investment is reaping rewards.*

Parker responds but not too convincingly, "That is my lighter. Obviously it's mine. It has my initials engraved on it, P...A...R." As he slowly speaks each letter, his index finger grazes each initial.

"The lighter was a graduation present from my dad a long time ago. I don't use it much though, barely at all, maybe only to smoke socially, once in a blue moon. I might have lit a cigarette or two with it a month ago. Is there even lighter fluid inside? Mainly, I carry it with me as a good luck talisman." Rambling on.

Nervousness building, noticeably trembling, Parker blurts out, "Look, guys, it's not me. It wasn't with Lars von Meester and not with Maxwell Brand either. I certainly didn't start a fire with my lighter." Very deep breaths, "And how did you get my lighter anyway? It was in the museum gallery with all my things." His voice starts to quiver.

"Let me get this straight"—O'Booker says as if he is winding up to tell a nice story—"First, you said you didn't see Lars at the restaurant. But you lied, because you did see him. Then you said the last time you saw him was when he left the restaurant. But you lied, because you were seen with Lars again at Lands End, which was right before his death.

"Your buddies already see guilt written all over your face. Many of them say they saw you at the lighthouse. And I am starting to think no, not the scene of the accident, but the scene of the crime. You were also seen trying to enter the lighthouse which clearly stated, no entrance. I think you got rid of the no entry sign, then busted the door open. That basically led Mr. Brand to walk in, knowing that the tower would be a tempting place to study the island. He then scrambled to the top. When you started the fire, Brand burned to his death in a few minutes."

Shenng says, "Yes, Parker, we found your lighter at the bottom of the lighthouse, and it has been easily determined that your lighter started the blaze by igniting a pile of old reports and debris stored under the entry steps."

O'Booker is reaching, but is convinced he is talking to the killer, twice over. "And you are saying that you had nothing to do with this lighthouse situation, or the death at Lands End? You are one lucky son-of-a—the heat from the fire made it impossible to get fingerprints off this lighter. Doesn't matter though. How is it possible that you are going to sit there acting like a boy about to wet his pants? You are a pathological liar, and a cold-blooded, two-time murderer!"

With zero response, Parker sits there frozen like a statue. He feels frightened and doomed, a very different reaction than the embarrassment felt when admitting the situation with Lars last time. Right now, Parker feels he has failed his master, failed his father, failed all his ambitions, past and present. Squandered the talents given to him.

Unexpectedly, a young boyish officer, freshly outfitted for duty, partially enters the interrogation room. Parker welcomes the interruption.

The officer leans into O'Booker and whispers, "Excuse me, guys. There is a very, umm, attractive female wanting to talk to you in the waiting area."

"I don't have time for a visitor right now. I don't care if it is a naked Miss Universe served on a platter."

But the young man explains, "No, not Miss Universe, but she says it is pertaining to the current questioning of an architect."

The detective is clearly perturbed by the disruption, especially as he just concluded his crime-story narrative. He grunts, stares at Parker, and states with an ironic voice, "Don't go anywhere."

Stepping out of the room, O'Booker tells Shenng, "I will be right back. Don't want to miss anything with our little architect. Don't start without me."

Shenng nods and stands there quietly. Like his first encounter with this suspect, the tall detective positions himself behind Parker, and breathes down his neck—a rhythmic wheezing of disturbingly warm breaths on the nape.

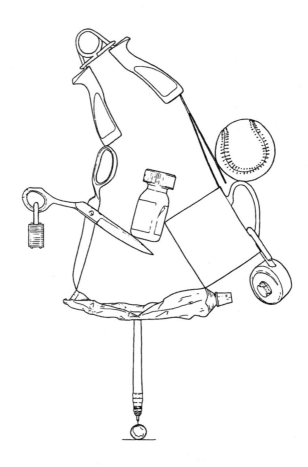

Death by Design at Alcatraz

CHAPTER 24

Capture and Release

A DOWDY AREA, the waiting area of the police station is more for the delivery of unfortunate news, than a respectable lobby to greet visitors. An eye-catching beauty, rarely seen in the precinct, greets detective O'Booker. Celadonna contrasts her surroundings, like an amethyst stone cradled in a heap of city garbage.

The gem introduces herself with a sparkle, "Hello, my name is Celadonna Kimm, Marketing Director for the WoMA competition, a new museum for Abstract art spearheaded by developer Magnar—"

"I know who you are"—interrupts the detective, agitated features expressing impatience—"and I know of Mr. Jones as well." The words that she started to say about a museum mean nothing to O'Booker— just a bunch of fancy terms and a confusing acronym.

He asks the obligatory question, "How can I help you, miss?" He tries his best to be courteous, but the contrived effort is unnatural, even comical.

The detective tries not to gawk at her orange knit top. Fitting too well, the yarn stretches to suggest the contours underneath. Her jeans are fashionably distressed, torn like an angry composition of art. The rips reveal enticing views of Pilates-toned thighs, and some tears are too high to be appropriately worn in the bright light of day.

Calmly in a casual voice and softened features, she says, "I understand you have our architect, Mr. Parker A. Rand, here at the station as a person-of-interest." She wants to add "again," but does not.

"Magnar Jones, my partner, has placed a call to the mayor, and in turn, the mayor has spoken to the police commissioner, who I believe is your boss." She emphasizes the word "boss," to deflate O'Booker's authority.

As if she is the decision maker at the station, she states, "You are to graciously release Mr. Rand to me, and he is to return to the design competition being held at a nearby building. Rest assured, alongside other architects, Mr. Rand has been and will continue to be sequestered and supervised. If you like, you can continue your interview with him when the competition concludes in two days."

He tries to be polite, but comments, "Look Ms. Kimm, I don't know anything about this. Why would I release Rand just because you say so? I would be happy to inform my 'boss'"—O'Booker counters with irony—"how Rand is a person-of-interest in a case, possibly two." The words "suspect in two murders" are unsaid.

"Listen darling, we don't have time. The situation was already made clear to your employer." Her composure compromises a little, as she loses patience like a child brewing a temper. She places a hand on her hip, and says, "FYI: Parker was with me the whole time at Alcatraz. He tried the locked door at the lighthouse. We did not break in. The sign was missing. Understand?"

Unwavering, O'Booker thinks how empty this attempt of an alibi is.

She continues with something more interesting. "And I am aware of his cigarette lighter."

The detective's brow furl, but he can't stop his mouth dropping open just a bit.

She adds, "Yes, that lighter is Parker's. I know. We know. He must have dropped it near the lighthouse. All the architects were scurrying around that morning. That cigarette lighter is a graduation gift from his father." She says this as if it means something to the investigation—as if there is some intimate familiarity between Parker and her.

Shenng, standing halfway out of the interview room, is listening intently. Door held ajar by a heavy foot, he hears his partner's voice raise, "I don't give a damn about this architecture competition, about architects 'scurrying around.' I don't care much for you or Mr. Jones. And how the hell do you know about evidence that our crime scene investigators just brought to our attention?" O'Booker's anger is rising, and his tone is accusatory.

Ignoring the question, she takes a few steps towards the open door to the room that holds Parker. Celadonna boldly leans forward, too awkwardly close to Shenng. She intentionally grazes his arm with the hint of her body. As he is holding the door open, he is stuck in this awkward position.

She points at the lighter, which appears to be glowing within the dimly-lit interrogation room. "If the lighter was used to start a fire, if there was any foul play, there is no possibility that Parker did this."

With a sense of finality, she adds with plenty conviction this time, "Since I was with him during the entire island tour."

Shenng demands, still uncomfortably standing there, "What's going on here, partner? What the hell is happening?"

At that moment, the police commissioner walks by with a troubled stride. Barely stopping at the group, he displays a bothered expression and posture of defeat. A silent gesture of his lowered chin to his two detectives signals Parker's release.

Deflated, O'Booker wants to protest everything Celadonna has revealed, but he understands the chain of command. He has no interest in disobeying the commissioner's command—his "boss."

O'Booker says, "Shenng buddy, we are done here—for now at least. Please let Mr. Rand go—for now at least." O'Booker stresses "For now at least," because that is his only thought of comfort. "Apparently, he has an alibi, and we have orders."

Parker gets up quickly from the cold metal table. "Am I free to go?"

Not even awaiting an answer, he paces out of the dank room coming face to face with Celadonna, as she leans forward to receive him. He looks back at his graduation souvenir on the table and recalls yesterday's humdrum words with this perplexing woman regarding the lighter.

In the lobby standing face to face, he asks her, "What are you possibly doing here? Are you the reason I am being released?" He whispers in the most quiet of tones, "I heard some of what you said. But we were never together on Alcatraz."

Very gently, she places two perfectly manicured fingertips on his lips. She hushes him, locks her arm with his, and starts their exit—their escape out of the police station.

As they hurry out, she only says, "You owe me. You need me."

The couple walks down Mission Street, and Parker finds himself inexplicably holding her hand. But she is leading and pulling him forward, more than cozily holding hands. Yet he looks down at their clasped hands in disbelief, then he looks at her exquisitely sculpted face as she only looks ahead and down the street. Then he looks back down at their hands—his palm clammy and hers silky.

At the Palace of Fine Arts, Parker only stood in Celadonna's presence at a ten-foot distance. His brain converted that ten feet to just two feet. Today, he is in her company, not ten feet or two feet, but mere inches.

As they walk briskly, Parker attempts to start at the very beginning. "Why did you email me the information about the list of architects months ago?" He probes, forgetting that he just walked out of a police station with her in arms.

She responds only with, "You need me," repeating herself.

One of Magnar's drivers is waiting at the corner in an imposing black car, either the same monochromatic statement from the press conference or, flaunting the developer's wealth, one of a fleet of similar automobiles.

She gestures Parker to enter the vehicle. He is being returned to the competition, to his studio to work, to his employees. She will not be joining him in the interior luxury of white leather and walnut trim.

He clumsily offers his hand for a shake, like a boy thanking his uncle for a nice afternoon at the park. Celadonna steps forward and reaches in. Her arms quickly embrace Parker. Her face against his.

The mere seconds of this embrace last for hours in his psyche, *Oh god. Don't let go.*

The cool morning juxtaposes the warmth of their skin, bodies too close. Parker's hands on her upper back, he explores for incomplete buttons. But her knit top offers him only soft cashmere.

She kisses him so lightly, a butterfly landing on his cheek grazing the corner of his unknowing lips. Surprising Parker, she returns the gleaming cigarette lighter, slipping it into his back pocket.

She says gently, "You forgot this," and the tone of her whisper echoes deep in his mind.

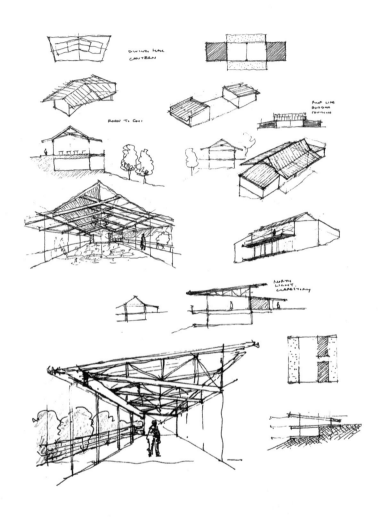

Death by Design at Alcatraz

CHAPTER 25

Architects Grueling at Work

T HE ARCHITECTS BUSY AT WORK, flutter around their studios. Exhilaration and brainwaves fill the atmosphere. Flashes of brilliance confront bouts of frustration. They draw, sketch, construct paper models. They input genius into computer screens. The act of designing engages each and every competitor like fish to water—like a boy starved for days before his Thanksgiving meal.

The public audience has not been disappointed in the creative activities they have witnessed. Dozens of spectators at each company's studio, totaling over two hundred observers—they behold demonstrations like no other, displays of genuine artistry.

Magnar Jones scrutinizes them all, architects and onlookers, with smugness and a glint of wickedness in his eye.

The work space of General Architects, Inc. is orderly. The architects buzz around with rationality of experience and composure of spirit. Johnny is aware that his WoMA competitors respect his technical expertise in designing museums, are even threatened a little. Unfortunately, he also knows of their disappointment in his lack of originality—how he applies formulaic ideas from the corporate library of predictable design solutions, as successful as such methods are.

But today, the Chicago architect no longer wishes to be complacent in his world of branch offices, subsidiaries, and company retreats. Johnny wants to stand taller, to wipe away the disdain from the others. Regardless of his impressive Cooper Union training, he does not possess the brainpower to debate with Boston's Chip and Ling or London's Margo. Regardless, Johnny Furnsby and his business cohorts are not shy of trying. If short of intellectual finesse, they do bring swagger and earnestness.

Self-assured, Johnny speaks to his three associates as if leading a roundtable retreat about a corporate mission statement. "Yesterday, we discussed many conceptual options. Today, let's focus in. We are all drawn to nature, right?" He straightens up, taking on a posture of haughtiness. "I have been reading a lot about something called Biophilic Design, and I think this can play into our design."

His colleagues are attentive, as are the mass of visitors who watch like an excited audience for an off-Broadway premiere.

Johnny says, "Biophilic Design refers to our instinctive association to nature and the resulting architecture that enhances our well-being. Let's apply this approach to yesterday's work, to the drawings already in progress. Let's add a generous use of landscape inside and out, abundance of natural light, organic materials and textures, good indoor air quality, and thermal and acoustic comfort."

The enthusiasm is moderate from employees and spectators too. Instead of the well-worn path of applying past successful ideas, Johnny is taking a risk, stepping outside his entitled bubble. But his design theme of nature, though accessible, is not stimulating enough, evidenced by only having a small handful of audience members nod in confirmation. Johnny spoke words that the public can easily understand, such as "lots of landscape and natural light," but he failed to ignite and inspire.

Abruptly, he tries again—this time speaking past his teammates and hoping for validation from the audience. "I got it, a second idea, a second layer of refinement. Color! Yes, color!" Johnny takes his time and attempts to establish eye contact with as many bystanders as possible, looking for encouragement.

"Alcatraz is an environment of monotonous grays, right? Also, museums are typically white to present artwork in a neutral environment. But in history, many European museums used rich colors in their galleries, deep burgundies and rich blue-grays."

For a brief moment, this Chicago architect thinks fondly of the deceased Maxwell Brand and his ample use of Mid-Century Modern colors: avocado green, mustard yellow, and burnt orange.

Johnny continues gesturing directly at the audience, "You have architects like New York's Richard Meier who primarily uses white, white, and more white. On the other hand, you have those Post-Modernists from the '80s applying vivid colors as an angry reaction to white Modernism and Abstract art. Our friend over there, Parker A. Rand, loves Post-Modern pastels and bright colors." Johnny points towards the PAR Designs studio and makes a disapproving face. Then smirks.

Though he is riffing on the spot, Johnny reaches a tipping point and impresses himself. "I got it. The use of color for WoMA is actually contextual, meaning it complements the context of San Francisco. This big idea for color recalls the city's famous "Painted Ladies," those late 1800 Victorian and Edwardian homes painted in a multitude of cheery and garish colors."

Johnny's senior architect finds an opportunity to jump in. He's been ready to participate for the crowd, and this nerdy individual is not short on words or enthusiasm. "Such polychromatic homes, called the 'Seven Sisters of Steiner Street,' launched the so-called Colorist movement. Like street artists tagging alleyways with vibrant hues, let's 'tag' our new museum with color, energy, and excitement."

Johnny jumps in, "Let's not have the typical, boring, vanilla, white museum!"

Whether the ideas are good or bad, Johnny Furnsby feels empowered, aware that his design directions will be backed by his army of corporate cronies. The audience is convinced both in part by the enthusiasm of General Architects, Inc., as well as the curiosity of their ideas.

In an adjacent work space, Chip Tooney and Ling Liang are bickering as married couples do. Regardless of the spotlight from a sizable gathering at their studio, the East Coast Power Couple argue forcefully. But know that this is their happy existence. Every morning and afternoon, husband and wife are debating architecture. Every night too. And the audience find their Harvard-trained banter entertaining.

Standing in the corner failing to hide from view, Ling proposes a radical idea. "It is uncommon to think of buildings as anything other than static. Architecture is the design of a fixed object, not something that moves. But why not?" She is looking at the current progress on the drafting tables and computer monitors and feels something is amiss.

Chip adds, no beat missed, "Let's do it, Ling: architecture as a kinetic thing."

"Is this possible for us, a building that moves?"

"We are not referring to a house that has a prosaic electric garage door, correct?"

Ling steps out of the corner, as if forward to an imaginary limelight. She elaborates, "Even for a massive new museum on an island, we can design the architecture to move dramatically, to change throughout the day according to the curator's or users' needs."

Chip has little discomfort when in the public eye. He stands proudly near the studio's entrance and cites an example. "It's like those popular Transformer robot toys. Our design will be a Transformer-inspired structure!"

Ling ignores the few giggles from the crowd. "Our architecture must be one that is in motion—"

"—staying in rhythm with a world that is constantly moving forward," he completes the sentiment.

Though many attendees have no idea what is being discussed exactly and can't possibly envision what such a building might look like, they enjoy watching these two artists brainstorm. It is as if an abstract sculptor plans to make modern sculptures from rusty plates of steel, and no one knows yet what will be produced. But the endeavor is riveting.

Chip and Ling awkwardly hug each other, a gesture odd for the cerebral couple. The insincere warmth is seen as putting on a show for the viewers—a proverbial bow to wrap up the discussion.

Across the way, Margo Hunter's company, Hunting Ground, forwards their designs, as well as reinforces their status as a band of big time movers and earth-shattering shakers. Dame Margo, like Magnar Jones, is never too busy to enjoy an audience. She hypothesizes a bold question, speaking arrogantly to the visitors and ignoring her employees.

"If Ludwig van Beethoven composed a tenth symphony, would he have changed the world?" She positions herself like a lecturer at an invisible podium.

"Nearly all classical aficionados agree that Beethoven's Ninth, his last symphony, is a perfect work of music. My reference to a hypothetical Beethoven's Tenth is to ask all of you, what is beyond perfection?"

This premise makes little sense to the dozens of witnesses or even her three teammates, especially as it relates to Alcatraz. But the confused stares do not temper Margo's enjoyment of pontificating.

"What defines a definitive work? How do you create something that is agreed by everyone to be perfection What about works that are so incredible that they surpass their own genre? What I mean is this: The Ninth Symphony is more than just music, just as Joyce's *Ulysses* is more than just a book, and the Sistine Chapel more than just a painting."

With typical intellectual bravado and her intimidating stance, she continues, "Architecturally, there are buildings throughout history that have become definitive works. The Empire State Building is more than just a skyscraper. The Taj Mahal is more than just a mausoleum."

Wanting approval from her employer, one of the associates from Hunting Ground speaks up, "The Pantheon in Rome is more than just a temple."

"Frank Lloyd Wright's Falling Water is more than just a house," says another associate.

Margo validates her employee's existence with a small nod, which implies that the boss concurs. But the concise nod also suggests that the associates should not interrupt.

Margo goes on, "All these projects have evolved far beyond being a mere building. These structures have earned the rare designation of a monument. Similarly with your own Golden Gate Bridge—isn't it more than just a span between two parcels of land?"

Her sermon-of-sorts moves full steam into an oratorial address. "Imagination, dreams, and visions collide to form a heroic effort. Beethoven, this furious artist only wrote nine symphonies. Nine, only nine!

Margo's finale, "WoMA will be *our* version of Beethoven's Tenth Symphony!"

Applause rings out. The audience is undeniably engrossed, though not fully certain of how this translates to a building design. Dame Margo Hunters's puzzled employees are afraid to ask what all her mumble-jumble actually means. Regardless, Margo has her sights on something.

One sweaty hand on his forehead and the other clutching his sketchbook, Parker A. Rand contemplates his design parti. Celadonna has been successful in his release, as well as sneaking him back into the frays of this competition. Barely missing a beat, he stands sure footed in the center of the PAR studio as if no time had been lost, as if he was not oddly missing for an hour.

He commands his PAR employees, "Discard the progress from yesterday and this morning. Let's try something different, folks, something fresh. Let's start anew, and test the fundamentals, not just of our architecture, but of life and art."

The teammates grumble, but only moderately so. They are accustomed to Parker's process, including his self-doubting, rehashing, and starting over.

Defiantly, Parker choses at this moment to veer away from his roots. "Everyone, say goodbye to our Post-Modernist agenda."

This San Francisco architect then asks his teammates an unexpected question, "What is beauty, my friends? How is it defined, described, and discussed—and even deconstructed?"

In intended earshot of the public attendees, he pretends to huddle with his three colleagues, and says, "One: The first form of beauty is man-made, meaning by the hands of a person. And its beauty can be at any size and complexity—from a gourmet delicacy to cantilevered steel beams fifty-stories high. For example, I love the artistry in seeing sushi being made, kind of like how all these strangers around us now are watching and enjoying our artistry."

An unexpected rant about gourmet food, he says, "Not only is the result visually appealing, but sushi's beauty is also temporal. The creations exist as beautiful, but for only a brief moment, as the juices soak for too long and discolor the creation, as the temperature changes how the food glistens.

"One of my favorite places on the planet is the 500-acre art park known as Storm King in Upstate New York. With immense scale, the sculptural installations are profound. No longer inhibited by the walls of a gallery like here at SFMOMA, the sky is literally the limit at Storm King. The man-made art is beautiful in the way it reaches up, out or down, and does so more ambitiously than anywhere else."

Parker picks up speed, swinging into full campus teacher mode, circling the gallery floor, "Two: I think that a second category of beauty is delivered through Mother Nature. I am fascinated by the natural stone formations at Devils Postpile in Mammoth Lakes. The basalt formations create hexagonal columns that start deep in the Earth and reveal their natural engineering at the surface. The beauty and structural logic of the hexagon is prevalent throughout nature.

"How about we look at Alcatraz for inherent natural beauty, like how the water crashes against the rocky formations? How does this inform the character of a new museum?"

Everyone is still. Parker's commentary has silenced the large attentive audience, and his employees too.

"Beauty can be obviously beautiful—or not so obvious. Three: My last thought is challenging. Perhaps beauty does not have to be pretty and attractive, but rather, sublime. This Steve McCurry portrait"— he points to the famous 1984 picture entitled Afghan Girl, pinned on the wall—"is universally considered to be one of the definitive portrait photographs in history, akin to the Mona Lisa in oil paints.

Yes, McCurry's work is exquisite. But I argue that photographer/artist Cindy Sherman, that I taped up over here"—he glides across to the opposite side of the gallery, directing attention to a collection of disturbing Sherman self-portraits—"has also captured beauty, but in her signature bizarre and deformed style.

"Philosophers have called this approach, the Grotesque, and I think this is also a form of beauty. I think with the horrific history of Alcatraz, we must find beauty within."

Parker is reeling in his teammates as well as the crowd of listeners. For this rare moment, His typically troubled thoughts are lucid, not labored with uncertainty.

"I think being that Mother Nature has given us this beautiful island, this grotesquely-beautiful island, our design shouldn't try to compete and yell for attention. To achieve true beauty, our human hands must collaborate with mythical and spiritual hands."

For this exceptional brief moment, Parker is at ease with himself—a rare occasion.

The massive audience has just had the unique opportunity to peer into the minds of these thinkers. Johnny Furnsby is exploring nature and color, as pedestrian as that might sound. Chip Tooney and Ling Liang believe a building should physically move and transform, though what that is and how it is engineered is the challenge. Margo Hunters is determined to compose an architectural Tenth Symphony. Such an abstract ambition is aspiring, daunting, and perplexing.

And Parker A. Rand hopes to define or redefine beauty. Good luck with that.

Magnar Jones's "Final Four" are now so deep in their heads, committed to a journey to unknown destinations. Whether gloomy or vivid, whether redemptive or victorious, there is no retreat, no point of return. Has architecture become a spectator sport?

Death by Design at Alcatraz

CHAPTER 26

Roundtable of Design and Ego

W ITH HIGHBROW BLUSTER, the architects have temporarily exhausted themselves. They take a much needed break, not just from their design work, but from the glaring eyes of the public. These competitors have waffled between showing off to the visitors vs. feeling trapped in this immense building.

Magnar's competition is not necessarily a prison, in that he has arranged group meals at the three-starred Michelin restaurant, In Situ, located on the first floor. The restaurant's name translates to "in the original place," and captures Chef Corel Lee's novel approach where he uses recipes "on loan" from celebrated chefs around the world. Magnar likes this concept, associating it with how his renowned architects are sort of "on loan" for his use.

Within the restaurant, the principal architects are gathering at a community table, while the support group of associates are scattered throughout the bespoke dining setting: a contoured ceiling, tables of thick wood slabs, chocolate-brown leather banquettes, and delicate pendent lights suspended like upside down black candles. This large assembly of talent is eager to indulge in more of the chef's creations. Today's specials: caramelized carrot soup with coconut foam, raw lobster with yuzu cream and Danish hibiscus, and chocolate cake with almond bubbles from Spain.

As lunch is being served, Parker quietly takes his seat, still reeling from his bout with the detectives, and more from his reverie-like encounter with Celadonna. Parker hoped that the design sessions with his team would shake him of the earlier events. He pinches himself then punches his arm, trying to wake up from a trance of confusion and desire—and clammy hands. No one cares to notice. The group chooses to view Parker as eccentric, or as Chip once commented, "just another odd duck."

Johnny Furnsby approaches those already seated at the central table and yells out, "What's up, losers? Just let me win already and save us all this waste of time."

Arms crossed defensively, Chip jumps right in, "Geez, Johnny, you are both a total ass and a dork."

Johnny grins with his false confidence. Neither take the exchange too personally, as they both understand smack talk.

As the culinary experience commences, Parker tosses out a topic, hoping that no one will ask about his disappearance earlier. Even his employees weren't motivated to ask. Parker tries an ice-breaking question, "What do all of you think about social media? I post here and there, but not incessantly like Johnny's company." He pokes at the Chicago architect.

Johnny defends, "It's not just about posting, Parker. Socials are critical to my organization's trade dress." Like the SWOT analysis previously, only this corporate designer would use the business term, "trade dress."

Parker resumes, "I've heard some of you earlier bragging about the exposure and the resulting followers and subscribers."

Margo Hunters says, gracefully holding a glass of wine, "Yes, but what is the currency of Instagram followers? Is there tangible value beyond bragging rights? I believe there is, and—"

"Margo, you may have a multitude of followers, but how real is that quantity?" Johnny interrupts. Most of the architects are aware that Hunting Ground has hundreds of thousands of followers. Johnny adds, "Did you know that some people actually purchase unauthenticated followers? So if anyone can simply buy fake followers, does it matter whether you have 1,000 subscribers or 1 million?"

Parker who opened up this conversation, gets tense in the neck due to the escalating tone. "I have participated, but only because I feel that I have to—keeping up with the Jones, you know? I hear that the WoMA marketing lady"—he makes no mention of Celadonna's name—"is constantly posting images of us working here. It's kind of embarrassing."

Ling Liang finally participates, tilting her body inward and speaking with eyes slightly closed, "Are our customers—the prestigious developers, big universities, and billionaire corporations—actually surfing Instagram and LinkedIn every morning looking at us? Probably not."

Parker complains, "One resulting evil of all this hoopla is when my clients demand, 'Give my project that Instagramable moment'— that one singular photograph that supposedly captures the essence of the project."

"Reducing all our work to one image is absurd!" Ling argues.

Chip concurs, "It is cruel to reduce the depth and layers of architecture down to a fixed instant in time—as in Instant-gram. Would anyone try to reduce an entire novel to one sentence?"

Ling adds, "The real problem is this: Bad architects design their whole project with that one superficial Instagramable image in mind, working backwards from what they want a building to look like in a single picture, and not applying critical analysis and introspection." She tosses an accusatory side glance at Margo, whose work is known to be about first impressions— more about the cover than the book.

Bothered by this claim and the previous one about fake followers, a guilty Margo tries to pivot, "Social media is just one tool, one of many devices. What about the handful of other instruments at our fingertips? Here's what I am positing: For most of us, the design voyage starts inside our heads. We are then challenged to extract that creative stimulus out of our brains. This is the progression that Mr. Jones is trying to exhibit to the public.

"While in our cages, our so-called studio galleries, we grasp at the tools of our trade to convert the design parti into some pictorial form of communication—be it a sketch on the back of a napkin or a crude cardboard model. We might choose to have our younger associates transfer our genius into the computer." She robotically glances behind her at her three loyal employees.

Feeling comfortable now that no one has asked about his whereabouts this morning, Parker speaks up, "But often, our ideas are grander, more ambitious, than any tool can capture—whether old school tools like a T-square, or new technology like a 3D printer. All tools have limits, whereas our artistic spirits do not."

"Nicely said, Parker," compliments Johnny sincerely.

Gathering gourmet morsels onto his fork, Parker continues, "A quantum leap in communicating design ideas arrived with digital technology. But here is where it gets scary. With algorithms, computers are not just communicating ideas that are in our heads but generating ideas without our heads."

Ling adds, "I worry about the morality of technology. Just because computers can capture our thoughts, even replicate thoughts on its own, should we build it in reality? Should technology replace the use of our brains and our hands?"

"—of our souls?" Johnny chimes in. "Not to put down my company, but my team can, with a few clicks of the mouse, generate dozens of ideas. I wonder if they are all good, all worthy of consideration. With this Alcatraz competition, we only have four days to do what typically takes months to complete. With or without technology, we only have the time to develop one idea thoughtfully and strategically."

"Your comments remind me of my figure-drawing classes in college," Parker asserts, feeling at ease, sipping some wine.

"What the heck are you talking about, Rand?" from Chip. A few chortles and expressions of puzzlement.

"Figure drawing helped me understand how to envision something, then execute the bigger picture. 'Thoughtfully and strategically,' as Furnsby just stated.

"As students in a figure drawing class, we had that moment when the beautiful model dropped her robe to the floor and stood there in all her naked glory, surrounded by us teenagers in awe and dropped jaws. Then our teacher said to study the woman and draw. Draw!

"As uncomfortably interesting as it was, we giggled and took in the nude figure before us. We learned to observe—have the details of the model's body enter our eyes and brains and come out of our hands. With charcoal pencils, we sketched this human subject five feet in front of us, onto newsprint five inches in front of us."

Chip says, "I sketch all the time. I observe and record. I draw regularly in my sketchbook—"

"Yeah, Chip, we don't care," Johnny dismisses the interruption. "Your current drawing activities are clearly for the audience, putting on a show like a circus animal."

Parker ignores the banter and continues, "What I learned most from my class was seeing the whole picture. In figure drawing, not seeing the whole picture can be catastrophic. The teacher instructed us to lightly glide our hand over our paper, imagining how we might capture the entire figure in broad strokes. And we are taught to not yet touch the paper with our pencils. As our hand gracefully outlines the figure over and over again without actually producing a visible charcoal line, our instructor finally commanded, 'Begin!' Without a break in motion, our pencils touch the paper, and the profile of the nude body is softly outlined."

More snickers.

"Don't laugh, friends. Though this sounds like art gibberish, imagine the disasters that could occur if we didn't follow this technique. An eager student might focus on the model's foot, carefully drawing each toe, highlighting the textures and shadows. As this eager student moves up the body slowly, drawing the legs, the waist, the torso, he might realize that there is not enough room on the sheet of paper to draw the model's head!"

Laughter of camaraderie fills the dining room.

Chip agrees, "If you spend these four days designing the perfect entry facade for this WoMA, you will have squandered your limited time, and not have a complete design in the end."

"Exactly," confirms Parker.

Waving her arms desperately, Margo wants the stage, "Speaking of the human body, I am thinking less about charcoal pencils, and more about the five senses."

"What the?" Ling reacts.

Margo quickly embellishes knowing that group critique awaits. "Whether a classroom building or civic center, my most successful works of architecture go beyond merely what it looks like." She tries to address Ling's accusation of the Instagramable moment.

Looking around intently, Margo says, "With a design for a restaurant bar, for example, my ideas surpass the exercise of picking things like the tile for the counter or fabric on the banquette. As a comprehensive and cohesive experience, design is more than the materials you see and touch. Architecture is a journey through"—she pauses for effect—"all the five senses."

Ling picks up on this theme instantly to show Dame Margo that her thinking isn't so profound. "Yes, sight. Selecting colors, textures, finishes. But we must keep in mind other aspects that an occupant sees, such as the lighting design. No, not just the look of stylish light fixtures, but what about Kelvins to lumens, fluorescent vs. LED vs. tungsten? What one sees goes even further, such as environmental graphics or maybe uniform design for the staff."

Her husband syncs with his wife's rhythm, "And there is touch. After the eye sees, the hand will take in more information. The visitor will touch the brick, for example. The texture might be smooth or rough. When seated, the body relaxes against wool cushions, and fingertips notice zigzag stitching. The body also feels temperature, such as the warmth of a carpeted living room contrasted to the cool stone floor of the kitchen."

Margo is perturbed her topic is quickly being appropriated.

Parker chimes in, "At the Chapel of St. Ignatius in Seattle, beeswax coats the interior walls. Not only providing a lustrous plaster surface for the eye to see and the hand to touch, but the walls also provide a sweet scent to smell."

Johnny can't wait to join in, diffusing Margo's attempt to grandstand. "I recall another project—a bagel shop that purposefully exhausted the oven's appetizing aroma into the street. The enticing smell of freshly baked goods attracted customers. There, architecture confronted one's nose."

Parker says, "Aside from smell, our Buddhist temple in Virginia involved sound. Our design transitioned the visitor from a grass path to an intimate gravel walk. The sound of feet shuffling on loose gravel slows the visitor to a meditative pace."

Wanting credit for a topic she started, Margo awkwardly rises from her chair and explains, "I am not talking about Parker's dirt and rocks. Architecture is sound indeed. Back to my design for a bar, everyone. I selected the music that accompanies the design, complementing the spirit of the space as it evolves through the day. Brisk music welcomes the early birds, even keel classical selections buzz for the professional at lunch, eclectic techno lounge greets happy hour, and jazz ballads play for the sophisticated diners. The architectural experience includes music."

Not impressed, Johnny asks, "What about the last one of our five senses? What about taste? I don't imagine someone visiting one of my office buildings and licking the conference room walls."

Chip responds, "For the design of a chocolate factory in Boston, we created tasting stations that presented the company's recipes and ingredients."

"Fine," Margo utters with barely an acknowledgment, not knowing whether to remain standing. She tries to wrap up the conversation like the end of one of her symposiums. "Through provoking all five senses, the sensual experience of architecture promotes emotional content that enlivens the human experience. Alcatraz Island is the perfect setting to capture the five senses: the salty air, the sound of crashing waves, crumbling concrete under our feet, the damp jail cells, the despair of forgotten buildings surrounded by bright sun and blue skies."

"Nicely stated, Hunters," concludes Parker with a mouthful of braised duck and fish flakes. For this brief hour, he is just another architect competing for a major project, participating in an exchange of ideas between peers. In this vacuum of intellectual exchange, he is not a person-of-interest in a double homicide, at least for the duration of a meal.

But the mind of this San Francisco architect meanders back to Celadonna. Earlier today, the enticing warmth of her skin boosted by the smoky scent of perfume left a scarring imprint on him. Now, with plates being taken away by restaurant staff, Parker remains immobilized in his dining chair. Everyone else has returned to their galleries to continue work, yet he slips into a regrettable despondent state.

Three words resound in his ears, over and over again as an audio loop—a whisper so close to his ear that the heat of her breath brands the message into his soul. She voiced so softly, "You need me."

GOLDEN GATE BRIDGE
1937

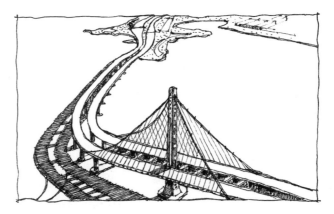

EASTERN SPAN
BAY BRIDGE
OAKLAND
2013

CHAPTER 27

An Outcropping

PARKER A. RAND, self-tormenting architect, sits on the floor in his Magnar-assigned workspace, a museum gallery temporarily transformed into a supposed architect's studio. Parker draws furiously in his sketchbook, a prized leather-bound memento from the Ponte Vecchio bridge in Florence, where he watched with excited college eyes, the leather craftsman engrave three gold letters on the spine, P-A-R.

Head and hands deep in drawing, the architect fretfully switches between a soft lead 314 pencil and his fat black Pentel marker. He sketches, scrawls, and scratches in search of design ideas, frantically flipping pages back and forth. He is questioning all the progress made over the last few days. Whirring around Parker are his three employees, who try to act diligent by typing madly on a laptop, sorting photographs from the Alcatraz visit, and tearing through old books and magazines. In actuality, they are doing little if nothing, as they patiently await orders from their great but suffering leader.

A museum staffer dressed in gray on gray enters the PAR Designs gallery. Brunette curls and overly applied eye shadow more suited for a night club than working at SFMOMA—attractive enough to startle Parker, she says in a quiet hush, "Mr. Rand, Magnar Jones requests your presence immediately."

As expected, the architect's mind unravels quickly. *More questions about Lars von Meester and Lands End? Further investigation into Maxwell Brand and the lighthouse? Does Magnar know about my encounter with Celadonna on the balcony? At the police station?*—and more importantly, their brief hand-in-hand walk concluding in a graceless embrace?

It meant nothing, Parker reflects to himself, *nothing happened.* But he has a woeful way of making nothing into something, and something into everything. The mere graze of a woman's beautiful arm accompanied by an intimate smile could be the end of days for this obsessive architect.

Befuddled, Parker asks jumping up to attention, "Why? Why does Mr. Jones want to see me?"

"Sorry, I don't know. Mr. Rand, please just come with me," a deadpan response.

Leaving the gallery with the woman, Parker gives token instructions to his team members, "Uuh, just keep working. Please…just come up with some ideas and drawings for discussion upon my return." The generic orders infuriate the employees who have been obediently and patiently ready for hours.

She escorts the architect down the elevator, through the lobby, and onto a warm sidewalk of this late afternoon. Citizens on the street smile, having completed yet another day of work. The momentum of city traffic flows briskly. Commuters on scooters and bikes pass one another, cars honk avoiding buses—all swimming downstream to either happy hour or happy home.

Parker notices one frozen object within the current of rush hour. He stands uneasy noticing the same black automobile with black windows and black trim into which Celadonna ushered him previously. The dark-haired museum attendant opens the car door, gestures gracefully with her arm, and he drops into the sumptuous white-leather interior—hopelessly expecting Celadonna inside. But no, she is not present.

The architect contemplates the lyrical Muzak that fills the cabin attempting to welcome him, put him at ease. But the selection does not soften the foreboding circumstances. Rather, it makes the commute more bizarre and chilling. *Who chooses this kind of music? What writes this crap?*

Saying nothing at all, not a hello or welcome, the driver launches the short journey. He is skilled at maneuvering through downtown traffic to rise up onto the Bay Bridge heading towards the East Bay. As Parker is transported over the bay, his critical eye judges the design of the bridge. He immediately concurs with a past conclusion as a college student when driving back and forth on this commute: The Bay Bridge is a far second place to the iconic Golden Gate Bridge only 20 minutes away.

Parker tries to take his mind off a displeased Magnar waiting at the end of the trip. He preoccupies himself thinking, *The Bay Bridge, a drab shade of army gray, is nothing more than a utilitarian double-decker commuting corridor. Whereas, the Golden Gate Bridge is a bright-red, one-mile-long suspension bridge, an internationally recognized landmark, declared as one of the Seven Wonders of the Modern World*

Traveling efficiently in the steel, glass, and rubber container, Parker crosses the halfway point, Yerba Buena Island. He now travels on the eastern span of the bridge, a relatively new structure. He argues in his head, *This project was recorded to be one of the most expensive public works projects in California history at a final staggering cost of $6.5 billion. The original budget was merely $250 million.*

He sneers, *And this disappointing design is infuriating. So clumsy, so inelegant. A total missed opportunity!*

He wonders how it is possible that in one area of the bay, architects created the breathtaking Golden Gate Bridge, but another area, the result is so unacceptable. He debates this as he whisks under the sloppy suspension cables of this new costly stretch of bridge.

Getting off the bridge turning left, Parker realizes that the driver is heading in the direction of uc Berkeley, his old stomping ground. *Why would Magnar want to meet me here? At least talking on my college campus is better than the police station.*

But the automobile continues past the university, heading north and upslope to the Berkeley Hills. The driver finally eases the big town car into a parking space on a precarious incline, arriving at a neighborhood spot, Indian Rock Park.

Parker recalls this public green, where he and his college crush, Adrienne Veley, once watched the sun set, and talked about a future as architectural partners. Thoughts of disappointment enter his mind now.

Indian Rock possesses a single massive rock outcropping surrounded by fields of grass. An optimistic setting, the park is a majestic and symbolic design of nature. The chauffeur steps out from the car, comes around efficiently to the other side, and opens the passenger door. Again without a word or even a sound, this ninja-like driver gestures the architect to exit. Pointing towards the top of the giant outcropping composed of Northbrae Rhyolite, the driver suggests the final destination of this mysterious journey.

Nervous to meet Magnar one on one, Parker recalls an old *New York Times* article that described Indian Rock as a "favorite make-out spot for couples…marijuana smoking, meditating and sunset-gazing." None of these activities could possibly be on Magnar's agenda. Parker notices the steep incline and the vertical rocky surfaces, and he thinks of von Meester falling off a big rock. He also thinks of Brand standing at a great height for the last time.

Parker walks uphill, more strenuous due to the mysterious circumstances than the physical challenge. Passing several amateur rock climbers, he finally arrives at the pinnacle. The panoramic view from Oakland's downtown to the Berkeley campus, from the San Francisco Bay to Marin County, amazes. This rare summit offers views of both the Bay Bridge and Golden Gate Bridge and reiterates his internal design critique.

As Parker marvels at this encompassing sight of dusk sun, a single soft hand reaches around his waist from behind. Surprised, he leaps forward and creates a safe distance from the stranger's reach. Turning around awkwardly and ensuring that his footing is steady, he sees not Magnar, but Celadonna Kimm. He is not sure which of the two would be less unsettling.

"Hello, Mr. Rand," greets Celadonna in her sweet voice. The welcome is warm accompanied by a short chuckle, her defenses down.

"You are not Mr. Jones. I mean, obviously. I guess I am sort of relieved, though I am not really...frankly, I am completely confused."

In this particular warm light, she appears more natural than usual, less makeup, flowing hair let down sloppily. With short cropped white jeans, she pairs a blue T-shirt that is worn to a wonderful level of broken-in softness. As the easy sun strikes her body, his nervous eyes spot vague outlines of lace trim under her shirt.

He studies her white Converse sneakers and says, "I don't know why, but I never figured you would own a pair of old school, Chuck Taylor, All Star kicks." He has no idea why he made such a detailed reference.

She does not comment, but gestures to the rock and takes a seat herself. Both seated atop Indian Rock's magnificent setting, Celadonna is gracefully poised like a scale figure in a Sunday artist's landscape painting. In contrast, Parker squats awkwardly—conflicted, constantly moving and trying to find a natural position.

She explains, her hand on one of his knees, "I only have twenty minutes," and she doesn't mean "about twenty," but precisely twenty.

With no time to waste, she jumps into a declaration previously rehearsed in her head. "I feel like my favorite song is playing, and you haven't asked me to dance."

An odd but clever metaphor. He continues internally, *Is this a game? Part of the design competition? Part of Magnar's role as a puppet master?*

To date, Celadonna and Parker have had no substantial conversations, only obscure exchanges, traded glances, and stolen moments. He fails at prompting a discussion, "We don't really know each other, but...well, what about that first email with the list? Why are we here, and—?"

Interrupting, Celadonna says awkwardly, "I am drawn to you, and you need me. You need me to win the competition." She says this as fast as she can, as if speed would make it less awkward for her. And efficiency can provide bravery.

What in the world? Parker is beginning to panic, hands perspiring. Ignoring that she just professed being attracted to him, he focuses more on the word she said, "drawn." He previously heard how he supposedly needs her, and yet, he drifts from confusion to analysis. His mind ready to implode with questions for kindle and doubts for fuel. *How will she help me win? By influencing Magnar's final selection?* he protests to himself.

An amiable woman revealing her abbreviated thoughts, she blurts out with great courage, "Parker, I am charmed by your naive charms, enticed by your sincerity and insecurity, and captivated by your talents. I have watched you for years now. You amaze me, and I adore all that is you." Her delivery is consistent and natural, and the message lands in his lap like Sisyphus's massive boulder. Does Parker push the big stone up the hill of Indian Rock, or let it roll down to the town car?

Though he has always wished to hear this kind of forward admission from a girl, a woman, he has never been so lucky, so blessed. With little experience in such matters of the heart and the opposite sex, he is unable to thoroughly process her words. Thoughts start to downward spiral, *What is happening here? This woman is the girlfriend, the lover, of my client.*

Parker's anguished mind falls further into an abyss of irreverent thoughts. *Am I on the brink of madness? Can I be both idiot and intellect, fool and artist, and—* he continues to unravel.

Celadonna watches the sun fade, as the air gets a brief cutting chill. She feels the gears rotating inside Parker, like a Rube Goldberg contraption. She actually believes she can hear his thoughts clicking through gears and cycling. Complacent, she has done her part for tonight. She stated her emotions frankly. She does not seek a reply.

"It's getting a little cold. I now need to leave you. But only for now."

He doesn't know what to say or do. But in a modest act of chivalry, Parker takes off his gray sport coat. His arms are instantly cold with only a short sleeve shirt on, but he is committed to his polite gesture. He places his jacket over her shoulders. She does not tuck her arms in the sleeves, because she enjoys feeling how this man's coat envelopes her.

She rises quickly, bends down towards the awkwardly-seated Parker. She puts her palm behind his head, stroking some waves of hair, leans in, mouths inches away. She whispers, "Farewell for now, my artist. I want you to win, and I will be your muse."

She offers an expression she once heard on a TV teen drama, "Let's just pretend that we kissed."

Suddenly, Celadonna Kimm darts down the big rock with sure footing like a cat on a New York fire escape. She races towards the black car that respectfully awaits, and opens her own door catching the driver off guard. Before the door fully shuts, the car is in motion, and leaves in a flurry of sounds from plastic and machinery.

Cold at this moment, but only in temperature—Parker places his arms around himself to stay warm. The view has transitioned from the Golden Hour to dark skies. The warmth of the earth's surface rises up into the bitter air and causes city lights to twinkle. He is unable to move. Like ancient stones and tree roots, the architect is petrified. His mind is swirling deliberations that he has no tools to process.

He doesn't know what is next for this day, for this competition. For his life. But for a brief minute, and only lasting one minute, he feels content—an emotion unknown to him.

Sisyphus's rock has rolled down the hill again. But this time, Parker stays at the top with no intention of going after the stone. For today, his job is done, and he is the mythical absurd hero. Having faced his own existence and accepting it, if only for a minute, today is calm, just today. Akin to Camus's character, if Parker's world lacks reason, then it is through struggling for meaning that might bring him happiness.

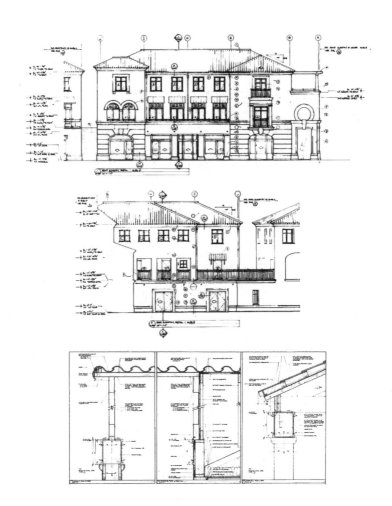

CHAPTER 28

Day Four of Four:
Flirting with Misfortune

C OMMON KNOWLEDGE IDENTIFIES the number 13 as unlucky. In Chinese culture, any reference to the number 4 is considered bad luck, because the Chinese pronunciation for 4 is similar in sound to the word for death.

Today is the fourth and final day. As decreed by Magnar, the contest for the new Museum of Abstract Art at Alcatraz concludes at 10 p.m. As the architects begin their dash towards the end, as they hone in on their final design ideas, winning fades a little. A small part within each architect just wants to have the day end. Like a cross country runner nearing fatigue, the goal is to have the honor of merely finishing—or with another mindset, to be put out of his misery.

Johnny checks in with his team, organized as ever—as expected. There is a stark contrast between the too logical, systematized creativity from General Architects vs. the other competitors whose studios are starting to look like a combination of a messy garage sale and a place where drawings go to die.

"Work with me, everyone!" yells Johnny forcefully gripping a clipboard, pen in hand held high, big strides throughout the gallery. "We have researched this type of building and its specific needs. We have discussed our typology of museums."

"Check, boss!" an associate responds with enthusiasm.

"We have investigated the site," Johnny says. He looks not-so-nonchalantly over his shoulder at his growing audience.

"Check!"

"After inquiry and debate, we authored our design parti."

"Yes, sir, check!"

"From there, the proposed building took its initial shape. We have diagrams and sketches, as well as design assertions and catch phrases."

"Check!"

"Today, we are following up with developed drawings, by hand and computer, as well as making big physical models. Not small." He claims, "Bigger is better!"

"Check," and the associates cheer.

"Lastly, as we refine our big picture vision, we are verifying all the technical components of the program, as in, how many galleries, how many elevators and fire exits, seating capacity of the restaurant, number of offices, and so on.

"Check, boss."

"We also researched city code requirements, and of course, the project budget."

"Check, Mr. Furnsby!"

Johnny tosses a self-congratulatory smile towards his team, then towards the observing members of the public. He has checked off with a big red marker his design to-do list, as if an artistic process could be so formulaic. He feels the gravity of his Cal Poly education over his Cooper Union studies. Constructability over creativity. City codes instead of design philosophy. Budget/schedule vs. the poetics of space.

Nearby, Chip Tooney and Ling Liang are more artists than corporate designers. Though their Harvard training instilled business-y platitudes, like "form follows function," their teachers require that imagination is foremost in their work. To widen their thinking, the couple engages their employees in an exhaustive debate on the responsibility of architects in society. Seated around a small work table, an hour passes of Ivy League-fashioned intellectual jousting. Such a mental break is part of ChipLing's process, and for today, it is part of their public performance.

Though enjoying the afternoon's intellectual back and forth, Ling finds herself needing a break. On her way out, she winks at her husband, unnoticed by anyone else. She doesn't mind that they have, after all their discussions, as yet to create their ultimate plan for Alcatraz. Only rough ideas so far, and this is day four. No worries. This is the kind of adrenalin-fueled, last-minute brainstorming that some architects believe brings forth great design.

Ling strolls the galleries which are dimly lit and empty—void of the public. The evening is not quite late yet. She finds peace for once, and appreciates the voices of past artists, not just the Abstract painters that Magnar enjoys, but also the Impressionist, Surrealists, and Renaissance masters. Though Alcatraz will become a venue for Abstract art, she feels that admiring only one period is limiting, like listening exclusively to orchestral works when designing a symphony hall. She thinks, *No, maybe some head banging, heavy metal rock might loosen up the thinking, might even relax my East Coast and Ivy League uptightness.* No one is listening to her self-judgment, as she sometimes finds her predictable Bostonian wifey-self distasteful.

Abruptly and unexpectedly sad, she realizes that her adoring husband and rigid education don't allow her to relax, take chances, or have mindless thrills. East Coast propriety runs deep, as she considers how Maxwell Brand's Southern Californian spirit provided him the freedom to be whoever he wanted, whenever he wanted.

Ling says to herself, "He really enjoyed his existence. He was boisterous and confident, rarely caring what others thought. He even dressed in those absurd plaid suits." Often, she would like to shed herself of her dogmatic teachings and the Ivy/Stepford Wife mold.

Having worked into the late hours of the past three nights, she is tired and gets giddy. Light headed, she rebels in her thoughts, *Many say sleep-deprivation impairs mental functions. But I disagree. I believe the fumes from my exhaustion fuels my thinking.*

Not drunk with alcohol, but drunk on exhaustion, she stumbles to a familiar setting, the fifth-floor bridge—the beautifully engineered glass structure that, on that first day, hosted name calling and accusations of murder. Suspended 75 feet in the air, the bridge's white steely frame looks like a bunch of bones. Ling leans her upper body over the edge of the handrail, and peers down to black and gray marble on the first floor.

She has no idea that she is being followed and watched from the hidden crevices of the building.

Disoriented and exhilarated, the Boston architect wonders if this is what Lars felt as he looked over the cliff to crashing waves below. She also tries to imagine what Maxwell suffered, and she pretends to see flames and smoke rising up to engulf her. She teases herself tilting her torso farther forward dangerously over the handrail. She realizes how this precarious position excites her.

Suddenly, Parker comes running up to her. In a panicked voice, he asks, "Ling, what are you doing?"

"Hi, Parker. Oh nothing at all." She is punchy and returns her body to equilibrium.

"Why are you leaning over the handrail? It's really dangerous." He gets ghostly white, as he thinks back to Maxwell's mention of a possible Lars suicide. Parker feels very ill all of a sudden.

Ling grabs the handrail and tilts forward again, feeling her heart accelerate, then quickly pulls back and catches her breath. She even giggles for a brief moment.

"What are you doing? Stop, please."

She realizes that she is flirting not just with death, but with this attractive man. Ling has noticed Celadonna glaring at Parker at the press conference, her standing at his gallery pleading for attention, and the two standing cozy on the balcony. Ling's female intuition senses something, not sure what, but she wants to find out what the fuss is all about. She wants to draw Parker nearer.

With hands gripping the handrail once more, she pushes up on her arms, locking them strong at the elbow, straightening them vertically like buttresses on a cathedral. Supporting her full body weight on her arms and hands, shoulders too, she pushes up enough to let her feet off the ground a tad at first, then a little more. As she hoped, Parker rushes close and grabs her by the waist, placing her back firmly on the floor of the bridge. Atypically, Ling is full of a zealous enthusiasm.

Parker yells, "What is wrong with you? Haven't we had enough accidents recently? Do you want to die or something?"

Her lack of sleep makes her playful. She places one hand on his, keeping his grip on her waist. The other hand reaches for his check, and she says, "Parker, my sweet lost architect, I am just messing around, just teasing." She winks, not too dissimilar to the farewell wink to her husband.

Releasing her waist, he steps back quickly. "Stop it!"

Parker is not used to these games. He has never found himself confident in the antics of flirtation or seduction, and especially with a married woman. He asks, "Ling, where is Chip? Don't you guys have work to do?"

"I guess my fun should be over. I should return to my protective husband and be at his side. I should be that predictably collaborative business partner and affectionate spouse."

Parker is shocked to hear this highly regarded designer, the likely better half of ChipLing, speak with such disregard. All he can think is that she must be drunk or really tired, or both.

"I am sorry, Ling. I have to go. I was just taking a break and wanted to walk around a little. Sorry, see you later." He is so confused that all he can think of is to be apologetic. Eager to return to this team, Parker leaves her side while mumbling to himself words of doubt and accusations.

Not long after, a shadowy figure moves out from the far corner. Extended swatches of gold fabric billow in the air and settle in front of Ling, startling her.

"Omigod, Celadonna! You scared the shit out of me creeping up like that," exclaims Ling.

Celadonna Kimm doesn't say a word as Ling tries to calm herself. "How's it going? What are you doing here?" Ling asks nervously.

Celadonna has been standing in the margins watching Ling this whole time as she first arrived at the bridge, then flirting with Parker. Celadonna hisses, "Leave him alone." Her voice drops lower and slower, "This boy is mine."

"I don't want any trouble, with you or Magnar. I was just playing around with Mr. Rand. I don't even know him. I don't even like him much."

"Stay out of my way, or—"

Ling doesn't hear an actual threat, but the effect is scary enough. She responds, "Lady, you are one crazy...leave me alone. I have work to do, work to complete for Mr. Jones. Who, by the way—isn't he your boyfriend, and not that nervous architect, Parker?"

Something snaps in Celadonna and unexpectedly, too quickly, the fatigued Ling feels a forceful shove to her side and finds herself losing balance. Celadonna is slowly but surely trying to push Ling over the handrail to a certain death below. She wants to scream, but her stomach is pressed hard against the steel top rail. From high above, her eyes take in the ground floor far below.

Ling barely lets out, "Help, stop," and her body partially folds over the railing like a doll that has seen too many years of childhood. But she has yet to fall to her demise. Remaining in a crumpled position partially bent over the rail, and at the mercy of Celadonna, Ling freezes. She thinks of Chip scolding her for the wandering around in an empty area of the building, sealed off from the public. Also, she wonders if she were to fall, how her colleagues will speak of her when found splattered on the marble five floors down. To the same group, she spoke so graphically and horribly of Lars's fall to death.

Celadonna, a woman determined to show who is in charge, holds Ling there for a few more seconds. Then to her surprise and relief, she is pulled back to safety. Both women crash to the floor of the bridge, Ling's face staring down through the glass pavers, reminded of what awaited her if she were to have been thrown over.

"You are in my way. Know that. Beware!" says Celadonna. In a single motion, she is up and walking off the bridge. Her long, gold dress flutters behind leaving a whiff of menace. One could almost envision Celadonna mounting a broomstick. Ling's short break ends with this sinister thought.

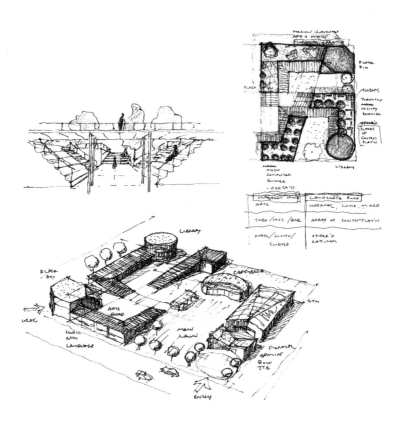

Death by Design at Alcatraz

CHAPTER 29

Any Last Words?

F OR ARCHITECTS, the term *charette* stirs a deep and arcane meaning. Charette refers to a concentrated session of designing. French in origin, charette translates literally to "cart." The word is known to have originated from the famed school in Paris, the École des Beaux-Arts. For over three centuries and counting, this institution has studied the architecture of ancient Greece and Rome, amongst other significant historical chapters.

Over a hundred years ago, during the conclusion of a frantic design assignment, the students rushed to produce final touches on their drawings and models. Enthusiastically, the professor wheeled a cart through the design classroom. He yelled, "Charette, charette!" indicating that the dreaded deadline has arrived. The word echoed through the panicked studio as a final warning for students, as they also chanted in succession, "Charette, charrette, charette!" This word sounded the alarm: Time's up. Turn your project in immediately. As the professor raced by each desk, the students placed their completed work in the cart—in the charette. Or in many cases, their incomplete work.

Presently, this ritual continues at many universities, and the trauma of a teacher yelling "charette" has the same intimidating effect on the students intensely working as the deadline ticks closer and closer. For professionals too, a frenzied final stage in the process persists even today, as one might hear an architect say that he is "on charette," or "charetting."

A pressure cooker of creative juices and half-baked ideas, this final evening on the fourth day of the Alcatraz competition is the charette. The competitors work at high speed, desperately sprinting towards the end of their journey. No one cares to ask where Parker disappeared to yesterday afternoon when he was asked to see the client, "Magnar Jones." The teams are furiously in production mode, game faces on, eyes laser focused on winning. Nothing else.

Ling returns, too embarrassed to say anything. Mortified of flirting with risk, death, and a fellow competitor, she post-rationalizes her exploit by accusing her lack of sleep, and hence, lack of judgment. An upstanding Ivy League alumna getting into a cat fight on a cat walk—she doesn't say a word about Celadonna either.

No one, not even Chip, notices a typically verbose Ling's atypical quietness. The ChipLing team are busy using technology as an extension of their bodies, eyes glued to a large monitor, hands on a keyboard and mouse clicking with determination. They mockup with Sketchup, then digitally model with 3DS Max, and applying the animation tools of Maya, create photorealistic visuals as well as fly-throughs. Though virtuoso computer work will likely steal the show, a small physical model is being meticulously crafted out of basswood and metal parts (?)—precisely cut, sanded, fitted, and polished.

Yet, Chip doubts the effort, "Is our model-making approach, its narrative technique, sympathetic to our artistic agenda? Our ideas are formed, yet what is its representation."

From a distance that provides little clarity, the crowd studies the wood and steel model in progress, and amongst themselves, they try to answer the philosophically vague query.

In the adjacent gallery, the Hunting Ground associates are drawing crude diagrams with Niji pens and Copic color markers. The child-like sketches indicate the organization of their design scheme—adjacencies of components like galleries to offices, coat check to auditorium. One of Margo's employees taps into the Grasshopper software to construct generative algorithms. The digital efforts result in graphic patterns envisioned to be water-jet cut from large zinc panels of complex compound forms that will comprise the building's exterior.

Hunting Ground also embarks on a large model with a highly conceptual approach. The mockup is made crudely from materials foraged from the island—literal sticks and stones, leaves and grass. Margo believes that a seductive work of abstract sculpture, rather than a scale architectural representation, will win points with Magnar who favors Abstract Expressionism.

Yearning for a past world of design, Parker and his associates from PAR Designs advocate old school methods. The principal architect believes his soul is better fed this way, than with a computer. The team has surrounded themselves with rulers, plastic triangles, and circle templates, as well as sticks of HB, H, and 2H lead. Nostalgically, Parker wants to recreate a romantic myth in his head, a Renaissance-like atelier setting in Paris or Florence.

Unpolished even makeshift, their architectural model is intentionally rudimentary. Rather than a realistic model with small cars and trees, the work is meant to exhibit progress, testing ideas over several days and still, ongoing testing. Adding and subtracting, the outcome is an expression, not of a finished idea, but of process—a creative path well-traveled.

Contrasting PAR Designs' artisanal efforts and antiquated devices, Johnny Furnsby and his members of General Architects, Inc. develop their design using AutoCAD, the industry-standard two-dimensional drafting software, and Revit, the industry-standard three-dimensional informational software. Predictable yes and not too sexy, but the team's speed and facility create a proposed design faster and more thorough than their competitors. Furnsby enjoys the resources of his company, using their desktop 3D printer and vacuum-forming machine.

Parker, aware of the sound of a 3D printer in motion, stands close to his associates and complains, "A soul-less device that only generates an object as cold as his computer files, as sterile as his designs for commercial buildings." Parker doesn't care if Johnny hears him or not, but the public audience certainly does, as intended. They titter at the competitiveness of this event.

This is a design competition and not a phase of work to produce the final set of construction documents from which to build, as in blueprints and technical details. Meaning, the proposal from each architect to be revealed tomorrow will be more about a preliminary vision than a fleshed out roof plan with gutters and downspouts. On the other hand, Parker convinces his employees that, "Even the meticulous analysis of water drainage is part of our design's poetics." Is this an accurate statement or more grandstanding for an audience?

With charcoal sticks in hand, he adds vague shade and shadow to an illustration and yells out, "Upon arriving at the island, what is the identity of our project, the personality and character, its essence?"

The public eagerly await a response from one of Parker's associates. A rare behind-the-scenes glimpse—the attendees stand at the edge of the galleries to watch how ideas might take their final shape in these remaining hours. As they observe and listen, so too does Magnar.

He and Celadonna sit in a small security office surrounded by monitors and cramped by voyeurism. She observes, "Mag, you have constructed a peeping-Tom peephole into the drama, and it is unfolding like the final dress rehearsal for a Broadway musical." She has returned to her roleplaying as the admiring lover.

"But better yet, darlin.'" He waves his hands at the monitors. "Look here. It's fascinating. The musicians are still learning their notes, dancers are tripping over each other, ill-fitting costumes are yet to be tailored, and the actors are only now studying their cues. I couldn't have imagined a more potent scene—architecture as drama, as theater. It is improvisational, organic, and unpredictable. That is why my idea is so genius."

His shoulders broaden and he smiles with too much satisfaction. "Is it unnerving? Yes. Slightly sinister? Yes. Is it magnificent? Oh indeed, yes, yes. People will be talking about this for generations to come."

As time ticks down, Parker is heard instructing his teammates as well reminding himself, "A client presentation must represent both our fabricated reality and the passion of our ideas. Our presentation must transport the client into a stirring imaginary world that was constructed first within our heads, then poured out, heart and soul, for the client to experience—and in this case, the public too."

He and his team realize that the final piece to the design puzzle of research, drawings, and models is the performance. Showmanship.

Besides the visuals of drawings, the expression of a great design must also be in words, a verbal demonstration to accompany the pictorial. As when they were students in a crit, these WoMA architects must deliver a convincing narrative, whether it is an elevator pitch of design soundbytes or the weaving of personal experiences and metaphors. The presentation, this final performance, is where all the ideas—from crafted verbiage to physical and digital artifacts—are exhibited in not only a coherent fashion, but a dramatic and theatrical one. The stakes are much higher than when in school.

They all learned outrageous approaches in their architecture education: an intellectual pedagogical speech or a bohemian poetry reading, a song-and-dance number combined with a county fair puppet show, or a sleight-of-hand magician with the desperation of a used-car salesman. The presentation of the designs, which Magnar has allocated 20 minutes to each team, is the culmination of not just four long days, but years and decades of life experiences that precedes them. Death happens to precede them too.

"Let's be stimulating and persuasive. Bring in the dancing elephants!" says Johnny half-jokingly. Then he looks desperately to the audience for an enthusiastic response. But their chortles are cut short as all heads turn toward the Hunting Ground gallery.

With no warning, Margo keels over screaming in pain, clutching her stomach. Sharp pains strike acutely inside her body. Her employees leap from their computer stations to their leader, now looking for the first time ever, quite powerless as she lay on the floor like a rejected work of Origami.

"What's wrong?!" an associate asks.

Margo yells out, "My stomach is in pain. Aaargh!" She tries to breathe. "Feels like I ate something really terrible." Tears of agony form in the corners of her eyes.

Her teammates help her up onto a drafting stool. It would have been better to leave her on the floor. One asks, "What did you eat earlier, that rich cuisine, like that bison tartar?"

With little awareness of the dreadfulness of the situation, another teammate offers, "Anthony Bourdain always gets sick eating fancy stuff traveling the world. He says it is worth it though, to give up comfort and health to taste the greatest flavors various countries have to offer."

"Shut up!" shouts the other.

Margo groans in total agony and says, "I don't know. I was socializing with Johnny and Chip a little earlier. They seem fine. We all ate the same dishes, didn't we?"

"What did you three talk about?" a team member asks trying to take Margo's mind off of the pain.

Still grabbing her belly and shrieking, pushing here and there like a doctor trying to locate the source of the pain, she waits for the jabs to subside. With short breaths, she responds, "Those two are oddball characters…they are still talking about…accidents, murders…deaths occurring at great heights…"

The London architect looks up with eyes big, like a cat looking around a dark bedroom in search of prey.

One employee says, "You don't think—?"

Margo's thoughts start to tumble. "I do," her voice deadly serious, and an octave lower.

"C'mon. No way."

She stares back solemnly and takes a deep breath so to speak forcefully, "Look at what has been happening. Look around us. Two architects dead, this weird Magnar-guy keeping us here like prisoners, extravagantly bizarre meals, the pressure of the competition—"

At this moment, she has the scary realization that someone might have found an opportune moment to continue enhancing the odds for winning: 1 out of 6 to 1 out of 5. Now 1 in 4. Possibly 1 in 3?

Margo freezes thinking a menacing thought. As horror washes over her body, she mutters, "Do you think someone tried to poison me?"

A cloud of threat descends upon their gallery. Severe cramps brings a scream of agony and reminds them of the terror present.

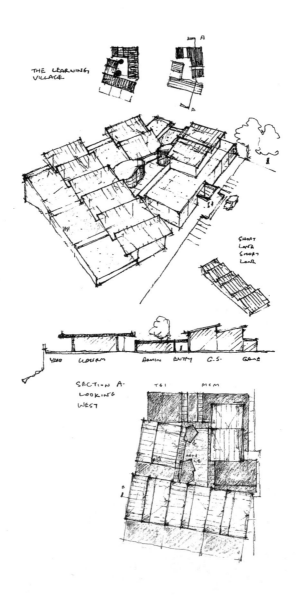

THE LEARNING
VILLAGE

SHORT
LANE
SHORT
LANE

YARD   CLDRM   ADMIN   ENTRY   C.S-   GAME

SECTION A-
LOOKING
WEST

CHAPTER 30

Tick Tock Goes the Clock

T IME TICKS BY. The clock's hour hand appears to move as fast as the minute hand. And minutes pass like seconds.

The architects decline their dinner break, their last supper—waving off the distractions of more highbrow banter and posturing. No to "textuality," "mimesis," and "Derrida." No, to wood sorrel in sheep milk's yogurt.

Margo pushes through the agonizing pains—sharp jabs that shoot through her innards, like a snake trying to snap his way out of a straw basket. She, too, decides not to eat a thing, not even a snack.

On the floor in the corner, the famed British architect is spent, but still has her wits intact and mental octane turned up several degrees. Even in anguish, she provides explicit instructions to her associates, as the team jumps from computer station to flipping through drawings for their immobilized employer to review. Whether nausea from a stomach bug or food poisoning, whether plain stress or an attempt on her life, Margo endures and snubs her threatening situation.

"Ladies, the design work is not yet up to par. Work faster. Work smarter. Work better. This isn't just about impressing our client. The city is watching me, watching all of us. I am soon to walk onto a world stage, and this design is so far apologetic."

The public is eager to see if Dame Margo Hunters will indeed compose through architecture, some kind of Tenth Symphony.

Nearing the conclusion of this architecture competition, the remaining four studios are a mess, a war zone of design disputes and battles scars—even lost limbs of an incomplete mock-up of metal, acrylic, and cardboard. Unsuccessful drawings litter the floor, aborted model parts are tossed across the gallery, and pages violently torn from magazines are haphazardly stapled to the walls—layers upon senseless layers. Pencils and pens of all sizes become tripping hazards like a banana peel awaiting its clown. Computer software crash due to immense file sizes, printers jam, and toners deplete as they always do when approaching a deadline.

And the principal architects rehearse their presentations. Sometimes, the choreographed performance is that of a well-oiled professional. Other times, it resembles a snake-oil peddler from a Western movie.

Attending the final hour is a rare ticket in town, a spectacular recital of showmanship and disaster. As model glue is drying with the accelerant Zip Kicker, as slides are being reshuffled in PowerPoint for the umpteenth time, onlookers absorb the antics and appreciate the determination of each architect. And the insanity too.

Chatter and rants between designers accompany the humming scanners, while plotter printheads rattle a helpless noise. Basswood is being trimmed and fitted for the models, while tired feet pace on discarded scraps gathering high on the floor. Despite the tragedy at the lighthouse, this fire hazard of discarded paper and kindle is of no concern to anyone in this home stretch. The competitors see, finally see, the definitive period at the end of a four-day-long sentence.

Seated, propped up more likely, on a stool, Ling Liang barely gathers enough breath to declare, "Model looks good, but we might need little trees and people, more details and texture, so that Magnar understands the scale." She takes another deep breath bracing her body on the seat with her shaking arms. "He has to be able to reference himself in our composition, otherwise it is too theoretical and nonrepresentational."

A fatigued Chip Tooney responds, "Damn it, we are out of those little green trees. Someone, anyone, make more mock trees out of the wood dowels over there. Or should we ditch them?" He points at nothing in particular, just waves his arms hoping his employees will follow through with something.

To his staff, Johnny Furnsby states, "Back home, headquarters will love this monumental presentation. Win or lose, there is so much PR value in this design. Win or lose, we will publish this competition story on our corporate blog and through all our media outlets." He looks closely at a computer monitor, "Keep working, try again. The dappled sunlight on the travertine plaza is crude—needs to be less cartoonish."

Nodding his head, the employee is already aware of the improvements needed. The rendering is still in the works after all. Biting his tongue, he is used to this boss prancing around giving superficial orders. The audience snickers, because many of them know an ineffective manager when they see one. They hear Johnny give another obvious instruction, "Make sure you do this well!"

Parker worries, *We still don't have a coherent about. We have pieces and parts of an idea. Yes, it's about beauty, but how is any of this a full design concept? There is no time left. What about, how does my discourse on the beautiful...I mean, darn it, what the heck am I mumbling...?"*

His thoughts trail off, and the employees don't say a word. They know when their boss is in a coiling trance. Do not interrupt his stream of consciousness. Similarly, do not wake up a sleepwalker.

The purge of Parker's thoughts begin again. This time aloud, "Beauty and ugliness can be the same thing. Pretty and deformity can collide. And it's uncanny when splendor is found in unexpected conditions, even disagreeable ones. Can we find beauty in the prison buildings on Alcatraz? But we are also exploring the influence of silence and elementalism, an architecture that is intentionally mute and reserved."

Parker snaps into attention, as his mind comes into focus. "Remember this, friends"—he stands at the front of his gallery addressing the citizens directly—"a simple design means it is simple, and not necessarily simplistic. A simple design can be more than meets the eye." Some attendees are warmed by such evocative words. Others roll their eyes.

For a brief moment, Parker's mind flashes to Celadonna Kimm, and he ponders his own naive nature. Literally pinching himself, Parker returns to the work at hand. "Let's keep at it, team. We need to complete our design soon—as in less than an hour, as in now. We are nearly there."

In real time, the last hour expires as 60 actual minutes. But during a charette, this final hourlong passage appears to vanish in mere minutes. Reminiscent of an episode of *MasterChef* where Gordon Ramsey declares, "Time's up," Johnny is the first to yell, "Times up!"

From the adjacent gallery, Chip hears this and adds, "And, pencils down, folks!"

With the concluding stroke of a pen, last click on the mouse, and the final exhale of drained architects—the four-day competition reaches its conclusion, its ultimatum.

With the utmost of punctuality, Magnar Jones marches towards the galleries, followed by Celadonna pushing a rickety flower cart, as if a remnant from the stage set of *Les Miserable*. The pair aim to be delightful as they try to reference history. In actuality, they appear to the public crowd as merely theme park-ish.

Parker looks to his employees and mutters, "Oh please. I hope Magnar doesn't say it."

Johnny hisses, "Don't do it, Mr. Jones. This would be so wrong."

"This would not be funny at all," begs Chip.

The quiet protests are not heard, and Magnar starts his ridiculous chant, "Charette! Charette!"

He bellows this potent word waving his arm as if he was one of the legendary instructors of the 19th-century Beaux Arts school. He is thoroughly enjoying himself, putting on a display of both commanding aura and comical showbiz. Pushing a faux turn-of-the-century "charette" does not suit Celadonna's typical grace and disposition. Yet, she appreciates being an extra in her boyfriend's theatrical production.

Exhausted nearly to tears, the architects are not amused by this dramatic sham. With little concern for his competitors, Magnar has had his fun. Eventually, Celadonna tires of this mock-charette escapade. Parker tries not to notice that there is no shirt under her designer jacket—just conceited contours of porcelain skin.

Magnar begins to make an announcement to the architects huddled at the front of each gallery, but instead directs his attention towards the public. Unsurprisingly.

Front and center, and ready to grandstand, he proclaims, "Architects, stop work immediately. My international contest has concluded. You are now free to leave and enjoy the rest of the evening in this great city of San Francisco." He opens his arms wide and glows before the audiences. "If you want to stay to straighten up and catch your breath, you are of course allowed to do so. But know this, no further design work will be accepted."

A loose threat for no reason other than effect, the Master of Puppets wants everyone to know that he is, as always, the authority figure. He adds, "If you attempt to add to your presentations, such actions will be grounds for immediate disqualification." No longer a loose threat.

Celadonna jumps in to diffuse his tense words, "Thank you very much for all your work, time and resources, and the perspiration of course."

And certainly no mention of two deceased architects, a near deadly fall from a glass bridge, and potential food poisoning.

"Have a relaxing evening. The restaurant is open for a final meal at sfmoma." Yet none of the architects are interested in yet another pretentious meal of tiny curated portions. Most certainly not Margo Hunters.

Magnar's closing instructions are, "We will meet at noon tomorrow in the ground-floor lobby with the public in tow. My staff will transport your presentations from your studios to the lobby and set everything up for you. Architects, please arrive rested and ready to present to me, my board, and the audience of this city."

As they depart, Magnar hushes to Celadonna, "I am impressed with it all, with them all. Let's head back to the penthouse to celebrate. I really don't have the energy to review any more of the tapes."

Disconcerting for the contestants, a large audience for tomorrow's presentations is anticipated. This assembly of hundreds of unofficial jurors will be surrounding the architects on the first floor, as well as gazing down from the upper lobby balconies, mimicking symphony goers in their private boxes.

Eager for tomorrow's conclusion, the public has witnessed the entire process from the announcement at the Palace of Fine Arts to this evening's final charette. But most still scratch their heads as to what each scheme is—how all the drawings and models will be presented as a cohesive design concept. They will have to wait until the presentations.

Most of the architects leave the building immediately, eager to get a drink, dying for a real drink—which is the opposite of the exquisite but unsatisfying selections from In Situ's wine list. Also, these designers desperately seek a hearty meal, a greasy Gott's cheeseburger or Little Star deep dish—anything, anywhere but within the claustrophobic corridors of sfmoma.

Parker stays behind to recuperate, to breathe, to gather his thoughts. He sits on the edge of one of the makeshift beds. The auto-timed spotlights begin to dim to a gentle afterglow, where one can only make out forms and shapes if squinting a little. In his vaguely lit area, he contemplates how his space now eerily looks like a back of house, gutted utility room. He weighs the consequences of losing, as well as winning. He hopes that if not victorious, triumph can still be found in having tried—and moving on to the next chapter, whatever that may be.

Outside on the street, the mood is celebratory. Though beat, the architects—Johnny, Ling, Chip, and Margo—find both the strength and sincerity to shake hands and hug, having braved a hard fought battle. The pretenses and bluster are gone. Instead of competitiveness, only collegiality remain if only for this brief moment in their collective existence.

"LEANING" MILLENNIUM TOWER
SAN FRANCISCO, 2009

LEANING TOWER
PISA, ITALY
1372

CHAPTER 31

Fall from Grace

"ONLY ONE OF US WILL WIN, and the rest, unfortunately, will lose," Margo states.

Except Parker, all the competitors have found a resting spot at a local pub—some drunk from a large consumption of celebratory alcohol, some exhausted from four days of grueling labor, and some senselessly anxious from the adrenalin.

"If I lose, I will feel like such a failure to my company," admits Johnny in a rare statement of vulnerability.

"C'mon, Johnny, without von Meester, you have always been one of the top contenders. I am actually envious," says Chip, also being oddly open.

Even with a victorious architect in the end, the group ponders the risks of winning—mainly, what would it mean to have the winning design of WoMA be a failure?

Johnny worries and asks, "What if I win, and my completed project is not well received by the media, peers, general public? Consider for example, the nearby famous, or I should say, infamous Millennium Tower."

The architects all nod solemnly. An immediate sense of disappointment occupies the conversation, as they consider the tallest residential building in the city. Containing nearly 400 units on 58 floors and completed in 2009, the Millennium Tower was designed by an international corporation headquartered in New York, colleagues of Johnny Furnsby. His firm, General Architects, Inc., competed for the commission, and unfortunately, came in a distant second place. Unlike Magnar's four-day competition, Johnny chased this high-rise project for two years, and in the end, failed to close the deal.

He takes competitive delight in hearing the project panned as a failure and officially deemed a hazard. Only seven years after the skyscraper's completion, the structure started to slowly sink into the ground. And tilt. If the tower collapsed, such a catastrophic failure would decimate entire neighbors—high-rises falling like dominoes.

Ling chimes in, "Clearly a design failure. The Millennium Tower has gone from a waiting list for the multi-million-dollar condos to a mass exodus of homeowners, from a celebrated grand opening to a project of scorn."

As of 2018, the sinking increased to 17 inches, with a terrifying lean of 14 inches at the top. These are no small numbers to laugh at. Though Johnny's shrewdness causes a smirk in knowing that the tower's architect face scrutiny and legal challenges, he does not relish in a situation that architects fear the most: No, not a bad design or public humiliation like Magnar's discussed *Jukebox*. An architect loses sleep over failing his social responsibility of providing a literal safe roof over the heads of the citizens. One design error, incorrectly drafted line, or numerical typo, and a building's integrity could be compromised. People could be injured or worse.

Chip remembers the oath with the American Institute of Architects, "protect the public's health, safety, and welfare."

Ling says, "I recently studied the forensic architect's proposed solution. She recommends underpinning the building with an additional foundation system of 52 concrete and steel piles that will be embedded 250 feet down. Exceeding $100 million in construction costs, this renovation will be the most expensive Band-Aid in history."

"Sorry, guys, I'm beat. Have to call it a night. See you all tomorrow at the presentations, and good luck," Johnny says with unanticipated sincerity.

Leaving behind festive drinks and jovial colleagues, Johnny Furnsby exhales a sigh of reprieve and takes in the pleasant night air. In contrast to the past four days of madness, this late hour is peaceful enough. Yet, he finds it unnervingly serene.

The Chicago architect chooses not to head to his nearby hotel, but instead down Mission Street towards the waterfront—wandering for the sake of wandering. Most shops are no longer open, save for a few bars and clubs. From the closed storefronts, interior lights behind expansive glass illuminate the sidewalk with ambivalent welcome. Thinking back to a brief visit during his youth, Mission Street was never so enticing. Then, the grit and grime, trash and drugs, defined an area where evening strolls were taken with caution. But tonight, he revels in the tranquility, its calmness misleading.

Coming upon a giant residential tower, Johnny looks upward at the 645 feet in height. He isn't sure whether the apparent leaning of the skyscraper is from his drunken stupor, or is this building tilting in reality? Even in his alcohol-induced daze, the architect realizes that he is standing at the doorstep of the Millennium Tower.

Johnny comments to himself, "Curiosity doesn't always kill the cat."

Curious to take a closer look, he is determined to see how the infamous design turned out. He mumbles, "With its precarious slant, we have ourselves a modern day Leaning Tower of Pisa."

Poised at the entry to the Millennium Tower, Johnny notices the cracks that have reared its threatening presence on the exterior. Litigious fingers have already been pointed in all directions: the engineer's foundation design in landfill, workmanship during construction, notorious bay mud and Colma sand throughout the area, and even new construction projects nearby that might have compromised the Millennium Tower.

He can't resist. He has heard the stories that if you place marbles on the condo floors, the marbles will race towards the other side of the residence. Though no marbles in hand, he wants to take a look himself at the fissures within the building and check out how uneven the floors are. Johnny wonders, *Is it true that the walls are crooked, that windows may fall out onto the street hundreds of feet below, that the elevator screeches as it travels up and down?*

The architect tries the front doors, but they are locked. Starting him, a soft buzz sounds, the doors click, and Johnny strolls into the swanky lobby acting as someone of importance. Facing a crimson-haired receptionist, the architect invents a story about working with city agencies, "to assess the structural feasibility of the proposed re-foundations and its impact on the existing surcharge against the upturned grade beams and underground shear panels, and—" His ploy makes no sense, even less so at this late hour.

The receptionist's eyes glaze over. At this tarnished address, the receptionist is to defend the tower against busy body gawkers, investigative reporters, and lawyers of all suspicions.

Having mastered his corporate-style coolness, Johnny is believable enough. He looks the part, talking and walking as some city-assigned architect would. As if a witless prey of a Jedi mind trick, the woman points directing Johnny towards the elevator banks.

She requests, "Please take that elevator at the far left."

Johnny moves quickly before she sees through the charade. He dashes into the beautifully appointed elevator. He recalls from his research that this residential tower only has 58 floors, yet the top button is 60. Under examination, he sees that the elevator is missing the call buttons for floors 13 and 44. These omissions are for superstitious reasons. In Chinese culture, 44 means double-death. He is not superstitious and finds such rituals absurd.

As the high speed elevator races to the top floor, the architect notices noises of metal scraping and steel cables rattling. He figures that with the building tilting a little, the elevator shafts may not be straight, thereby compromising what would typically be an exhilarating and silent journey upwards.

For amusement, he asks himself the question that so many anxious passengers wonder and fear: *Would an elevator ever fail, fall, and crash down to the earth?* Like kids scaring themselves sharing ghost stories, he now finds himself eager to step out of this claustrophobic steel box. Upwards, the elevator communicates through lit buttons, 45, 46, 47, as floors pass on by, forebodingly so. As the elevator reaches the very top, Johnny calms his nerves, and the doors open.

An elderly woman in a black crochet shawl is standing in the foyer. She speaks in a low voice, "Oh no, no, you shouldn't have taken the left elevator. It is supposed to be shut down. With its shrieking noises, I think the elevator ride sounds like small animals being tortured. Sometimes I think the elevator shaft is possessed by evil spirits." Sounds like she is telling her own ghost story, and it immediately haunts Johnny to his core.

All he can say is, "What? Who?"

She says slowly, hauntingly, "I imagine someday an angry spirit will put an end to the screams by cutting the elevator cables. The cab will then fall out of the sky, dropping 1,000 feet to the ground, delivering sounds of screaming people as they realize their descent is falling faster and faster each and every second—to their deaths."

Johnny is clearly agitated, hands in his pocket but shaking. Who is this old person? What is she stammering about?

Another resident steps into the hall, a youthful active woman in yoga clothes. She immediately questions him with an aggressively extended arm, "You don't belong here, do you? This is our floor. There are enough suits, investigators, and reporters coming up here. You clearly don't belong here. I am going to call security!"

Before Johnny can even compose himself, even step forward, she adds with disbelief, "You rode the left elevator? Are you insane?!"

The elder individual repeats, "Will fall out of the sky...screaming passengers...to their deaths...the left elevator..." Her chants chill Furnsby into a terrified figure, a mere shadow of an important architect. In his eyes, the old woman wrapped in black knit is looking more and more like a witch trope.

The night is late, he is inebriated, and he has found himself in a surreal setting with two random people circling him. Wanting to only tour the building for a few minutes, he has instead found himself a participant in a bleak de Chirico painting. He doesn't have any more Jedi mind tricks in his pockets.

The nervous architect turns around and positions himself with his face very close to the elevator doors, with his back intentionally towards the approaching elderly woman. With tremendous pressure and urgent rhythm, he pushes the elevator call button. Then again. And again and again. A useless habit that most people do, regardless of the fact that they know only one push of the button will do.

Finally, the elevator doors of refuge open. He steps in, not looking back at this uncanny old lady. He can't wait for the elevator doors to shut on their own. He hastily pushes the "close door" button. Over and over again, he does this. Though again, one push suffices.

As the wood-lined steel cab doors start to close, he hears the warning from an ominous voice, "Not the left."

Johnny gets his last glimpse of the woman who is standing inches from the closing doors. She now looks more like a ghostly apparition than someone's grandmother. Through the diminishing vertical slot, he hears for the last time, "…will fall from the sky to your demise…"

Doors tightly shut, the elevator cab starts its escape, and Johnny breathes a little easier. But then, the scraping metal sounds start again. On the elevator's descent, the sound is more piercing. The noise resembles a train braking as it approaches a turn too fast—metal against metal determined to stay on its curving track and not fall to disaster. He covers his ears, as the screeches start to sound human, like screaming—like the elder woman mentioned.

Because of the wretched noise, Johnny hasn't realized until only now how fast the elevator has been going down, falling faster and faster. At this moment, the plummet is sadly clear to him, as the lit-elevator numbers shuffle by, indicating the astonishing speed as he passes by each floor. Sounds of steel cables snapping and whipping within the elevator shaft invade the falling cab—and assault his ears in turn. Clearly he is in a free fall, his body nearly levitating in response. He knows that he is now falling to his death, trapped within a steel cage.

He pushes the buttons, any button, all buttons. But with no success, the elevator continues to plummet out of control. The elevator has become a rocket ship with engines blasting, but facing downward to the granite of earth, not upward to the majestic moon. The cab containing one unfortunate architect accelerates as it plunges to its doom—and takes this man to his death.

The impact of the steel cab hitting the concrete makes an explosive sound heard from miles away, by Parker in his SFMOMA gallery, by his competitors toasting their nightcaps. Precious stone lobby floors shatter into powder, windows explode outward like shrapnel into the streets, and chunks of concrete bust through the ground-floor walls. Clouds of dust and debris instantly enshroud the neighborhood. Unlike the city's early morning blanket of fog, this white haze is not peaceful or cleansing.

As firetrucks arrive, neighbors gather in the dusty street. They speak three words as both a question and an explanation. Saying dreadfully, "The left elevator?"

"But how is it possible? It's supposed to be shut down," an unknown voice responds.

The receptionist has already left her station, calmly walking away from the calamity. No one gets close enough, but it doesn't matter. No one would recognize what remains of this architect who has fallen from the sky. Elevator remnants spread over jagged chunks of a building's bones. Johnny Furnsby lays motionless within a growing cloud of fog-like white and smoke-like black. Only the elevator cab prevented bloody Johnny fragments from being scattered into the neighborhood.

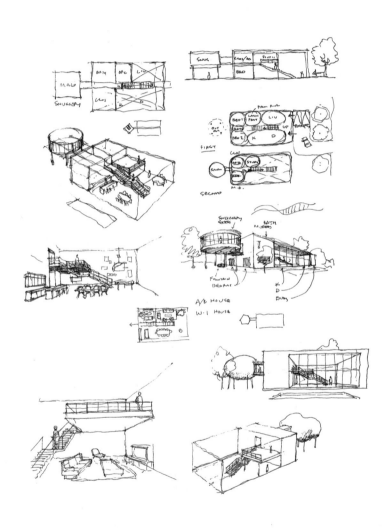

Death by Design at Alcatraz

CHAPTER 32

Celadonna's Dalliance

T H E PARENTS OF CELADONNA KIMM named her after the green glaze of Asian ceramics, known as Celadon. Originated in 25 A.D. in the Chinese coastal province of Zhejiang, the jade-color glaze was enjoyed for its mysterious translucency and signature small cracks of beauty—a befitting origin for their daughter's name.

Growing up in Seoul, Korea, Celadonna watched American movies, and particularly obsessed over Hollywood's portrayal of architects. Within movies and TV, whether accurate or not, she viewed the architect as thoughtful, cultured, and artistic. The young Korean girl fantasized that such traits should make up her future lover. Unfortunately, such traits do not exist much in her current keeper, Magnar Jones.

Always prepared for another viewing of any one of dozens, Celadonna loved her library of films about the architect protagonist—dozens and dozens, movies from the '50s to the present. She was fond of them all: from the stately Henry Fonda to the sexy Wesley Snipes, from the adorable Tom Hanks to struggling Woody Harrelson, and from the Parker A. Rand look-alike, Keanu Reeves, and lovable Steve Martin—both playing architects twice—to Matt Dillon, three times.

As compared to films with cops, bankers, and lawyers, her celluloid architectural heroes are sensitive and idealistic, not corrupt or hostile. In her eyes, an architect is the ideal man, and it just so happens that her Magnar has a list of architects—a catalog of romantic partners for Celadonna to peruse. Conveniently, a roll call of lovers was at her fingertips, like a glossy shopping catalog for a frustrated housewife.

She had set her sights on Parker A. Rand long before the introduction at Starbucks or the big event at the Palace of Fine Arts. As she pondered her options, she assessed that Maxwell Brand is gay, Ling Liang and Chip Tooney are married, Margo Hunters is not her type, and Johnny Furnsby is, in Celadonna's eyes, asexual and a big company nobody. And well, the dashing Lars von Meester, though a potential candidate, was found as a corpse floating in the ocean.

Parker is talented though fragile, assured but not overbearingly confident. This architect has always been tortured by his ambition, troubled over what he should be doing and what he is not—the missed opportunities. That day in Morrison Hall's piano practice room, he left many of his musical dreams, and other dreams as well, behind when Adrienne Veley found his original melody only mildly entertaining.

Like a dog sensing fear in people, Celadonna senses Parker's insecurities every time she places her body near his, or even tosses a minute expression. Their past encounters have been slight for her and clumsy for him. Tonight, a brief passage of time before the morning presentations, she will have her architect.

It is 4:30 A.M.: SFMOMA is still and calm, awaiting the design presentations and the selection of a winner. The lock down is another rule, yet another circumstance of control, from Magnar—though he suggests it is to protect the architects' work. Parker did not join the festivities of his colleagues. At times like this after a grueling charette, he prefers to be alone to contemplate, to uncoil.

In his design gallery, a studio surrounded by the remains of an artistic process, he tries to relax on his Magnar-provided temporary bed. He lays exhausted from the final effort of the competition, but he doesn't sleep. In fact, he rarely sleeps well. It is not simply insomnia, but a mind that can't stop designing, worrying about his world, or maybe his grocery list and credit cards—pondering where and how his life will end up. Parker tries to rest in his half slumber, but his brain is in full throttle.

With access throughout the building, Celadonna casually finds her way to a barely-asleep Parker tossing restlessly. In a fuzzy haze, he is not as startled as he should be when she opens the curtains. Under the last light of the Moon beaming through skylights, she approaches. He is not alarmed, because he doesn't know if she is a dream-state spirit or flesh-and-blood. Is she actually here, and if so, driven by attraction, curiosity, or contempt? During these wee small hours, the sun is rehearsing its soon-to-arrive sunrise.

Celadonna speaks no words, eager to advance. Standing self-assured, she removes her topcoat dropping it carelessly to the floor, revealing a fitted dress that leaves little to Parker's already active imagination. He studies her like absorbing the aesthetics of a Grecian temple.

She leans forward and murmurs delicately, "Hello, Mr. Rand." Faint perfume enters his psyche like fog rolling over the cliffs.

Hands shaking nervously, the anxious Parker's only thought is to ask a circumstantial question, "What are you doing here?"

"I am at my best at this hour," she whispers an enticing response. She laughs softly.

His innocence wants to respond with, *I have no idea what you mean by that*, but he actually has some idea.

She seats herself joining him on the edge of the mattress, as he sits up abruptly. For the moment, he ignores the fact that this woman is the significant other of Magnar Jones. The architect glosses over such context. As it was with other encounters, he has no defenses against her small gestures, a wry but pleasant smile.

Reluctance passes, and he accepts her approach. Parker flashes back to his unrequited infatuation in college which represents so many lost opportunities that followed. Time to make up for past failures.

Celadonna's mouth reaches out to briskly touch the side of his neck. Her anxious lips grace his face. He wants to say no, but he cannot help his selfish arms that reach forward, ready to partake in intimate treasures.

The architect questions in a soft undertone, "Is a kiss ever innocent, ever not stolen? With the greeting of lips, secrets and sorrows are passed between two mouths." He makes no sense to Parker's early morning participant. She ignores his words.

Their two mouths lock, no key, and their passions are released like a deck of cards tossed into the air. In the vaguely lit room, their eyes barely see, but their ears hear the faint racing beat of hearts. His hands grip her back tightly leaving subtle imprints as if God's breath on desert sands. Their noses catch a scent of delirium, and the tip of the tongue takes a trip of three steps. Parker taps a pulse inside a realm where only imagination feasts.

Even if I live for a flicker of such a moment, then at least I lived, he senselessly responds but with no audible sounds.

He continues in his mind, *All that I want is, for once in my existence, to reveal my hopes and wishes to a kindred soul and see if I truly matter.*

He starts to move more insistently. As she claims his body, he claims hers as well. They cannot breathe without each breath tethered to their naked souls. Lying next to each other on a small cot, the union of desperate gasps heightens to a point of fervor. He releases his deserted spirit from his body, this delicate shell. Both their worlds pump nervously a tribal dance that some unknown teacher once taught them.

Celadonna enjoyed her coy liaison, but she has no idea of the deliberations that have entered Parker's head. She also has little concern for or even recollection of Magnar.

For Parker, this confrontation was not an act of intimacy. The encounter was an internal struggle, as he says aloud this time, "If this event of truth brings about my demise, if this act kills me, let me die. Let me scream and cry a monumental death."

Baffled and uncomfortable, she pretends not to hear, and gently separates their embrace. But hands now, not their lips, still lock together—a gesture even more cherished than what transpired only moments before.

The world continues to rotate, and nothing else matters to Parker at this moment— nothing other than to know that someone, this stranger named Celadonna Kimm, is near him, with him.

The naked beauty with her porcelain skin enjoys this brief measure, despite some unknown war waging inside the architect's head. He begins to drift wanting his limbs to be interwoven with hers. His mind wanders into shadows much deeper than simply sleep.

Parker asks of himself, *My angry imagination wants to know, if God created this earth, then what am I to create in return?* His thoughts drift further into an abyss, *If there are creative works that have stopped the movement of this world, then what is to be mine? Constantly, the desire to be great haunts me.*

Celadonna hears none of his internal doubts and wanderings, because no words are explicitly said. She lays there next to him unsure as to whether she should embrace him or leave.

His brain floats deeper into a chasm, as a flock of birds fly noiselessly by. And he imagines that only moments ago in their bare bodies, they were soaring with these birds.

Through the skylight, an innocent ray of sunlight illuminates Celadonna's bare shoulder. She feels a searing warmth. They place their laying bodies closer for a brief instant, then rise and walk towards the window. Sun now warms all parts of their slender souls.

Aloud this time, Parker looks intensely into her eyes and says, "If I were to fall through this glass to the street below, my fragile body would shatter, exploding, all my secrets made public, like a piñata struck by a child wielding a broomstick."

Celadonna is both amused and apprehensive. She wants to ask but doesn't, "What in the world are you babbling about?"

He can't help himself, and his outpour becomes her burden. Holding her tightly from behind, he rants, "The sounds in my head are like those of skeletons making love on a tin roof, or like Glenn Gould's piano sonority. Thelonious Monk too, ripped open sound, baring all treasures—the timbre of natural scatterings."

Disturbed by his outburst, Celadonna gradually steps out of his embrace and gathers her topcoat from the floor. Not at all what she imagined, this meeting has ended, and the moment is now oddly tender and alarming as well.

Parker feels the need to gather all his broken dreams into a small pouch that dangles from his heart. For him, what has occurred is a random happenstance in a majestic world. He thinks only this, *I do not know if I was ever closer to God.*

Celadonna swiftly leaves him in the gallery, and he retreats to a pile of journals, frantically jotting down design notes.

She sought an evening of adventure and escape, maybe even of conquest. She tries to digest his thoughts but has no idea what just transpired. The architects in her movies were not this Parker A. Rand, a man so brilliant yet flawed, a man of both genius and madness. Her night turned out to be both an affirmation and a denial.

As Celadonna walks outside the building, she watches the morning breeze move the fallen leaves on the sidewalk. With each gust, leaves tumble forward, rolling past one another. Unwillingly, the leaves are going somewhere that is a far place from where they came.

This early morning, Celadonna is certain that, akin to the leaves, she knows she can never go back. Trees do not take back their fallen leaves.

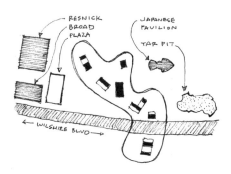

RESNICK
BROAD
PLAZA

JAPANESE
PAVILION

TAR PIT

← WILSHIRE BLVD →

ZUMTHOR'S LACMA 2023

CHAPTER 33

Design is Everywhere, People!

A SUBSTANTIAL AUDIENCE of design fanatics congregate in
the lobby. Noon, finally—Magnar stands outside, ready for the
conclusion of his four-day spectacular. Those who have not arrived
early enough gather on the upper atrium floors, where the terraces
look down upon the big affair.

From the restless crowd, a growing hum is heard as background
chatter, as well as felt as actual physical vibrations. Some visitors
are sacrificing their valuable lunch hour for this event, while serious
attendees take off the early afternoon to fully enjoy the architects'
presentations. Architecture students arrive with sketchbooks in hand,
ready to take notes and jot down sketches of inspiration from their
heroes. A few visiting tourists, art hobbyists, and museum members
happen to be here at SFMOMA today to view the museum's permanent
collection. They have stumbled upon a bonus exhibition, willing to
join whatever is in store.

Local and national reporters along with their photographers are
present, and British media hopes to bring home good news of their
famed architect. Magnar has also invited the city's most powerful
political figures and cultural impresarios. Most have accepted the
invitation with graciousness, and the rest, not so graciously and
somewhat reluctantly. Celadonna, as the marketing director, added
her contacts of promoters, agents, and influencers to the guest list.

The staging, lighting, and overall production value is extravagant, with Celadonna enlisting help from her friends at the nearby famed Orpheum Theater. Adding a Hollywood-caliber AV system, the room sings. Large banners with Magnar-branded graphics hang from the upper terraces of the lobby, as well as plaster the building's exterior. On each banner, the acronym of WoMA is boldly presented in a Supergraphic, white, block-ish font on a cool-gray background. A second line of highlighter-yellow serif letters read, "Magnar Jones Delivers the World Museum of Abstract Art on Alcatraz."

With a contrived celebrity factor, Celadonna produced headshots of each architect as enormous posters. She enlarged the standard 8-by-10-inch portrait to a heroic 8-by-10-foot print on canvas. With no smiles on grainy, black and white faces, the look of seriousness presents architects deep in thought. For each, such big scale graphics do not stroke any egos. They are embarrassed by the large format, cartoonish photographs.

On the sidewalk, Magnar and Celadonna await the exact moment to enter that will bring the most fanfare. Then they stare intently at each other. He gives a quick wink. With the drama of a back-lit bride entering a French Gothic cathedral, this regal couple bursts through the lobby doors. At the nave are the competing architects, already seated. No lucky groom.

Between Magnar and his architects sits an enormous and dense pack of guests, hundreds, even a thousand perhaps. As the Puppet Master and his lovely companion start their procession through the swarm, the crowd parts—a cinematic scene like the legendary parting of a sea. The host and hostess take their time to wave, insincerely shake a few hands, and most importantly, fuel Magnar's narcissism. In his self-admiring mind, the audience gathers today, not to hear the presentations of hard-working architects, but to bask in Magnar's glorious ego. His boots are a rich-black lizard skin to match Celadonna's black on black on black ensemble. His khaki suit is unexpected, off brand. Regardless, he carries off the attire nicely, and the casual fabric does not downplay the electricity in the atmosphere.

Staring at the banner-like headshot of Parker, Celadonna searches inside herself for a description of what transpired mere hours ago. But only blank eyes of the large photograph stare back, and she shudders a little in both hesitation and confusion. She tunes out the crowd for a second to ponder whether with Parker, there will be more.

The presidential pair, developer and girlfriend, finally make it to the stage, leaving behind the assembly of guests as they take their seats. Magnar's team built a large platform three steps high, painted blank white to accompany the museum's cool setting. He walks towards his stage, this neutral canvas awaiting the brush strokes of his vanity and arrogance. His few steps up are so assertive that his air current leaves Celadonna swaying behind. He does not look back, or care to look back, to see if she has situated herself.

On the front edge of the stage, the lead architects are seated in black, steel folding chairs—in a precisely organized row, several feet apart from each other: Margo, Ling and Chip, and Parker. Though sitting patiently and appearing calm, Parker's hand wrings nervously. Cheering on the fearless leaders on stage, all the employees are placed on the floor in the front row.

But the stage presents a single empty chair. A haunting image of a lonely black chair in a sea of white plywood—Johnny Furnsby's seat is noticeably empty. He is assumed to be running late due to a night of festive libations.

Behind the row of the renowned architects is an impressive collection of material: large drawings of all mediums attached to freestanding panels, laptops and projectors focused on giant screens, physical models big and small carefully poised on side tables, and various artifacts of the creative process: books, stacks of sketches, material samples, and so on. As the architects learned in their school presentations, the display of one's design must be a spectacular extravaganza. The audience eagerly await how the compilation of creative output will take form.

The WoMA developer raises both arms already feeling victorious. The audience does not cheer quite yet, for there is not much to cheer for at the moment, but they do provide an even-keel applause. Magnar's triumphant arms slowly wave and drop, as if asking the crowd to quiet down—as if the crowd was out of control with enthusiasm. Delusionally, he imagines this.

He begins an introduction without, as usual, any obligatory niceties, like a "welcome" or a "good afternoon." Consistent with his opening at the Palace of Fine Arts earlier in the week, he launches into a tale of design, to bring the audience into his world—to show off his token knowledge of art and architecture.

"Architecture is everywhere, people! Whether decorating your little homes, building a city hall, or master planning a university—design is the epicenter. Design is everything from cake decoration to a hybrid engine, from make-up and blow outs to websites. And yes, even the ergonomics of a toothbrush handle." It's a catchy introduction and an accessible one for the audience.

Magnar feels the momentum building in the lobby, and he barely stops to take in oxygen. "Architecture is the nexus of everything around us. Consider this. There are 100 million viewers per month of HGTV, $1.5 trillion comprising the U.S. construction industry annually, and 100,000 members at the American Institute of Architects. And such numbers grow daily.

"Print and online, there are countless design magazines—over one million subscribers to *Architectural Digest*, and another one million to *Sunset* magazine. So many books, websites, blogs, showrooms, lectures, and conventions. The design of a new building headlines the media, and architects are iconic figures in an endless list of movies and TV shows."

Celadonna grins.

Magnar is a locomotive train picking up inertia, not wanting to slow down, "DIY everywhere, prefab homes, style-as-content, going green—it is all part of an omnipresent movement. In recent decades, retail stores placed design on an approachable platform and within the reach of consumers, with stores literally called, Design Within Reach. The traditional Crate and Barrel offered a new hip and youthful company called *CB2*. Pottery Barn inserted their own design studios within their stores. Each of these retailers sold design as a lifestyle, not just a commodity.

"Even in the tabloids, though it was a few years ago, who could forget how Brad Pitt praised his own love for architecture, then designed housing for New Orleans after Hurricane Katrina. Didn't he also criticize how Jennifer Aniston, his then-wife, had little understanding of modern design? I believe she countered with how his sense of design was cold, and that she preferred warm and cozy."

Magnar attempts humor, softens his posture, "Was her comment about his design sensibilities or her husband's personality?" A few snickers resound.

"Mr. Pitt even once shouted, 'I'm really into architecture, structure and design. Give me anything, and I'll design it!'"

Magnar defends the seriousness of architecture and his event. "I say, 'Gimme a break.' Recently, Brad Pitt provided questionable Hollywood cache at a public hearing for Peter Zumthor's proposed LACMA, a controversial new museum for Los Angeles that will span over eight traffic lanes. Interesting yes? But worry not, my museum at Alcatraz will be greater! And I don't need a celebrity wannabe-architect to speak in support of my project. Hollywood cache is nice for PR, but do I need it in my world of artists and designers?

"I ask this: When did design move out of the privileged Renaissance world that commissioned architects Michelangelo and Palladio. With great fury, design moved into our everyday: weekend warriors at Home Depot, and domestic goddesses wielding Martha Stewart paint swatches. And who isn't watching Li Ziqi's YouTube videos?

"I welcome this movement that has delivered design to the general audience"—he steadies himself for the big finish—"and the world is prepared to welcome in the highest level of progress that civilization can handle. We are building an unforgiving empire of creativity, people!"

He says "people" like the crowd is his people. And this time around, the audience cheers for his inspiring words. He ignores the reality that the attendees did not come for him, but rather, to see the work of world-class architects.

Nicely choreographed, Magnar side steps and Celadonna, already in motion, takes to the microphone. They exchange a well-rehearsed peck as cheeks pass—a hollow gesture just for show.

In a robust voice, "Thank you Magnar for a wonderful introduction. And thank you all for attending this incredible event." She does much better at delivering the appropriate welcome.

"We are eager to share with you four design proposals from our selection of great architects. Each presentation is a very different vision for the new Museum of Abstract Art at Alcatraz. We fondly call our project, WoMA."

Ever so discreetly, she casts a glance in Parker's vicinity hoping to fish out a reaction. Yet the only response is an anxious architect looking down at his hands squeezing one another.

Magnar gives her a subtle dismissive hand signal, she is confused. Did he notice her attention shift from the San Francisco crowd to the San Francisco architect? Or is he suggesting for her to stop? Confused, she winds down quickly. "Please relax everyone for a few moments. We will return after a 10-minute break to introduce our architects." The audience is also confused—an intermission already?

Magnar stomps over towards her and grumbles not so quietly, "Where the fuck is Johnny Furnsby?!"

She sighs in relief that his disruption has nothing to do with Parker. Magnar and Celadonna both drag themselves over to the architects seated on stage.

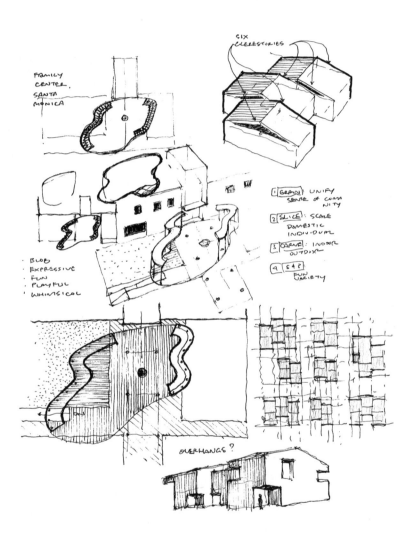

FAMILY
CENTER,
SANTA
MONICA

SIX
CLERESTORIES

BLOB
EXPRESSIVE
FUN
PLAYFUL
WHIMSICAL

1 GRAIN: UNIFY
SENSE OF COMM
NITY

2 SLICE: SCALE
DOMESTIC
INDIVIDUAL

3 CARVE: INDOOR
OUTDOOR

4 S+S: FUN
VARIETY

OVERHANGS?

CHAPTER 34

WTF?

S TARING DOWN AT THE COMPETITORS, he repeats in a threatening whisper, "Where the fuck is Johnny Furnsby?!"

His facial expression is screaming, fists form at his side, and he demands, "Where the hell is he? I thought, sure, maybe a little late. But fuck this! You better find your little friend."

The architects believe they actually see steam coming out of Magnar's ears, like one of those furious cartoon figures. Celadonna remains still like a classical statue. She knows better than to try to diffuse the situation with some humanity.

Though this group is trying to appear normal for any attentive audience members, Magna's cowboy boots stamp on the hollow stage, sounding booms as he demands an answer. "Where is Mr. Furnsby? How could he not be here for this big day, his big day, my big day!?"

Margo replies uncharacteristically weak, "We last saw Johnny when he departed from our potations at the establishment late last night."

"Drinks at the bar"—Chip jumps in—"we were celebrating the wrap up of the charette."

Clearly, this is not the answer Magnar is seeking. He turns to Johnny's three employees, his corporate sidekicks from General Architects, Inc. Magnar's glares down from the raised stage at the nameless company men seated in the first row. He doesn't even need to ask the question. His intensity and forward-leaning posture voice plenty.

These middle-management associates stay seated, afraid to stand for fear of appearing to challenge Magnar's presence. One brave individual speaks up, "Sorry, ummm, Mr. Jones, we haven't heard from him since last night. We already left a few messages. He has been MIA since the end of the charette,"—a ridiculous use of "MIA."

With the developer getting even more upset, this Johnny crony tosses out more irrelevant information, "Maybe our boss is stuck in traffic, or can't get a Lyft, or got lost in these streets."

Being lost is a ridiculous suggestion. Magnar gesticulates wildly, which draws some attention from the nearby viewers. He says, "That's preposterous since the neighborhood is a simple grid and the north-south streets are numbered in sequence, you idiot! How can anyone 'get lost in these streets'?" Magnar ridicules the architect's squeaky voice.

Another Furnsby employee shrugs and adds, "You know there was that huge disaster last night around midnight? Some elevator fell from the top floor of a condo tower, crashing down with an explosion, shutting down block after block. Just around the corner from here—smoke, debris, dust everywhere—it's a real mess. Johnny could have gotten hung up in the traffic from that. Emergency services are still sorting out any missing people, and building officials are saying the clean-up could take months."

No doubt, Magnar has already heard of this catastrophe, a nuisance of a news item that already had taken up some of the reporters he'd expected to cover his ceremony today. Had it also delayed one of his competitors?

Johnny's employee says with a misplaced authoritative tone, "It was that outrageous Millennium Tower, the one that has been leaning since it opened. The elevator fell from the 60th floor straight down to the street level."

"Enough!" says Magnar. "I don't need a recap of the morning's headlines. I just want to know where my competitor is?"

He then turns angrily to the principal architects on stage, also glowering at an innocent-looking Celadonna, and says, "Fuck it! It's Johnny's lost. I don't give a damn! I knew I had to start with a long list of names, because most people don't have the fortitude to make it to the end. Of course, some would withdraw. Your three final presentations are fine."

Parker wonders, *Did Magnar actually refer to the recent accidents, murders, food poisoning, and a missing architect as a 'withdrawal'?*

Looking out to the crowd, Magnar notices impatience rumbling. He says softly and decisively, "No, we are not calling off this contest. Not postponing either, just because one architect got lost on his way to the presentations. Lost the nerve to win."

This master of ceremony hastily walks away from the architects, stands beside Celadonna, and pulls her in forcefully, giving instructions. He then gestures to the crowd with one arm partially raised to grab attention. She takes center stage again, gliding to the microphone with her easy movements.

Magnar intentionally chose a microphone and sleek stand, rather than a bulky wood lectern, because he wanted the audience to appreciate his Cowboy boots, as well as covet his lovely girlfriend. Both are treasured possessions he has collected for this day.

Celadonna looks out, one hand shielding her eyes from both the spotlights and the public gawking. She notices that the audience has grown larger having gathered late comers.

She requests, "Please everyone, take your seats. We are ready to begin." She waits for just enough silence and says, "Today, we have three design teams to show us their proposals for the new World Museum of Abstract Art at Alcatraz." She makes no mention of a fourth participant, and clearly no mention of a fifth architect. Or a sixth one either.

An audience member wonders quietly, "What happened to the other architects we were following these past days?"

Providing a proper introduction to his extravaganza, Celadonna explains, "Museum developer, Magnar Jones"—she waves at him endearingly wanting the audience to see the gesture—"has made all the political and economic arrangements with this welcoming city of San Francisco. He will re-envision the legendary and often tragic Alcatraz Island. I don't need to tell you about the infamous bank robbers and murderers imprisoned there, the Island's first lighthouse, or its operation as a fort, then military prison, and then federal penitentiary.

"And no, I don't think the Rock, as the Island is often called, is really haunted. At least, I haven't seen any ghosts myself. But maybe someday, a ghost will show up and give me a personal tour of the Island—and even some fashion tips from the '30s."

She smiles in a girlish way and receives a few giggles. If not for her natural adorability, the remark would have fallen flat.

Enjoying the mild reception of her comment, she announces, "Magnar, his board of directors, and many generous patrons of the arts have made this museum possible. We also thank the city's planning commission and civic leaders." Many of which were bribed into conceding, as is not uncommon for development in any big town.

"A few months back, Magnar and I"—in reality, she actually means just Magnar—"created a lengthy list of architects qualified for our project. We traveled the world, met some of the most honored architects, including Pritzker Prize recipients. Having interviewed a final handful of candidates and visited their completed works around the globe, we authored a short list of the talented architects you will hear from shortly." Three, not even close the original six.

Constantly and not so tactfully this time, she glances over her shoulder to ensure that Parker sees her. Unfortunately he does not, as he looks blankly and nervously into the crowd. Slightly rattled, she forces herself to stay focused.

With a contrived smile, she says, "Without further ado, I am eager to make the introductions again. You all may remember these distinguished architects from our formal announcement at the Palace of Fine Arts a few days ago. The architects are as follows: Dame Margo Hunters of Hunting Ground, far from home, from London, England; Mr. and Mrs. Chip Tooney and Ling Liang of ChipLing from the East Coast; and last but not least, our very own Parker A. Rand from PAR Designs, based right here in this city." She ignores the awkward fact that she introduced the full band of competitors only four days ago: six competitors.

With forced excitement, Celadonna stated these three entities like she is announcing the nominees for Best Actor at the Oscars. She also introduced the renowned architects with the delusion that she is of equal importance, similarly to how a wedding planner thinks the big wedding day is about her, and not the bride.

Celadonna continues, "As many of you are already aware, the architects were given only four days to create their design presentations. And here's the interesting part, they worked in an assigned gallery space in this San Francisco Museum of Modern Art. Yes, all the competitors—each principal architect accompanied by their three most trusted associates—stayed here in this building the whole time. They ate here, slept here, and of course, here they designed their most creative vision for a museum on Alcatraz.

"Add one more challenging layer, an intriguing idea from none other than our Magnar Jones." She turns to throw him a wink. "As the architects worked hour by hour, they were exposed to the eye of the public. Many of you have visited over the past few days, standing at the studio entrances, witnessing the genius behind art and architecture—even listening in on their conversations as they searched for design ideas at all hours of the day and night. I saw many reporters scribbling down stories in their notebooks.

"After hearing the three presentations today, Magnar and his colleagues, me included," –she smiles in her way and tosses a curtsy—"will announce a victorious architect this afternoon. This winner of our competition will sign a contract for what you all have already heard as the commission of the century."

Two items: it was Celadonna and her marketing spin that gave the project its sales pitch of "the commission of the century," and everyone knows that Magnar's "colleagues," his token board members, have nothing to say in the selection of the final architect.

She is really owning her spot-lit storytelling, but the architects are weary of all this fanfare. Sitting impatiently, they are ready to stand up, and present their ideas. Also, they struggle with how they got to this final chapter. The architects contemplate the deaths of Lars von

Meester and Maxwell Brand, and now, the disappearance of Johnny Furnsby. Ling tries not to think about her fight with Celadonna, and Margo still feels sharp stomach pains.

Eager to get on with the show, this song-and-dance routine of ego and creativity, the architects are ready to conclude this competition-turned-circus.

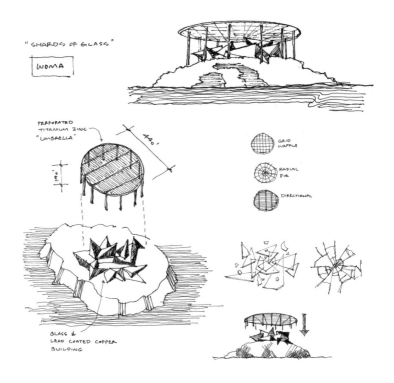

"SHARDS OF GLASS"

WOMA

PERFORATED
TITANIUM ZINC
"UMBRELLA"

440'

GRID
WAFFLE

RADIAL
PIE

DIRECTIONAL

GLASS &
LEAD COATED COPPER
BUILDING

CHAPTER 35

Hunting Ground: Shards of Glass

M ARGO'S AMBITION BATTLES her aching body. Adrenaline counters any poison. And arrogance rejects her suspicions of murder. She awaits her name to be called.

Celadonna prepares the audience for the first competitor, "Let's get started, and welcome Dame Margo Hunters, founder and principal architect of her London-based company, Hunting Ground. Her international projects of soaring shapes and signature use of materials have captivated the media for decades. From skyscrapers to performing arts centers, corporate parks to resorts, Margo's unflinching design vision truly excites us all. And we can't wait to see what she will be presenting. Everyone, I give you Margo Hunters!"

Effective architects tell stories. The art of storytelling should be both creative expression and sensible communication. To capture an audience, the explanation of a design must be like a persuasive speech. Or sermon even, like a theatrical monologue.

Whether a design is for a lawyer in her office, students at a university, or citizens visiting the state capital—in all cases, the architect has to present to his specific audience. When an architect is designing a house, the family might want to hear about the envisioned Thanksgiving dinner and the warm environment created for them. If designing a new school, the architect should not only talk about the square footage and number of students in each classroom, but she should also explain how the design relates to the teaching methodology.

For the proposed museum on Alcatraz, the three upcoming presentations must be more than a discussion regarding the size of the art galleries on each floor or the number of rooms in the administrative wing. Instead, the presentations must not just be about the *what*, but the *why*. A good storyteller should also be personable and relatable—and even full of surprise and delight. Lastly, for this audience, the architects will plant emotions and perceptions, so to ensure a winning design.

Applause welcomes Margo as she moves from her seat to center stage. Predictably, the British press provides the most enthusiastic of receptions.

For a few seconds, Margo stares at the floor, still and in complete silence. A gray cape-like jacket enshrouds her. Drama.

She then looks up, spreads her arms and cape, and starts with a claim, "Our design for WoMA will stand alongside the Seven Wonders of the World!"

No, storytelling doesn't have to start with, "Once upon a time."

Margo's brash statement is consistent with her assertion made to the public two days ago. Then, she declared to her team, and the eavesdropping public, that she would create a design that surpasses the musical perfection of Beethoven's Ninth Symphony. In theory, she wanted to compose the Tenth Symphony.

Towards the audience, Dame Hunters nods and persists, "The Colosseum in Rome, Great Wall of China, and Giza's Pyramid—these monuments of history will pale in comparison to what I will present to you today."

Her grand standing is off putting, but captivating. Magnar is pleased to see that his event launches with a very conceited bang.

The London architect shifts her weight to one side and her body moves aside to show the design behind her. The concept has been in the works for viewing over four days, but this final form, its staging, the pitch—Margo's presentation has come together in an unexpected reveal. Before the audience sits an architectural model on a table large enough for a family reunion. Huge at five feet by twelve feet—her model is a remarkable work of architecture, sculpture, and art. This composition is not the typically delicate architectural model with scale bricks, plants, and little people. Instead, a blue-ish sheet of acrylic represents the waters of the bay and dramatically reflects the overhead lobby lights. The rough terrain of the mock Alcatraz Island, made from rocks and dirt from the site itself, sits within the blue waters.

Even at first glance, it is clear that Margo's design eliminates all the existing buildings of the prison. "I find no reason to be nostalgic, no reason to look backwards. First step: All old structures on the island will be demolished to make way for my vision." She actually means for her glory. "The island will be razed clean as an empty canvas for my design."

Magnar is intrigued by the idea of a clean slate, a similar approach for the Abstract artists and the Bauhaus.

Her hands wave above the model like a chef drawing in the aroma of simmering soup. On the model, over the heavily textured island hovers a thin disc of bright metal. She proclaims, "Appearing to float in the sky, I propose a circle of perforated titanium zinc, 440 feet in diameter, bigger than a football field, and supported by thin-steel columns 140 feet tall. That's fourteen stories up." She doesn't care much for Chinese superstition against the number four. In fact, the numbers are intentional.

"It will be the world's largest and most incredible sunshade. From the sky above, from arriving airplanes, my museum will be seen in conjunction with the nearby Golden Gate Bridge. This will be a rare setting of not one, but two Wonders of the World."

The audience responds with literal oohs and aahs, even a dramatic wow from Celadonna. The eyes of the crowd now follow Margo's hands as she directs attention to what lies beneath the thin-metal disc. Under the circular element sits an assembly of two dozen buildings, violently collided, one on top of another, no right angles, just tilted planes and jagged corners. The viewers squint with one eye and raise an eyebrow with the other, as they see acrylic chunks representing glassy buildings smashed together.

One viewer in the crowd whispers to another, "Is this for real? It's wild and beautiful and dramatic, all at the same time."

Another asks, "Or is this ugly and confusing?"

Margo continues presenting, "Each gallery will be structured in robust steel trusses, then the buildings will be entirely wrapped in a combination of plate glass and lead-coated copper panels. Yes, I am employing sheets of copper dipped in molten lead. Each gallery building will have its own unique shape, its own character of angles and twists. Together, all my structures collide with great force, with no fear. My composition for this museum will appear like natural formations of crystal. But instead of a small handheld jewel, my quartz structures are 100 feet tall!"

Her excitement is contagious, as she says, "Furthermore, with its millions of tiny holes, the perforated disc above will allow sunlight to dapple onto the crystalline surfaces, reflecting and refracting as natural quartz does. Throughout the day as the Sun's rays move across my museum, the look and feel, its weight and personality—all will change, and change again. From any side around the island, even from the wharfs of San Francisco or the docks at Sausalito, one will witness sunlight reflecting off the glassy surfaces. My glistening design will call out, like the historic lighthouse that once stood on the island."

She certainly is not going to make mention of the lighthouse fire that took Maxwell Brand's life.

Margo further explains, "To contrast the shimmering quality of my design, there is lead-coated-copper panels on portions of the exterior, a material that weathers with grace intersects the clarity of ageless glass. The metal panels will age and become more beautiful each year. As the saltwater meets the metal, its surface will patina. The colors will transform from a shiny gray to a soft textured dark gray, and the green copper will glow through the lead coating, like a bride's smiling face behind a wedding veil."

Yes, make the presentation relatable.

Margo speaks to her fascination of aging buildings. "Architecture should not deteriorate and fall apart, then require a costly renovation to bring it back to its original appearance. As I have done with my past award-winning projects, I believe in applying what I call, Living Materials. Architectural materials and finishes should not deteriorate. Rather, they should evolve, should mark the passage of time, as do our bodies and the cities around us—and look more amazing each year."

Magnar leans towards Celadonna and admits, "Margo has outdone herself...the model, the island made from actual fragments of Alcatraz. And the collision of glass and metal forms, all under a UFO-like disc hovering in the clouds."

He couldn't be more pleased, though he wonders if this design will work in reality. He puts on his business hat and construction helmet, and ponders, *Can it be implemented?*

Celadonna is no architectural critic, but she understands beauty, risks, and sensuality. "Mag, how will the other architects top this? Margo might have been a tad ego-maniacal in her introduction, but her design is so powerful."

Standing proud, Margo's head inflates. Seated in the front row, her employees are beaming in full support. But the audience is not fully sold, as with all courageous and innovative ideas unveiled to an ignorant crowd. As with the Eiffel Tower and its shaky start, many new ideas are despised for their newness.

Some members in the crowd are eagerly praising Margo's design.

"Pure genius."

"A game changer."

And "RIBA-worthy."

She absorbs these praises like a hungry lioness feasting on her prey. To her disdain, she also overhears other phrases.

"Pretentious, student-ish project."

"Ridiculous, unbuildable, expensive."

And "Looks like several cars crashed together under a large umbrella."

But Margo does not waver. Posture defiant, she believes she has written her Tenth Symphony and is already basking in her own genius.

Over the decades, this royal architect had little concern for what the public said of her work, whether complimentary or insulting. Margo had never been one to view architecture as merely a client-based service. For her, the Golden Rule of "the customer is always right" is severely tarnished.

Wrapping up, Margo adopts an academic tone. "I have always loved the works of Étienne-Louis Boullée, Claude Nicolas Ledoux, and Jean-Jacques Lequeu." Her French is flawless. "Their heroic visions from the Age of Reason changed our view of the world, yet these architects never had the opportunity to build their ideas. We only have their masterful drawings."

She looks explicitly at Magnar and requests, "I ask you today to accept my challenge. Do not be timid. Do not be meek. Build my museum. My design will house the bravery displayed in the works of illustrious contemporary artists, past and present. My design is not for the weak minded or weak knee'd. My work is for the fearless, for those that stand taller than others around them, for individuals that have the boldness to change lives. My design for the World Museum of Abstract Art is not just for all of you today, but for future civilizations to come."

And taking in a deep breath, in a rare tone of graciousness, "Thank you, everyone."

Applause rings out from most, and questions remain from others. Regardless, Margo Hunters stands in the spotlight proud of her presentation that exhibited both creativity and will power. Any attempt on her life is now a distant memory.

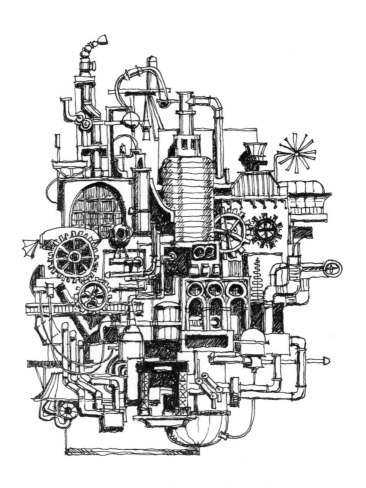

Death by Design at Alcatraz

CHAPTER 36

ChipLing: Machine for Art

B EFORE APPLAUSE FADES FOR MARGO, Celadonna Kimm, prances to the microphone. Rhetorically, she asks the audience, "Wasn't that design amazing? So evocative. Let's give another round for Margo Hunters and Hunting Ground."

This time around, the clapping is contrived. Wanting to keep up the pace and not wanting to be desperate for applause, Celadonna announces the next architects on stage, with considerable congeniality—overcompensated even.

Standing formally, hands at her waist, she announces, "Let's say hello to our second competitor. We are fortunate to have the husband-wife team, often referred to as the 'East Coast Power Couple,' Chip Tooney and Ling Liang, from their office, ChipLing of Boston. The duo's projects display the rigor of their Bauhaus Ivy-League training, and they are the go-to architects for the most prestigious projects from D.C. to New York. I believe that Ling and Chip are here today to bring their Modernist Minimalist discipline to our mysterious Alcatraz Island. Ms. Liang and Mr. Tooney, please take the stage."

The architect pair take their time to find their positions, gathering their thoughts for an intellectual rally, or perhaps battle. No, this is not a TV reality show or singing competition, but Magnar has effectively created a dramatic stage for rivalries waging war on the battlefield of abstract ideas and creative weaponry, with a prize so big that victory would be a game changer—that perhaps the ends would justify the means.

273

Her face very serious, one hand on her chin, Ling begins with academic coolness, "In the early 1900s, a Swiss-French architect by the name of Le Corbusier"—nods of acknowledgment from attentive members—"suggested this: 'a house is a machine for living in.' And so, Chip and I evoke the same sentiment. Your new museum for Abstract art will be a machine for appreciating art and sculpture." She emphasizes the curious descriptor, "machine."

Heard in the back of the room, "What is she talking about?"

"Aren't machines kind of unfriendly, sort of impersonal and mechanical?"

"Well, machines are actually mechanical."

Ignoring the chit chat, a casual Chip steps over next to his wife. With his self-assuring smile, he jumps in, "A machine has moving parts, and our design—museum as machine—will also have moving parts. The building will have enormous, bold-faced moving parts." His voice accelerates. "Building components, limbs, and entire sections will change and reposition before your very eyes!"

The Boston architects hold the audience's attention, as they wonder, "What kind of moving parts?"

"An elevator? Loading dock?"

"I don't understand."

Hearing the side whispers, Ling answers immediately, "No, not the obligatory parts of a building that move, such as elevators or escalators. Instead, we propose a design inspired by the art movement of kinetic sculptures—large scale structures moving and twisting in the air."

Chip declares, "Our museum will have moving floors, moving walls, and moving roofs. Providing maximum flexibility, gallery rooms and whole building wings will be manipulated, customized to suit the needs of every artists and their works of art. The experience of our architecture can evolve into thousands of permutations, physically and experientially."

Ling adds, "Every museum director asks that the architecture provide a blank space for each artist to display their work in the best light. Yet empty walls and adjustable lighting do not make up a space of adaptability. To do so, we need walls that can stand straight or tilt, roofs that lift high or be removed, like a giant convertible car. And we need floors that can rise and fall, even warp as needed."

The story is enticing, and the crowded audience believes that they understand the architects' presentation. They have seen pieces and parts, but not yet, the whole. Chip and Ling have not revealed their total design, not quite yet as they continue to build anticipation, like a good storyteller.

Faintly heard from the upper balcony, "I get it. This building is like one of those Japanese toys, the small metal robot becoming a car, then a jet."

A response hushes, "But a museum is no child's toy. Can a museum actually change and move?"

"Is such engineering possible?"

Magnar grins as he points out to Celadonna their recent visit to New York City. "Remember that project we toured by architects⌧, ⌧Diller Scofidio + Renfro? They designed that massive performance building that could change to provide various sized events. The gigantic structure transformed like a telescoping machine on wheels."

"I remember, dear, and I love where ChipLing is going with this. It is such a different approach than Margo's sculptural work."

Finally, the design being unveiled, Ling and Chip each split to one side, well-practiced, no longer blocking the large screen and projector flanked by drawings. With a click of the small remote in Chip's pocket, a video of their project plays for the attentive crowd. Through a 3D-computer animation, the screen displays their proposed museum, and the audience is on the edge of their seats. The bizarre looking proposed building is actually moving, rotating, and shifting, then getting taller, then shorter, becoming wider than skinnier.

For those followers of ChipLing who expected one of their crisp white, contemporary Cubist buildings, this daring scheme is startling. Chip then stops the video and shifts gears carting their physical model to center stage.

Under hot spotlights, he waves his hands over this model, yet the audience is more confused and amused than impressed. The model is merely a wood base, a carefully crafted representation of the island, but blank, no prison buildings, no lighthouse. Nothing.

Someone jokes, "Is this some kind of Minimalist joke?"

Ling eagerly pushes forward another cart, her charette. A large vintage steel box, exposed rivets at the seams, glows for the audiences. The size of a pirate's treasure chest, the box's weight causes a sticky rubber sound from the cart's wheel on the wood flooring. She pushes with all her might, while trying to maintain a professional demeanor.

Having opened the heavy creaking lid with both hands gripping tightly, Chip reaches in and pulls out something resembling a refurbished car part. He gently places it on the wood model and yells, "Mechanisms!"

He then gets another part from the box in his wife's arms. This time, sort of an antiquated lever from a vintage sewing machine. He shouts, "Apparatus!" and places this item on top of the first. She hands him what appears to be components of a wall clock.

He says, "Gadgets and devices!" positioning the several new elements with the others.

"Instruments, tools, and contraptions." Chip steadies more and more parts as if from a disassembled dishwasher.

Chip's bizarre performance mesmerizes the audience, possibly even more than when Margo presented her model. The husband-wife team engrosses the crowd through a display of process, involving them in the making of a building.

As if a clown car, more comes out of the box than makes sense. Chip continues, piece after piece, chanting machine-like words, shaking his fingers, nodding his head, having an enjoyable time—like Julia Childs whipping up something that the viewers can't wait to taste.

The audience starts to see beyond a collection of random metal parts, cogs, and gears, delicately assembled on a platform of wood. A persuasive building appears before their eyes, a beguiling design vision.

The East Coast Power Couple then step farther to the sides of the stage, and their arms direct attention to the humongous drawings. Consistent with the model, the illustrations provide a blend of technology and science fiction, the retro past with futuristic fantasy. The depictions are executed in sepia ink and capture the steam-powered machines of the 19th century, an appropriate inspiration for the architects' design ideas.

They don't need to announce it explicitly. An audience member does so for them, as he blurts out to his wife, "Steampunk!" Clearly a fan of this genre.

The wife responds, "Wow, I have never seen such a museum design that combines ideas from Europe's Industrial Revolution with the romanticized science of the Victorian era."

With enormous building sections that can be manipulated and repositioned, this WoMA design is less of a building and more of a contraption, a compilation of repositionable elements on the scale of a five-story building. The drawings display curious structural components: large gears 30 feet in diameter, a giant web of galvanized ductwork, pistons of a fantastical engine, and glass elevators that travel on the outside of the building, appearing ready to launch into the atmosphere like Willy Wonka's transport.

The Ivy-League architects smirk, having discarded their righteous education of "form-follows-function" and "ground zero," of mute white concrete boxes. No longer purists, they are simply having fun today. The ghosts of Gropius, Mies, and the Bauhaus do not haunt them any longer. They are pleased to take risks and shed the teachings of their Harvard professors. Chip and Ling's ground-shifting thinking results in a building that is provocative and sexy, like a vintage Indian motorcycle showing off all its gleaming chrome parts.

The other architects are listening intently. Perhaps out of envy, Parker starts to fuss. He turns to Margo quietly saying, "Kind of kitschy, right? Isn't the design just a ridiculous Steampunk theme park?"

With rare respect for her competitors, Margo responds, "I think Ling is offering a thrilling view into the future of buildings and cities."

"But c'mon. It's absurd. Slanting walls and moving floors are impossible. It's just a mess of metal parts, not coherent structural engineering. Even if these kinetic ideas are possible, the building is still ugly and unwelcoming."

Celadonna shoots a hush-informed stare his way. Parker recoils and looks to the floor.

Seeing a smiling Magnar, Chip is encouraged to continue the presentation. "Our design is not just a building, not a conventional institution for art. Our design is not just about movement. It is movement. Our project is about change and transformation. Evolution in history was about motion: first crawling, then walking bent over, to standing upright, finally running tall. Man and woman evolved through the need to move and adapt."

The Harvard architects are talking too much, but no one seems to mind. Ling elaborates like a teacher to students. "Consider your old Candlestick Park in nearby Bayview Heights. One day it was a square-ish stadium for baseball. But the next day, the building was a rectangle for football."

Feeling that the audience is getting saturated with their words, Chip transitions into the finale, bringing forward the last drawing on a movable panel. At first glance, it appears to be one of those Dyson Vacuum ads where all the parts of the vacuum cleaner are separated apart but graphically laid out to show how the components come back together. This encore drawing, created in Revit then airbrushed by hand, captures their thinking in a single image.

Chip wraps up philosophically, "Buildings are made of parts. Like a car, the parts inform the whole, and the whole informs the parts. We want your new museum to be appreciated not just as a single composition, but as a collection of a million parts. And these parts move to create the everchanging whole."

One hand on her chin again, Ling concludes, "Please allow me to end our presentation by citing an excerpt from American poet, Robert Francis.

"From segment, fragment, he can reconstruct
The whole, prefers to reconstruct the whole,
As if to say, I see more seeing less…

Gives something unglassed nature cannot give:
The old obliquity of art, and proves
Part may be more than whole, least may be best."

There are respectful cheers and applause from the audience that has been intuitively set out to disapprove of this presentation from the East Coast. Up next, the last architect.

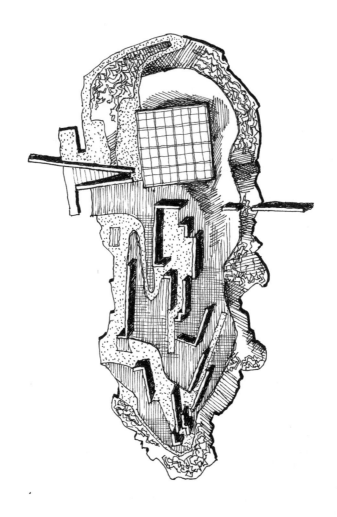

Death by Design at Alcatraz

CHAPTER 37

PAR Designs:
Keep It Simple, Stupid

C ELADONNA'S INTRODUCTIONS appropriately honored the previous two companies, but for the final competitor, she brings a personal interest. Over the course of four days, Parker A. Rand has become aware of her fascination with him, alongside the unsolicited support. Starting months ago, she wanted him to win this competition. Yet, the architect doesn't know if this fixation was because she respected his talent and therefore deemed him the best man for the job, or something else. This something else troubles him, and so far, cannot be defined.

Taking the stage again, Celadonna boasts with an easy smile, "Now we will hear from our friendly neighborhood architect, our final presenter, Parker A. Rand, based here in the Bay Area. The portfolio from his boutique studio, PAR Designs, demonstrates the most thoughtful and site-sensitive solutions. With his praised Post-Modern projects for universities and corporate clients, Mr. Rand has been showered with honors and rave reviews."

She can't wait to add some spice to the otherwise generic introduction. "His tremendous reputation as the thinking man's architect makes him the design voice to follow. The poetry of his work, his dedication for the environment, and the passion for—well, enough said. Frankly my friends, I am definitely a fan. I am holding my breath to see what Mr. Rand has in store for us—" She stops herself from embellishing too much, from gushing.

"Everyone, please welcome to the stage, professor at UC Berkeley, author of several books, and a published memoir already, our very own Parker A. Rand!"

As the San Francisco architect clumsily gets up from his seat, the hostess flashes him a flirtatious smile that finally hits its bullseye. Not to be distracted, not to downward spiral into reckless thinking, he disciplines himself to target the topic at hand: winning this competition.

He gracelessly lifts the microphone from the stand, causing the irritating feedback noise that occurs at nearly every event. He positions himself in front of his presentation with a posture not as confident as it should be. His gentle poise is more that of an introspective spirit, and less of an entrepreneur prepared to sell his vision and close the deal.

Parker has armed himself with numerous pencil drawings mounted on panels behind him, all neatly drawn by hand. Oddly, some of his illustrations are so refined—executed with such a light touch—that the enigmatic drawings appear hesitant, barely evident to the naked eye. Yet, this was the architect's intent, to present a quiet scheme—a design meek, mild, and modest.

He thinks to himself in preparation, recalling the presentation where Margo claimed her own design to be greater than the Seven Wonders of the World. *That was so bombastic. So arrogant.*

And ChipLing's ideas of moving buildings, *Gimmicky.*

Parker also recalls the only other thing he learned from his childhood Bible classes, beside the Talents parable.

Running through his mind is the Book of Matthew, *Blessed are the meek: For they shall inherit the earth.*

He is vaguely religious and doesn't care much for deciphering the Scriptures. For this one short verse, he doesn't analyze the words as spiritual. Rather, he reads it literally. This Biblical excerpt about meekness provides him complacency in a world that rewards those who speak the loudest and too much, like Magnar Jones, even Margo, Ling, Chip, and Johnny. Yes, and Lars von Meester too.

Standing proudly at a large model of his design, all white made of crudely cut foamcore sheets, Parker begins with a squeak in his voice, "Many have heard the instructional 1960s acronym from the U.S. Navy: K-I-S-S."

Hand on his chest, clearing his throat, he attempts to pull the audience in, "It stands for Keep It Simple, Stupid." A few laughs and several claps of affirmation, as if a sigh of relief from the previous two overly complex presentations.

"These days, this pithy recommendation is delivered by anyone in the role of doling out advice, from architecture professors to life coaches, from advertisers to political campaign managers. But life gets complicated and keeping things simple is not so easy. So what do we do?"

He directs the question to the entire audience, making sure he has made the required eye contact with as many people as he can—directly front, far back, side to side, and high up on the terraces.

His voice is stronger now. "We all want to keep things simple, but to achieve this level of simplicity—the desired purity and mindfulness—one has to work hard at making it look easy. At PAR Designs, we call upon our analogy of a duck."

The audience chuckle in amusement.

"The feathered animal glides so smoothly across the lake, but beneath the water's surface, little webbed feet paddle furiously. But please don't underestimate the rigors required to achieve simplicity, whether a work of architecture or a duck leisurely floating in a figure eight."

The viewers are perplexed, entertained so far, and eager to hear a punch line.

"Minimalist architect, Mies Van Der Rohe, gave us one of the most impactful phrases in design and in life, 'Less is More.'" Knowingly taking a line straight out of Ling and Chip's Harvard-Bauhaus script, Parker glances in their direction with a soft smirk.

"With this three-word philosophy, we present to you today a project of sculptural austerity recalling the roots of Alcatraz. Our composition will posit lucidity and precision. Autonomy and self-referentiality comprise the unapologetic purging of the conventional beliefs for adornment."

These fancy words mean very little to the crowd, but Parker's competitors listen, understand, and are shocked. They realize that the local architect is no longer promoting his roots in Post-Modernism, no longer applying charming colors and abstractions of classical forms, no more cuteness and humor in buildings. No, not today, this San Francisco architect is suggesting something very different.

He peppers his presentation with terms like, "minimalistic," "humble," "ascetic," and "clarity." Then Parker flips quickly through, but in steady timed pace, a slide show of images from his visits to the East Coast sculpture park, Storm King. He has selected black and white photos of what is known as Earthworks. With this art movement from the '60s and '70s, rural earth was shaped like sculpture, as if from the hands of God. At Storm King, an ecological experience of textures, shadows, and abstract shapes were provided at a magnificent scale of soccer fields.

Unlike Hunting Ground's and ChipLing's decisions to demolish all of the prison buildings and start anew, Parker has made the decision to keep a number of the existing structures, but in a surprising turn, remove the roofs and even some floors.

Standing at his mysterious illustrations and cool white model, he says, "We view these remaining building walls and the island's topography as a starting point in which we knit in new walls, floors and roofs—all to be a soft gray, board-formed concrete."

The model has an impression of a small village, not an overbearing building complex. The musical sequence of walls—new ones next to old ones—delivers the feel of a beautiful Roman ruin.

Magnar's keen eye for Abstract art immediately understands the understated monochromatic campus, and he is captivated.

For the audience though, without spending a lengthy amount of time studying the pencil floor plans, one can barely tell where the existing buildings stop and the new one begins. "I am having a hard time separating new from old."

Parker understands this challenge and argues, "The subtleness is exactly the objective."

"Very clever, restrained, effortless," Magnar comments to Celadonna in an uncommon respectful whisper. "A design of new structures seamless with the existing prisons—island and buildings cohesively one. Parker's ideas sit gently on the surface, resting on the land like a feather. The proposal is a sculpture of abstract shapes and landforms, no longer a prosaic building with walls and windows. Elementalistic and primitivistic." Magnar tries a few fancy words to impress his lover. They don't.

Scratching his head like a college professor might, Parker provides commentary on the provenance of Alcatraz Island. "Also, we explore our fascination with the philosophy of the Grotesque. As we examine such a polemic on beauty, we speak not about the unattractive prison buildings, but the alluring history and myths. The legends are beautiful because they are provocative and even notorious. The existing prison is beautiful through being uncanny. And we want to work with the old buildings, not against them."

Continuing with such ideas of modesty and restraint, his design approach suits his personal demeanor, as his posture softens, and shoulders relax. Even an easy smile forms. "I don't want a building that fights for attention, fights for the splash page of a website or magazine cover." He coyly directs this attitude to fellow competitor Margo.

With his chin down and closing his eyes for a few seconds, Parker says, "It's not about me and my legacy. If you wonder what makes our design special, maybe that is the goal: for you to always wonder. To look. To seek answers. If you are unsure where the building ends and the landscape begins, then we have done our job. If you are confused by what parts are new and what parts are existing, then relish in this state of perplexity. The past seamlessly exists with our present and the future. If you ask about the Big Idea, then we would say there might not be one. Maybe our proposal is for both the conscious and the unconscious."

It is subtle, but noticeable to attentive attendees—Parker has replaced his competitor's use of "I" and "me," with "we" and "us." The shift in jargon supports the noble ideas that he is presenting.

Intentionally not directing attention to his drawings or model yet, he speaks with growing conviction. "If you are seeking a self-congratulatory, indulgent design statement like Gehry's Walt Disney Concert Hall, or maybe one of my competitors' designs, well, then our composition of unassuming beauty is not for you." Parker makes this direct challenge to the other architects, and the audience is his jury. The advantage of Celadonna scheduling him last provides Parker with the strategic position of context and criticism.

Still examining the model, Magnar suggests, "This design is so elegant and delicate. It's pretentiously unpretentious, and I like—"

Celadonna interrupts and asks, "Dear, what was that project that you took me to in Leca da Palmeria?"

"Exactly, the enchanting public pools Alvaro Siza. Upon arriving on the structures, we saw almost nothing, just the ocean and some concrete retaining walls. But that was the objective: The project looked like nothing. It placed itself so delicately within the earth, it was some kind of anti-building."

Parker ignores the chatter and continues, "Our proposed design for WoMA is meant to be silent. Like much of Abstract art, the visitor assigns values and emotions. For example, a red painting by Barnett Newman might be about anger and fury, or maybe a hot day in summer. Or maybe it is just about red paint. It's up to you. We respect you, and for this Alcatraz project, my ego will not write your script, the buildings will present the art, not detract from it."

The architect is weaving a relatable story, and his face shows excitement. "Not only are we respecting the history of the existing buildings on Alcatraz, but we are also suggesting ideas that are powerfully introspective and confidently content." He says these words as if he is arguing for his own disposition in life.

"Being spare in design moves takes a lot of work to be successful, as I mentioned with the duck." Abruptly Parker states, "Enough of philosophy, folks. Let's look at our proposal in detail."

Parker reaches over the model and waves his arms at the drawings, dashing from right to left, side-stepping between each panel.

"The proposed new structures sit very low to the shifting grades of the island. If our buildings go up, they are only one story. By design, many of our buildings are underground. Certain galleries are to be intentionally without sunlight to protect the art from ultraviolet rays, from discoloration and oxidation."

He leads the eyes back to the model and points out a big crevice-like cut in the landscape. "The entry to the proposed museum is this large opening in the earth, a single slash in the island. You descend down a long concrete ramp, slowing your pace, leaving the worries of the outside world behind. As you pass through a softly lit transition, bright natural light finally welcomes you. And the visitor arrives at the lobby 25 feet below the surface. But not a cavern. You are under a massive flat glass roof on thin-steel trusses—so minimally detailed that you will think there is no roof at all. Also, the glass roof is coplanar with the island's surface. When approached from afar, it appears as if the glass is a giant Zen-like reflecting pond.

"Underground galleries are lit by dramatic beams of sunlight coming through various-sized skylights. And at the surface of the island, arriving visitors will come upon each skylight looking like small tranquil bodies of water. The visitors are unaware until later that galleries are underneath these shimmering patches of light."

He continues with stories and impressions of each major area of his design, filling the audience with emotions and sensations. The architect references history, nostalgia, and even epic tales of lost empires. Parker tells a powerful story, as he moves the audience through his design, tapping into their imagination and transporting them into the architecture.

As his time is up, his arms reaches forward as if a welcoming embrace. He delivers his final statement, "We urge all of you to think about your lives, and how exhausting it is to work so hard to be noticed, to constantly strive for the front of the stage. We should all relax and stop trying so hard.

"Our design for WoMA consciously defers, stepping out of the limelight. Our design does so casually but with strength."

He lowers his eyes quietly and combines his final words with an unintentional anecdote for his life, "Our design is wonderful because it is authentic. It doesn't need to shout to everyone that it is worthwhile."

A roar of finality arrives through resounding applause and hails, not just for Parker A. Rand, but for the heroic and ambitious efforts of all three presentations. The proposed visions for WoMA are indeed elaborate and impressive: an aggressive composition of acute forms from Hunting Ground, a daring machine-like building from ChipLing, and PAR Designs' mesmerizing statement of reticence.

But if one is to seek a winner, how does one judge genius?

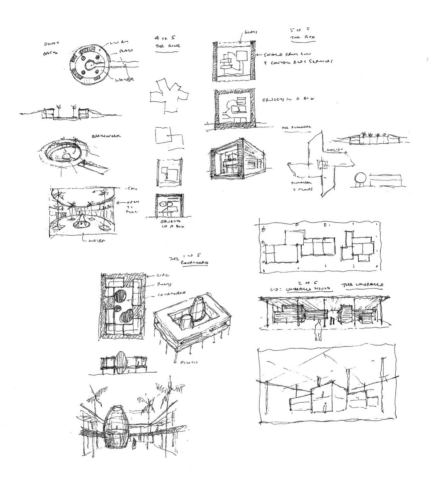

CHAPTER 38

Judge and Jury

A STARK SILHOUETTE of decision-making authority, Magnar Jones confronts the three architectural presentations on stage. This developer, a self-proclaimed visionary, grasps the design intent of each of the architect's concept. He appreciates that blood has been squeezed from a stone for him—and in only four days. Announcing a victor is no leisurely undertaking. Judging the designs with the goal of selecting the singular best is challenging as well as disheartening.

At the mic, Celadonna announces, "Thank you everyone for being such an engaged audience. And most of all, thank you to our three WoMA finalists." She asks the audience rhetorically, "Weren't the presentations simply amazing?"

She continues "Magnar Jones, our gracious host and design aficionado"—internally she struggles with the latter description provided to her—"will be leading the judging process. Within the hour, yes one hour, the victorious winner will be announced to 'y'all' here." She tries Magnar's Texan accent for fun. "Mingle. Grab a plate of the delightful hors d'oeuvres from our farm-to-fork restaurant, right here in the museum. The finest cases of refreshments have been flown in from the nearby wine region of Napa Valley. No expenses are spared for this Magnar-produced affair.

"For now, please stay off the stage, so to give Magnar and his board members the space to review the designs in detail. We will inform you when they have completed their assessments. Then you are all welcome to browse the presentations close up. We only ask that you be very careful. The works are artifacts of true genius, a testimony to the artistry within the human spirit." In a flirtatious tone, "See 'y'all' back here very soon!"

Already on stage and brooding, Magnar asks himself, "Amongst these top-notch architects and their diverse ideas, is there really a clear winner, a second-place runner up, and an unfortunate third-place loser?"

He carefully weaves his large, intimidating frame between the presentation drawings and models, as his business associates come near the edge of the stage awaiting their opportunity for closer evaluations. The audience has now dispersed around the museum. Fine china holds exquisite finger food to entertain them as they await the decision.

Only a few times in his life has Magnar been troubled like this. At the front of the stage, he steps near Celadonna who is now on the lobby floor. Looking down at her but mostly over her, he debates, "As with art, architecture is subjective. Beauty is supposedly in the eye of the beholder, and I, me alone, am the beholder. But is beauty really the goal? Mozart wanted his music to be beautiful, but Beethoven, this mad composer, was less concerned about composing beautiful-sounding music. Instead, he reached deep into angry emotions, and produced challenging textures, and percussive rhythms of rage and fury."

Celadonna is used to these deliberations. Her role is not to participate, but simply be a sounding board—a silent one at that.

Being appropriately hostess-like, she finds the opportunity to slip away and give Magnar his breathing room. She heads over to the members of the board, patiently and uselessly waiting in the sidelines. She decides to be a mouthpiece for her deep-in-thought boyfriend. She explains, "These proposals are conceptual only, created in a short time frame—an intense burst of creatively. Please understand there will be several years of work after the selection of the winning scheme. The chosen architect will be developing the design, refining details, and then finally commencing construction."

She speaks articulately enough, informing the directors of what to expect after today. But more importantly, she keeps the group preoccupied so that Magnar can be alone on this stage with his thoughts, and not bothered by corporate antics. He does not want to pretend that any of their voices matter. This developer has no interest in what anyone thinks, especially not his trophy lover or a group of individuals assembled merely for the trivial construct of a corporation.

These mock board members, a dozen women and men outfitted in expected garbs of navy suits and white shirts and blouses, circle the edges of the stage going through compulsory motions. Keeping a safe distance from their CEO Magnar Jones, they eye the architects' drawings from a distance and with little comprehension. Adding stale commentary, figureheads all of them, they are aware that they are merely for show, that the decision lies completely in their boss's hands.

Celadonna too is now standing back far from the stage. She watches her man run scenarios in his head, and she does not dare to even place a foot onto the platform—knowing well that she is merely a girlfriend, nothing more. And if she has a job to do right now, it is to run interference for the board and keep the audience and press at bay. That's all.

Magnar understands the gravitas of this decision—a gift to the city. This project has been made possible by his passion for Abstract art and his personal wealth, supported through his political maneuvers. But this afternoon, he does not concern himself with origin stories, nor the pragmatics of the upcoming technical phases of architecture and engineering, or the logistics of construction. Today, he seeks poetry. Like Salieri judging Mozart, Magnar is no true artist, but he can judge and is aware when in the presence of creative virtuosity.

The architectural finalists left the stage a while back, very anxious to have done so. They stand huddled together near the coat room. No words are spoken during this hour. They stand as a tribe, though each in their private domain of creative decompression. This is the fog-like calm after the storm of a charette and public presentations—after Magnar's contrived antics. Patiently the contestants wait to be called back to the stage and think of the past few days as already a lifetime ago.

Audience members and reporters sniff out the exhausted architects to offer compliments and congratulations, questions and criticism, and/or votes of confidence. Though the architects typically enjoy the limelight after a successful presentation, they are in no mood. Simply drained, they are too weary to socialize, market their companies, or network relationships. The growing horde around them understand. The architects are not rude, not stand offish; they are simply spent. And the sympathetic pack dissipates, leaving the world-acclaimed competitors to claim what's left of their spirits.

The minds of these individuals brood over recent occurrences—from accidents to murders, from a cliff to a lighthouse, a brawl to poison, even an elevator falling to its ruin, and from death to design. Parker in particular adds to his check list a face-off with Lars, visits to the police station, and chance coupling with Celadonna.

But preoccupying themselves with one-track thoughts is something most architects do after a presentation, Here, they wonder if their design could have been better. Each presenter asks himself/herself: Was their design good enough, how should it have been better, was the presentation articulate enough, what word choices fell flat, what drawing was incomplete? And so on. This is the self-torture and self-critique that all talented architects instill, not just a typically doubting Parker A. Rand. All architects, and maybe artists, writers, and musicians as well, are cursed by the insecurity that their creative work is never done, always in flux.

No matter where the designers are in the journey of making architecture—beginning, middle, or end—they are constantly aware that their ideas could be better, should be better. The ambition to be better—this pursuit of greatness—is but a plague.

Even when a building has completed drawings and is finally constructed—even with rave reviews, many thanks, handshakes, and congratulatory pats on the back—the architect finds himself standing alone in the finished spaces thinking, judging, and condemning.

Parker thinks back to his design of a local library, *Damn, eight more inches to the width of the window would have created a better relationship between man and nature.*

Such a curse burdens the artistic spirit. When a building is done, when a book gets published, or when a piece of music is premiered—the creative process is a path with a clear cut beginning, but unfortunately no distinct end. Just an affliction to chase perfection.

Magnar paces in search of guidance that no one is able to give. He stares at Margo's alluring model, a courageous work of sculpture and creativity—glass-like shards under a parking lot size umbrella. He then moves to Chip and Ling's Steampunk contraption, buildings as machines with moving parts and all. Finally, he views Parker's white model of simplicity and sensitivity. Then this decision maker goes back and forth, and back and forth again, like a slow motion tennis ball in a Grand Slam tournament.

Atypical for his exacting presence, Magnar is mumbling aloud. "Is the design attractive? All three do attract me. But is the design supposed to be attractive?" He does not usually spiral, nor does he tend to second guess. But he feels the weight of this challenge.

"Is it functional? How do I judge function? How much will the design cost? How long will it take to develop, have city permits, then build the whole damn thing?"

He contorts his mind, twists his body, and continues thinking, "Yes, I can see that there are the required number of galleries of various sizes. I see a big lobby. It looks like there are plenty of restrooms, but so what! Is the overall design a good one?"

Magnar ponders the critical question, "What is good architecture?"

He plunges his hands into his jacket pockets for just an instant, a habit when he is deeply stuck in making a decision—a habit Celadonna has observed many times. In anticipation of this moment, she slipped a piece of paper into his pocket earlier in the day. He finds it now as he stares at all three presentations. Immediately, he recognizes the handwriting of his partner, and a familiar fragrance from this perfumed letter that pierces his senses.

On the parchment envelope, it reads, "For Your Brilliance and Your Love of Brilliance: For Your Love of Great Words from Great Minds," written in dark-red ink and accompanied with a child-like cartoon heart. He stares at the gift, not coming upon any conclusions. Then puzzled and exasperated, he opens the envelope hastily, pulling out a small ivory card. Celadonna scribed a quote from the 19th-century Russian writer, Leo Tolstoy.

"Art is the uniting of the subjective with the objective, of nature with reason, of the unconscious with the conscious, and therefore art is the highest means of knowledge."

Magnar reads this to himself, then mutters it softy, finally stating it clearly on the third try, concise word for concise word. Celadonna has been eyeing him, awaiting the appropriate reaction that she knew such an offering would stir. She stands ready.

As expected, Magnar rushes to the front edge of the stage, and urgently gathers Celadonna and token board members. Not even waiting for this small group to settle in, the impatient man recites the quote one last time. He speaks proudly as if he authored the profound statement.

At this very moment, as afternoon sun delivers its insistent company through the glass ceiling of the lobby rotunda, Magnar has chosen the winning design of his international competition—handpicked his triumphant architect. He imagines the soft clouds above parting and blue skies opening up to illuminate him with brilliance. To the few around him, Magnar Jones whispers very slowly, "I have made my decision."

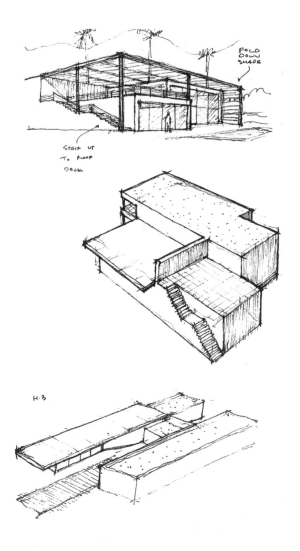

CHAPTER 39

Apprehension in the Lobby

W ITH BARELY A NOD, Magnar signals to his lover.
"Finally," Celadonna declares in a low voice. Though she rushes towards the stage, her movements are as exquisite as always. Mic lightly held by three fingertips, she calls to order, "Everyone, please return to your seats. We are about to get started."

Throughout this event, cameras have been flashing away documenting this design affair like it is a paparazzi-fueled gathering of the city's most envied socialites. Audience members have followed in stride with their phones capturing images and videos—filtering and adding hashtags, posting to social media.

As Celadonna addresses the hustle and bustle erupting through the lobby, the urgent public trying to find their way back to calm. Her excitement level begins to breach through her serene composure, and she announces with increasing pace, "I am so thrilled to let you know that Magnar Jones will be making the announcement you have all been waiting for. He will declare the champion winner for the new World Museum of Abstract Art at Alcatraz!"

She roars towards the huddle of architects, "Please, all of you, we would love to have each and every one of you back in your positions on stage." They look more like a pack of awkward middle school students at their first dance, than seasoned professionals.

Finally, the audience seats themselves, as some find this the last opportunity to horde gourmet munchies onto tiny plates. Reporters and photographers return to their assigned spots in the sidelines, like cages that read, "Do Not Feed." The principal architects shuffle in an erratic fashion to their seats next to Celadonna at the microphone, and all the design employees scurry to their front row seats. Each team of associates cheer and prop up their valiant boss in hopes of winning the big museum contract, which would secure jobs for each employee for years to come.

Celadonna calls out, "Let's bring back museum developer and our host, Mr. Magnar Jones!" Her voice cracks from the adrenalin. This final time with a buzzing hum in the room, he receives his due applause, an enthusiastic welcome for a man who has captivated a city with his dedication for a new arts institution, daring to re-envision Alcatraz Island, and the unconventional venue of the competition. Magnar takes to the stage, standing haughty and too proud. His narcissism stills his body so that he may absorb as much glory that is being given to him at this moment. He is like a desert succulent in a thunder storm—not a drop of rain to be missed. His broad frame is positioned symmetrically, balanced with precise equilibrium—both in his physical body as well as his vanity. He is already thinking of how this WoMA tale will embellish his legacy.

He decrees with no casual commentary. "We have made our decision."

The "we" is, as before, only a considerate gesture to his perfunctory board members, as well as his souvenir girlfriend. Though he struggled with making a selection, he shows none of the internal battle now. The crowd is mostly noiseless, prepared to hear the grand conclusion of a four-day design circus.

The architects sit apprehensively at the edge of their seats, each person already tasting the juicy "commission of the century" or preparing themselves to lick their wounds. Each architect, even in their fatigued state, is re-energized at this one moment. With the win, each candidate envisions humbly accepting the Pritzker Prize and being named one of the greatest architects in history.

Magnar starts again, but this time rephrasing his words in terms he wants the people and his legacy to acknowledge clearly, "I have made my decision."

He leans forward, mouth grazing the mesh surface of the microphone, and his breathing rumbles low. Magnar waits motionless, extending the suspense to entice the audience into his world. The silence of eight seconds isn't long, but long enough to ensure that the atmosphere is charged with static. No one is speaking or even moving, maybe not even breathing.

As he inhales a dramatic breath to then follow with the name of the victorious architect, four police officers erupt from the street barging through the lobby doors. The raucous startles the crowd. The drama has an effect on a previously soundless lobby of sounding like an explosion.

Looking over their shoulders, the audience see at first only the bright sun outside the windows. But as hundreds of pupils dilate, they see police in glaring contrast to the light, only a blur of dark figures at first, but eventually forming an intimidating group in black and blue. The four officers surge their way through the crowd, as many start to rise from their seats panicked.

The front officer commands, "Please, everyone, calm down, and stay seated."

"Stand down!" yells another cop militantly, and such a phrase adds to the growing panic.

The audience cannot ignore how the right hand of each officer is resting on their city-issued firearm. One moment the crowd was looking at harmless architectural drawings, and the next, the setting has flared into chaos.

In organized unison like a muscular ballet troupe, the team of four police maneuver their way deeper and deeper into the lobby towards the stage. They now confront Magnar at the microphone, and he shows no indication of concern. Confounded, the architects' most recent aspirations of fame suddenly go on hold. A pin, a nail gun actually, has burst their balloons.

Parker starts to tremble as he recognizes the uniformed individuals from the first day of the competition. Then, that group of officers hauled him to the station regarding the murder of Lars von Meester. Parker's posture slumps immediately, his head nearly in his lap. Exhaustion from the competition, anxiety from the earlier encounter with Celadonna, and now this, armed police storming the occasion.

He worries, *Von Meester, Brand—please, no more talk of Lands End, of a burning lighthouse, of my cigarette lighter.*

Parker's mind warps into an abyss of dread, so debilitating it is nearly enough for him to finally stand up and beg, *Officers, I beg of you. Get this over with and arrest me for the murders. Put me out of my misery!* But he keeps to himself.

One cop breaks from the line. The female officer, compact and sturdy and not to be challenged, walks distinctly away from the architects. She approaches Magnar with a few accelerating stomps, but only to chuck a disapproving glance at him. Instead, she approaches Celadonna, who is standing off to the side.

Her graceful beauty does not wane, not yet, as she hears the officer announce, sounding almost like a recording played back in slow motion, "Celadonna Kimm, you are under arrest for the murders of Lars Von Meester and of Maxwell Brand. Please come with us."

These words ring plainly, and the audience reacts with thunderous confusion. The Mayor and his political cohorts scan the room, seeking the most efficient path of flight. Other members of the audience stand from their seats to better take in the action unfolding at the front. Like seeing a car accident, one can barely turn away. Within the commotion, most observers are staring at a young woman who appears to have spent more time accessorizing today's outfit, than scheming a murder. Or in this case, two.

Under the theatrical spotlights, the other three cops join the first, and surround Celadonna. She remains still like a classical marble sculpture in Rome.

"Please come with us, miss." The female officer steps behind Celadonna taking hold of her, grabbing securely her arm. The officer's other hand is placed on Celadonna's shoulder, and she feels the sturdiness of this short woman, a female type that is diametrically opposed to the cut and silhouette of Celadonna. Metal clangs and handcuffs strike her slight wrists. She cringes, but only a little—again, keeping her composure.

Even with arms locked behind her back, even with the cloud of a double murder, the lovely hostess appears to glide effortlessly off the stage through the lobby, accompanied by police on either side, one in front, and the compact one behind. The mass of people, accented by the flashes of photography, separates for the spectacle of navy-blue officials and a porcelain-perfect woman to pass by.

While being hurried forward, Celadonna only hisses, "I didn't do it. I didn't kill Lars. I didn't kill two architects." Inexplicably she is passive. Indifferent to this particular walk-of-shame, her polish does not tarnish.

Most people are taken aback, the politicians have already and conveniently vanished, and journalists continue to push through. Commentary within the crowd is tossed out to no particular listener.

"Is this for real or part of the show?"

"She killed two people in cold blood?"

"Shit show!"

"The best lunch break ever."

While pacing towards the exit with her guards, Celadonna looks around the room, apparently with no sense of urgency. She looks intently for Parker, but he does not look up from his slouch—his face still in his hands, his stomach still in his throat. He barely knows what to do, what to think, as he peers through his clammy fingers. Total dismay immobilizes him, as he thinks, *What the hell is happening around me?*

The other architects stay seated but get shifty. No longer focused on the competition decision at hand, they watch firsthand the senseless activities surrounding them: police making an arrest; a bound damsel in distress; spectators, politicians, and gawkers pushing and yelling; and media with their cameras. The architects know Celadonna as: an accessory for their client; PR consultant; hostess for the day; and vapid lifestyle blogger on make-up tips and hotel recommendations. They cannot bring themselves to see her as a killer of two of their colleagues.

The police and their captive get part way down the lobby. Celadonna looks over her shoulder and calls out, "Magnar!"

His assertive voice is accidentally picked up by the nearby mic. The police and the entire lobby hear his command, "Stop. Please stop."

He approaches Celadonna, standing close to the police but ignoring them completely. He stares at his lover, his trophy, his prize. One officer warns Magnar, "We know: So-called friend of the police commissioner. We don't care."

Continuing to dismiss the officers, Magnar faces his lover with an unexpected look of no concern. He nonchalantly stares upon her as if assessing whether a bruised fruit in his kitchen should be tossed into the trash.

She gasps, "Magnar? What?"

Though still very much composed, her eyes desperately calls for his aid. He steps even closer to her, nearly penetrating the human layer of police between them.

As the cops reach out to restrain him from moving any farther forward, Magnar utters in the most peaceful of undertones, two sounds, "I know."

There is a brief pause after his deliverance—a pause for her mind to shift into the appropriate gears.

"Know what?" Panic in her voice, as she is aware of what is coming next.

"Last night—"

The police urge Celadonna to continue walking. But she freezes and asks in weak defense, "Last night?" There is a void in her mind, as she stands motionless awaiting the next impending words.

Magnar clarifies, "With Parker. With Parker A. Rand."

And the mention of that name finally defeats her, sending her instantly into a calamity of tragedy and ruin. It doesn't take more than a few seconds for her to recall how Magnar arranged for the security cameras to monitor the creative process in the architects' galleries, at all hours of the day and night—a continuous loop of sight and sound documenting all that has transpired.

For the first time since this entire competition started, maybe for the first time in her life, her poise is lost, and her gracefulness leaves her like the 21 grams of one's soul. Celadonna's body crumples forming a frail scarecrow supported by flanking officers. Her face turns to an expression of dread, all enchantment gone—her composure finally devasted. She is no longer Magnar's romantic partner, no longer a figure of universal attraction and envy.

Uneventfully, the officers escort her out of the building and into a police vehicle, while the audience diminishes, then dissolves entirely. Magnar Jones and his architects are already gone, staggering into the underbelly of this massive building.

CHAPTER 40

If You Build It, They Will Come

T HE COMPETITION, from five years ago, is a memory whose once
vivid colors have faded into a forgotten past. Now excitement
builds in town for the soon-to-be completed World Museum of Abstract Art at Alcatraz. With construction underway for three years
now, the project edges towards a glorious finish.

The celebrated San Francisco architect, Parker A. Rand, stands
proudly on the rocky terrain of Alcatraz Island, taking in the construction progress of his monumental project. With a Roark-ian outline,
he contemplates his triumph of winning the WoMA competition,
and he happily acknowledges the incredible professional and personal
successes that have since followed.

Five years ago, museum developer, Magnar Jones, selected Parker's
visionary design out of three remarkable proposals. The client's decision for this local architect was based on aspects from pragmatics to
poetics, from presentation to personality.

At a press conference held a month after the conclusion of the
competition, Magnar highlighted why he selected the design from
PAR Associates. Through a quad of speaker clusters taller than he,
Magnar spoke to the crowd. "These are good questions, people. Parker's
design respected the history of Alcatraz, preserving then transforming
the existing buildings into something breathtaking. Yes, the prisons.
Parker honored the myths and legends reaching deep into the islands'

antiquity, then added a new chapter while respecting the past ones."

An ambitious reporter chimed in, "But Mr. Jones, the other two schemes were much more creative, more gutsy. More the kind of thing you have been known to build."

Taking an aggressive forward-leaning stance, Magnar retorts, "Hunting Ground's or ChipLing's scheme would have suited me just fine. Extraordinary indeed, but the self-indulgence of those two designs lazily sought a blank slate for their grand ideas. Without a second thought, Margo, Ling and Chip's proposal demolished every part of Alcatraz Island, its very soul, from the structures to the hills—to the notoriety. A starting point of demolition, of total annihilation, is reckless. Parker's strategic restoration and re-envisioning—subtraction and addition—was cleverly bold, an approach that did not require the violent amputation of a major limb of San Francisco." Though an unexpected comment, the audience appreciated Magnar's rapport to their cherished landmark.

"Part of my success stems from juxtaposing vision with intelligence, genius with pragmatism. I saw immediately that Parker's design is buildable, as compared to the inexplicable 'Tenth Symphony' or the outrageous 'machine for art.'"

From the back row, an argumentative journalist asked meekly, "So your selection was based on practicality?"

"No!" Magnar barked; eyes narrowed. "Let me be clear: I sought a groundbreaking idea, literally, but one that was insistently simple, a simplicity that is cerebral and rational—a poetic solution that is fundamental yet commanding." Just indulgent words to some.

From another reporter, "A lot of people don't get it, don't understand the design. What is this Rand architect getting at?"

Trying to hide his displeasure of the public's ignorance, Magnar says, "Let me be clear, people—"

He was rudely interrupted with, "We can't even tell where the new buildings are, or what exactly happened to the old buildings."

Magnar got impatient with the small mindedness of his audience but was determined to educate *his* people. Calming himself, he stopped from calling the crowd out as imbeciles.

"Parker's vision found strength in restraint. His design was potent in its silence, stillness, and subtlety. I was initially infatuated with the thrill of the other two schemes, but I value the approach that will make my museum quietly yet powerfully timeless."

As Magnar further proclaimed his opinions and defended his decision, the reporters held up their recording devices even higher, while throwback journalists furiously jotted down notes.

"In life, as in art and architecture, brash notions may attract the most attention at first, but there is more value in authoritative resolve, in being in control. My clarity in leadership comes from my gut, my tenacity, my determination. And with this competition, my gut told me who to pick."

He growled a few more sentiments, as the crowd winded down—some moved and enlightened, others still baffled by all this architectural babble, and a few tired of such a display of vanity. Parker was not present at this gathering and didn't need or want to be. He was already working hard on the WoMA design. From the pack, there were no more questions—astute, asinine, or otherwise.

Shortly after the press conference, Parker signed Magnar's contract for architectural services. There was little debate over the legal mechanics.

Magnar said, "You don't mind do you, Parker? My executive team of attorneys will iron out the agreement"—of course in the favor of the developer. "Parker, I don't like to get my hands dirty in legal this-and-that."

In predictable contrast, Parker had his uncle, a retired paralegal, provide counsel on a few items in the agreement. Ignoring this David vs. Goliath setting, the entrepreneurial architect found all this lawyer banter boring in comparison to being awarded the job and starting the official design process.

Similarly, the design fee that Magnar paid to Parker was not a fair amount of cash—not enough to provide the boutique practice of PAR Designs depth in the coffers—but the money was abundant enough to keep the studio afloat and pay off business loans. Despite a low payment, Parker optimistically viewed this project as a monumental opportunity, something to capitalize on for decades to come. Appreciating his promising future that lies in Magnar's hands, the architect stated, "You are right in terms of prestige, Mr. Jones. Someone—I forgot who—did once coin this project as the 'commission of the century.'"

With barely a breather for Parker to celebrate his win, design work at PAR Designs started with an explosion of activity. Parker and his three trusted associates hired more talent and moved to bigger quarters. Similar in vibe to his original brick studio, Parker's new warehouse was no longer off an alley off an alley, but instead had a ground-level South Park storefront with a view of ironically, his much despised Bay Bridge. Staring out nostalgically at the colorless bridge with a vague recollection of being chauffeured across it once, Parker doesn't bother to dig further into his memory banks for more details as to why, who, and when.

PAR's team of architects eagerly took the conceptual ideas from the winning presentation, and developed them, refined them into a fleshed out work of architecture. Parker commanded the computers and tech that hum through his firm. Only he, the sole veteran architect, still drew by hand—expressively with a pencil on vellum under a tired drafting lamp.

For additional technical expertise, PAR Designs collaborated with several consulting companies to help turn his sketch ideas into a real building. Though the competition was so long ago, Parker queried his structural engineer, "How in the world would Chip and Ling have made their ambitious ideas into the real thing? C'mon, a moving building?"

Parker's design team continued to expand its roster: electrical engineers, acoustic technician, historical preservation expert, waterproofing specialist, even a horticulturist. Parker's many architects investigated a host of design topics, i.e.: the strength of concrete, details for the skylights, species of wood, the auditorium carpet, etc. Reminding his staff of one significant aspect of the process, Parker spoke in a perturbed tone, "A museum of this complexity, especially one that sits on a 22-acre historic island, is not easily approved by the numerous city agencies."

"Don't we just go through the city for a permit?" said a new intern.

Disappointed in such naivete, Parker responded, "No, there are dozens and dozens of officials to meet with, to get sign off from— for example, the Department of Building Inspection, Public Works, Mayor's Office on Disability, and so on. Good thing we have Magnar Jones's political relationships in our back pocket—"

Someone blurted out, "You mean bribes?" and a few laughs filled the room.

Well aware of who his client is, Parker warned, "That's enough. Do not bite the hand that feeds you."

The commencement of construction revealed the challenges when only having access by boat, transporting building crews, materials, and equipment—wading through pea soup fog across rocky bay waters, and no operational lighthouse for guidance. Even with construction crews working day and night, the project fell behind schedule.

The architect commented to his patron, "Mr. Jones, if I may"—Parker submitted gingerly— "I want my design, your design, our design to be incredible—and this takes time. I apologize for the delays. I am trying my best to deliver a project on time and on budget, as much as that sounds so trite. Essentially, Magnar, I want you to be a satisfied customer, and I am doing my very best."

Magnar smirked with satisfaction. He knew his architect as a man of integrity, an entrepreneur of dedication. Magnar appreciated the earnestness. Also, this developer didn't mind being catered to, fawned over even. Ego stroked.

Since the win, Parker discarded the burden from his hopeless interpretation of the Parable of the Talents. He now focuses on the only other verse he knows. Every day, facing uncompromising circumstances or easy challenges, he tells himself, *Yes, indeed, the meek shall inherit the earth.*

He is not interested in examining this sentence for more profound Biblical meaning, since his literal reading of this excerpt provides contentment and confidence enough.

Though less so these days, Parker's usual anxieties still dart around his brain, like an endless Pachinko game. But today, this day where an architect can stand like a king viewing the building of his nation, he celebrates from the top of a reconstructed lighthouse in progress and salutes his accomplishments.

Surveying his design from this elevated vantage point, he peers down upon the expanse of the island blanketed with cranes, fork-lifts, and builders, hundreds and more. The nearly finished museum faithfully resembles the original model created for the competition, and Parker is more than pleased. At this moment in the sky, he has unearthed a rare peace of mind—enough at least to bring upon his face saturated by a setting sun, both a grin and a smile. Finally.

Death by Design at Alcatraz

CHAPTER 41

End of the Line

LIKE A LITTLE BOY WITH BOOTS and raincoat stomping in puddles, Parker does similarly with his industrial boots on rock and dirt. After this rare moment of joy, he allows his mind to drift back to his third and final visit to the Mission Street police station. For the first one, the detectives questioned Parker about the murder of Lars von Meester. The second, the murder of Maxwell Brand. This last visit was Parker's voluntary confession.

Decidedly, Parker A. Rand had returned to the station that morning, shortly after leaving the haze of Celadonna's enchantment and prior to the WoMA presentations at noon. With well-adjusted conviction, Parker sat with both detectives O'Booker and Shenng for one last conversation. He had no awkwardness this time, no fear. And he did not hesitate to ask for the familiar officers investigating a double homicide that seemed to involve him.

At the same steel table, fluorescent overhead lamps buzzing, Parker stated with surprising composure, "Celadonna Kimm and I were not together at Alcatraz two days ago. Mr. O'Booker and Mr. Shenng"—he said with respect—"I have no idea why she fabricated the story, that alibi that got me released that day. I apologize for going along with it; I was focused and desperate to get back to work. And I barely even know her."

This last part concealed what happened only hours earlier in his bed. Even as he sat in this frank conversation with police officers, he was still reeling from the aftereffects of a dream-like incident—an act of both desire and bewilderment.

"I know this new information could make me look bad—that I don't have an alibi, that my cigarette lighter was found on the island."

He squirmed a little in his seat as he thought of the horrific flames engulfing his California colleague. Parker pleaded, "But please believe me, sirs, I didn't kill anyone. And Celadonna's attention on me before and during the competition was peculiar. She was peculiar. She stated a few times that I 'needed her' to win."

To Parker's relief, his admission did not garner a nod or any reaction that indicated the likelihood of him being even more a person-of-interest. For the detectives, Parker's information had peripheral impact on both the investigation at Lands End and at the lighthouse.

A day earlier, evidence arose that already dimmed the spotlight on Parker. At the cliffs where Lars von Meester was pushed to his death, investigators discovered numerous small footprints in the dirt. The tiny impressions were combined with large footprints easily connected to Lars's European construction shoes. The staccato pattern of the two types of footprints supported the previous story that a struggle with the Flying Dutchman occurred. But this was not a story that involved Parker.

The petite footprints not only matched Celadonna's exact foot size, but also her Converse All Stars shoes with the iconic diamond pattern on the soles. Though such information was inconclusive at first, eyewitnesses came forward.

That morning of Lars's death, construction workers were routinely documenting their work with images on their cameras. From one photo, the detectives had no difficultly identifying an attractive petite female in the fog as Celadonna Kimm. A white baseball cap held back her flowing hair, but this cap was not enough to disguise her—to cloak her in the whiteness of innocence.

One worker asserted, "I saw those two men brawling at first, but when it was over, the scrawnier one just walked away like a beaten puppy leaving Mr. von Meester, who then walked over by the cliffs by himself."

Another early morning observer also remembered the athletic shoes. "Clean bright shoes like hers just stood out for me. No one sees that trudging through mud, nails, and debris."

The detectives also obtained insights from Parker's colleagues during their interviews. With Ling holding Chip's hand, she admitted, "Celadonna and I had this cat fight on the lobby bridge. She mentioned Parker like he was her lover or something. That bitch was trying to push me over the guardrail!"

An additional comment from Margo Hunters confirmed more, "I am sure I was poisoned. It is not the meal I ate, because we all ate the same thing over four days."

One significant event disarmed even the powerful Magnar. Just an hour before the architects' presentations, he watched his so-called "security footage," which was less "security" and more a voyeuristic act. The following moments would hit him like a sledge hammer.

During the evening that concluded the competition, he warned his architects that no further work would be accepted. So Magnar's viewing of the afterhours was nothing more than routine. The developer had expected to fast forward through the videotape and find absolutely nothing. But a numbing jolt sent his body into shock, even dread.

"What the fuck?!" To his disbelief, Magnar found himself frozen in awe and disgust. His viewing revealed the sexual encounter between one of his architects and his girlfriend, a perplexed Parker and an assertive Celadonna. Magnar slowed down the tape to assess this carnal meeting, because he didn't believe his own eyes. Unfortunately, the reduced pace also extended his agony, as he forced himself to watch frame by frame.

In the dark security room, the slow-motion scene illuminated his despondent face and a forming fist. For a commanding man who has destroyed business rivals time and time again, it was this brief passage displayed on a small TV that paralyzed him. The Puppet Master had no strings to pull here, and he could not decide which emotion to accept as reliable: rage, jealousy, aggression, denial.

He found himself walking into the same police station that Parker left only 30 minutes prior. Magnar made no effort to protect his now ex-lover. Bursting in on O'Booker and Shenng at their desks, he blurted, "I heard from the commissioner that you have been looking into Celadonna Kimm, my girlfriend no longer." He said, "no longer" with extreme clarity.

"She was with me on the visit to Alcatraz that day. But she did leave my side at one point."

O'Booker chimed in, "We know already. Seen by a few of the architects, she was hovering around the base of the lighthouse."

Magnar revealed, "I gave her a simple assignment: to display a placard prohibiting visitors from entering the lighthouse, which was at the request of the island's caretakers. They stated that the lighthouse would not be safe for groups of architects going up and down the old wood stairs or ogling off the top platform. Celadonna claimed that she did attach the sign."

Shenng explained that there was no sign attached to the lighthouse when Maxwell entered, that their timetable showed Celadonna at the lighthouse only minutes before the architect found a welcoming door. "We found said sign floating in the bay!"

Magnar responded, "In her twisted mind, she probably took delight in catching a fish in her net. I thought it was odd how she instantly appeared back at my side as a fire was burning. She was agitated, but disturbingly calm too. At the time, I didn't think much of it…" His thinking trailed off into anger and nonchalance at the same time.

The museum developer contemplated the attention he bestowed upon Celadonna, also the unnerving security footage with Parker. Magnar, an individual familiar with manipulation as sport, viewed his ex-girlfriend as either a misguided little girl or a socio-pathological woman.

"I merely borrowed the lighter, boys," Celadonna bragged when in police custody, held on one murder charge and suspicion of a second. "I'm happy to talk about the lighthouse. During the evening before the Alcatraz tour—yes, I took Parker's treasured cigarette lighter," she contended with a mad glint in her eyes, a sneer of darkness creeping out of her voice.

She continued, "I was simply drawn to this lighter and Parker's tender story about a good luck charm from his dad. I just wanted a small piece of the architect. I was entitled to this memento. It was a tiny price of admission owed to me—for me to steer the commission towards Parker."

It didn't take long at all for Celadonna to confess her wrong doing, because she took pride in her actions. After Maxwell entered the lighthouse, with much less effort than Celadonna anticipated, she ignited materials and debris stored at the bottom of the stairs. With no remorse but delight actually, she watched as a fire rose up to find an unlucky architect at the top.

Parker did not have his lucky charm that day, and so it was not he who dropped the lighter. In her rush, Celadonna accidentally dropped the stolen object. For this brazen woman, it was not about murder. It was nothing more than just fun and games—as effortlessly as a child winning at Tic-Tac-Toe. She viewed her activities as simply part of a good day's work, securing the commission for her would-be lover.

Parker's denial of the alibi, the All Star footprints, eyewitnesses at Lands End, Magnar's information, and other collected facts stitched together a tale of conceit, madness, and ill-advised desire for a particular architect to win. The beautiful Celadonna Kimm was charged in the murders of Lars von Meester and Maxwell Brand.

At the time of selecting a winning architect, Magnar faced a difficult test of resolve. On video, he unflinchingly watched his lover intimate with one of his architects, Parker. At first, the developer was fueled by protectiveness of Celadonna. Then came distrust and fury as his mind replayed their history together. But to his relief and a nod to his determination, such responses of resentment faded quite quickly. His museum, this great addition to his legacy, needed his attention. It was no surprise that his focus and ego allowed him to discard his trophy lover in 15 minutes, allowing him to stick with his gut in choosing Parker.

After the competition, the client and architect began a ritual bonding process. A significant admission came over Sunday evening drinks. To Parker's amazement, Magnar said, "Know this: I hold no grudge against you for your participation in the escapade with Miss Kimm. To be frank, I found her actions predictable and tedious. You are such an agreeable man. For Celadonna, you were more a target than a participant, more prey than a romantic interest."

The architect found his judgment prickly, but also accurate. He did not look back at Celadonna with any fondness, but rather remorse and the sickening feeling that he was just a mouse for a cat with which to amuse herself.

After Celadonna's conviction for both murders, Magnar and his architect never spoke of her again. The lass was no more than a trifle. Not much needed to be said between two men who embarked on the promise of the greatest museum in the world.

Standing at his construction site on Alcatraz one afternoon, Parker enjoyed watching concrete being poured deep into gray soil and steel beams erected high into blue skies. He tried not to think about the competition—the four days under the scrutiny of faceless viewers, Celadonna's unsolicited help, her intrusion into his bed, his third and last visit to the police, the thrill of the presentations, and finally, her arrest and sentencing.

He also tried not to contemplate the loss of three well-respected colleagues. The body of Johnny Furnsby, or what remained, was discovered folded into the debris at Millennium Tower. The mystery around his sensational death trended through a few news cycles, until whatever new headline struck.

Beyond Parker's most hopeful dreams, the finished museum delivered world acclaim to PAR Designs. For Magnar Jones, the media, for better or for worse, did not provide the accolades that his ego so desperately craved. This developer wanted to be thought of as a creative partner to Parker, yet the public was not so generous. Magnar was credited as the developer, merely an astute businessman who pulled political strings and funded the project—nothing more, no recognition as an architectural visionary, the way he viewed himself. Of course in interviews and his press releases, he told a different story, weaving a wild tale for his legacy.

After a brief time of sulking and even considering legal action against the newspapers and journals—wanting to "set the record straight," Magnar moved on to his next world-shattering project, as well as his next "Celadonna."

That chapter in Parker's life, long gone, had been a roller coaster of exhilaration, as well as nausea and regret. For today, as he clomps his boots in the dust and stares up at the grand opening of the final wing of the museum, he knows he arrives into his skin. He leaves behind the skeletons in the closet, fantasies, and fugues. This afternoon, he is the darling of the design world. Perseverance and resolve has indeed offered Parker A. Rand the world as inheritance. And so it is for now.

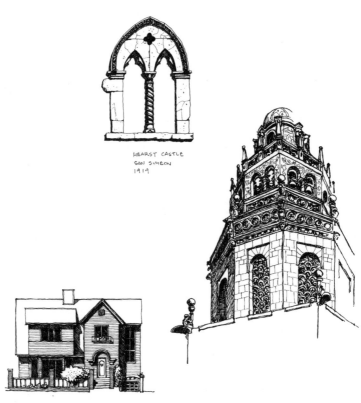

HEARST CASTLE
SAN SIMEON
1919

2820 VALLEJO STREET
JULIA MORGAN
ARTS & CRAFT, EDWARDIAN
1928

CHAPTER 42

"Honey, I'm Home"

A BOVE THE TRANQUIL SPLENDOR of Indian Rock Park, architect Parker A. Rand arrives smiling at his home perched high in the Berkeley Hills. Entering his Julia Morgan-designed residence, he returns from his reception in Shanghai, where he was bestowed the Pritzker Prize. He is only the eighth American architect to be a recipient of what is commonly known as the Nobel Peace Prize in architecture.

Several years prior, the World Museum of Abstract Art at Alcatraz held its grand opening and the associated fanfare surrounded Parker. The architect and his award-winning firm, PAR Designs, went on to design two other museums. Housing art from Australia's 19th-century Heidelberg School, Parker's design floats in the harbor like a massive ship docked near the Sydney Opera House. In Italy sits his other design, a transformation of the Roman Coliseum of 80 A.D. into an arts institution of Rococo chiaroscuro.

Shutting the hand-carved door behind him, Parker breathes easily as he walks through his foyer. A cliché but endearing expression, he shouts towards the kitchen, "Honey, I'm home," a surprising sing-song tone from this notable architect.

Stepping out of the kitchen with his two-year-old son in arms, Parker's wife appears. The stylish and sleek figure with short red hair dons a Kimono-like, gray house dress. He wraps his arms around his wife and son—a bear hug followed by a warm kiss on her lips.

Parker compliments, "Ms. Adrienne Veley, you get more and more gorgeous every day."

"Oh darling, stop your nonsense." She blushes.

"Each time I see you, every moment—"

"Stop, please."

"—I realize how fortunate I am to have won your heart, and this little gift is our child." He picks up the napping infant with a construction grip used in handling samples of precious stones, exotic woods, and rare metals, gently kisses his forehead, then places him in his crib.

He strolls over to the mantle where he proudly places his Pritzker Prize: a bronze medallion hanging on a thick red silk sash. The honor brings him great elation, as his fingers feel the embossed delicate patterns. The turn-of-the-century architecture of Louis Sullivan, often referred to as the "father of skyscrapers," inspired the embossed details of flowers and vines carved into the bronze.

He flips his medal over to read aloud the inscribed Latin words, "firmitas, utilitas, venustas." Like the architecture teacher that he is, Parker speaks in a mock professorial tone, "From the ancient Roman architect Vitruvius of the 1st century B.C., his words translate to firmness, commodity, and delight."

Adrienne gives him a sweet peck on the cheek, and replies, "I know, sweetheart, you have told me many times—and always in that ridiculous teaching voice."

She really doesn't mind hearing it again, or the past dozen times. She enjoys seeing her husband happy, so pleased with himself. Adrienne likes supporting him and his successes over the many years. She finds it empowering, amusing at times, to watch over this architect's evolving legacy—like a devoted wife's pet project.

After dinner, Parker stands again at the mantle, at his Pritzker, and reminisces, "Remember in college, we talked about being together. Well, here we are, my sweet Adrienne." His beautiful wife presents a loving but sarcastic smile.

Unaware of the subtleties, he continues, "Who knew we would end up exactly as I once envisioned?" Again, a smile on her face, this one more forced.

"It's all so thrilling: our life, WoMA, the Pritzker, new commissions—"

"Enough, dear," Adrienne halts his train of self-congratulatory thoughts. She adds, "You took your own sweet time."

Tone deaf to the off-remark, he continues, "Do you recall how I wrote you that silly love song? You weren't swooned at all, were you? Your rejection really stuck with me—for years, even decades after."

She bites her tongue, then her lower lip. In college, Parker was too eager. He had too many plans bursting with naivete. He was sweet and determined, but she, at 20, wasn't ready to plan her whole life—husband, house, business, and child.

Adrienne says, "Parker, I am here with you now to ensure that nothing will ever compromise what you set out to do." She is edging with more to say, yet he continues his self-indulgent reflection and jaunt down memory lane. Her words would be ignored, like background music to his self-important sense of accomplishment.

Not long ago, he realized that he did not need to do as Sisyphus did so valiantly, yet so absurdly. As soon as the ambitious Parker stopped pushing the fallen rock back to the top of the hill, he found peace. He simply had to let his shoulders shrug, let his imagined burdens fall, and envision that Camus's tragic character does finally figure it out—that he can leave his boulder at the bottom of the hill. Parker's shoulders relax, and a satisfactory smile lights up his face. He is unprepared for what is next.

She nudges him with a gaze, then sneers, "My darling husband"— her tone dry, sardonic even—"yes, it took decades for you to arrive here with me. You were going nowhere fast. Would still be. For decades, it was like watching a sad, injured turtle."

Parker's mouth slowly opens, but stays silent, as she now has his full attention.

"If I hadn't taken the reins, well…" Adrienne winks with bewildering nonchalance. She explains that after graduation, she consistently tracked his blazing trail of architectural successes, as well as his hiccups and shortcomings. But for all the accolades and progress, she knew it was not enough for him. And certainly not for her. She patiently waited for many long years for her choice in men to become her man of choice.

Parker interrupts, tries to downplay his early apprehensions, as several of his historic insecurities begin to rise within, like a sleeping volcano slowly awakening. "I finally found myself with the WoMA competition," he asserts as much to himself as to her.

She shakes her head no, and goes on, "Of course, the WoMA competition was the threshold for you to cross, for you to advance your career in one giant leap."

Adrienne's voice deepens as the words seep from a shadowy darkness. "I wanted you to win, but the odds were much against you. Lars was the frontrunner. Johnny, or maybe Margo, were also likely shoe-ins."

Parker just stares at his wife, mouth falling open more with nervousness. Her usual cheery tone continues to shift, and her voice sounds an uneasy growl. "You had to win that competition. You had to."

She adds three words, "You needed me."

Taking two steps backwards, he is startled, frightened. It has been many years since he has heard such words. Adrienne's short phrase transports him painfully back to a person he has long hoped to forget: Celadonna Kimm.

He attempts to lighten the conversation, tries to shift gears and drive this conversation onto smoother terrain. He doesn't have the courage to ask, *Why did you just say those three words?* Actually, he doesn't have the fortitude to hear the answer. The once magical evening becomes melancholic, then utterly disturbing. He has no chance to brace himself for the final round of comments from his wife.

She is now an eerie force, no longer the gracious mother of his child, nor the adoring wife. She adds to his racing heartbeat, "Isn't it peculiar how all three deaths of your colleagues related to high places and in famous locations?"

"What the heck are you talking—?"

She observes that Lars was pushed off a cliff, Maxwell burned at the lighthouse, and Johnny fell from the top of the Millennium Tower.

Adrienne's voice drifts now, her eyes focusing on nothing in particular, as if she doesn't need her husband as audience. Yet, these bleaker words are for him. "Maybe, such deaths are symbolic of an architect's ambition. You are such creative but fragile individuals— soul-searching, over-reaching, and miserably self-centered animals."

Parker struggles to make sense of his wife's assertions and symbolism.

Adrienne tosses out coolly, "Oh, wasn't she pretty, that Celadonna Kimm?"

He tries on a veil of forgetfulness, but "Who?" is not convincing. Parker's mind whirls at her words, her calm; he needs to defuse the situation. "Nothing ever happened with me and her, Adrienne. She was crazy. And she is in prison right now convicted of two murders."

Adrienne pulls the pin out and tosses her grenade, "Two, you say?" She demands all of his attention now, "It was only one."

Parker is at a complete lost. Adrienne glares, her features harden. Parker has never felt such a force of intimidation from his otherwise dutiful wife.

"Your cute girlfriend only murdered one person. Yes, she lit the lighthouse on fire, burning Brand to his death. She even boasted about doing so. But here is the unfortunate thing: That single murder was all she was capable of doing. This sexy, mindless kitten—oh, she had no drive, no consistency. She wanted you to win, but she lacked vision. I don't."

He fears her next round of sentences. Perhaps it was something he sensed for some time.

Adrienne confesses words of revelation. At SFMOMA, she was present in the crowds over all four days. It had been a decade since graduation, she was not easily recognizable. She had also even been at the Cliff House café the morning of Lars's death, only two tables away, and overheard Lars's infuriating dismissal of Parker's plan.

"I, too, have white Converse sneakers in a petite shoe size. It was so convenient that these workers thought I was Celadonna. I needed to get Lars out of your way. Out of our way." She explains how easy it was, so easy. Lands End was foggy, and Lars was already unsteady on the slope.

"Then there was Johnny Furnsby."

Parker's panic increases, "No, Johnny died in an elevator accident."

"Yes, he did." On the last night of the competition, Adrienne followed the architects to the bar. Lurking in the background, she overheard the conversation, particularly the comment that without Lars, Johnny was a likely candidate to win. She had turned her sights onto him there and then.

When Johnny left, he headed in the direction of the discussed Millennium Tower. Adrienne shadowed Johnny as he strolled through the city in a drunken daze. When he arrived at the residential tower and began studying the exterior, she slipped into the empty lobby.

Convenience and happenstance dictated the rest. Unlike Parker and his colleagues becoming renowned design architects, Adrienne's technical studies chose a different path for her, that of a forensic architect. After the foundation issues began at the Millennium Tower, the owner hired her analytical team to assess the structural situation. She had the entry codes, entered the lobby, and stationed herself at the vacant reception desk ready to buzz in a buzzed architect. No security guard for this late hour, just a welcoming receptionist.

With no plan in mind other than to entertain herself, Adrienne let Johnny in and directed him to a particular elevator. In addition to being intoxicated, he was exhausted from the contest, and did not notice the sign near the designated elevator that clearly said, "Entry Prohibited."

Parker shrinks back into the living room corner, as Adrienne takes a few threatening steps closer towards him.

Smugly she admits, "I thought maybe Johnny would get trapped in there, delayed, maybe miss the presentations. But the result was so much better. Fortuitous, wasn't it? The right place at the right time."

She shrugs, "And Margo? Surprisingly, the Brits seem to have a stronger constitution that I anticipated."

Adrienne steps back, a soft smile for her husband now, and concludes, "And yes, I would do it all again, because I love you. You needed me to win that competition. You need me now."

Adrienne Veley's last words twist affection and ambition, conceit and insanity, and echo in Parker's head with no fading over time, no end.

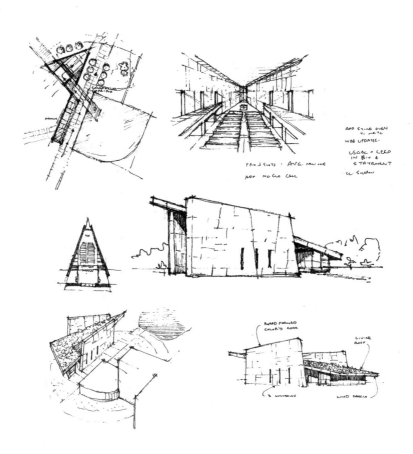

Death by Design at Alcatraz

Glory and Grief

F OR SEVERAL YEARS TO FOLLOW, as Parker attempts to fall asleep each night, he prays for peace. Cycling through doubts and regrets, he demands answers. Yet, no responses are offered—no resolution.

Anguish is tethered to him like an unwanted shadow. The San Francisco architect tries as best he can to revel in his string of accomplishments, but the burden of knowledge eclipses all of it. Within Adrienne's construct of absurdity and madness, all his good fortunes have become an affliction.

Inside his home, his child sleeps soundly as Parker never can. Adrienne hums a cheerful jazz standard in the kitchen, perfectly syncopated. And Parker faces the living room's fireplace, staring into flickering flames.

He tortures himself. *I failed so often in my early years. Now, so many accomplishments, but none based on my talents, but rather, death and manipulation. Would I have won WoMA if I competed in a fair competition? Would the Pritzker have been mine? How far into history has Adrienne been engineering things in my favor? Have I sold my soul and to whom?*

Parker clenches his Pritzker prize tightly against his chest, and he feels his triumphs fade, as quickly as waking from a dream where the recollection is only apparent for seconds.

He stands slowly, lifting his body out of the chair—a body's weight that is immense, dragged down by a gravitational pull of guilt. Pritzker medallion in hand, he looks casually at the inscription one last time, his fingers rubbing over the bronze. He glances in the direction of his son's bedroom, then the kitchen, and throws the prized medal into the engulfing fire—red silk sash flailing in embers and smoke.

And no one notices. No one cares about the glory, grief, and torment of this acclaimed architect. Yes, he had become the darling of the design world. But it had been not at his own perseverance and resolve, but by Andrienne's murderous hands that Parker A. Rand had indeed been offered the world as an inheritance. An empty legacy with a price paid from a foundation of death by design.